The year is 1899 . . .

The kitchen stove burns wood or coal. Clothes are scrubbed on a washboard. Soap costs four cents a bar, coffee retails at twenty cents a pound and a plain gold wedding band can be had for $1.50.

The eighteen-inch waist is the ideal for women, whose corsets are made of canvas and steel. Men use petroleum jelly to mold their handlebar mustaches and keep their hair in place.

Suitors escort their ladies fair to nickelodeons for an evening's entertainment. And chaperons cool the fires of young love.

It is a slower time, a time almost vanished from memory—preserved only in sepia-toned photographs and the treasures of Grandma's attic.

It is a time of gaslight—of grand dreams and great loves.

It is the time of Lucie Kolska and Jamie Kelly. . . .

Dear Reader,

Have you ever looked forward to those visits with older relatives when they pulled out faded photographs and told you the stories of their youth? Of the days when motorcars vied with buggies and "talkies" became the greatest form of entertainment. When the Depression pulled families together. When soldiers danced at the USO and women wore seamed stockings. When TV was a novelty. When they fell in love with handsome John Kennedy and the miniskirt was revealed. When they marched and sang political ballads. When Armstrong took that historic step for mankind and Nixon lost 18 minutes of tape. When *glasnost* came into our vocabulary and President Bush promised a kinder, gentler nation.

If you enjoyed those times, you'll love the Century of American Romance, a nostalgic look back at the 20th century—at the lives and loves of American men and women from 1899 to the dawn of the year 2000.

Beginning with this book, and in one American Romance each month over the next year, you can relive the memories of a time gone by and sneak a peak at romance in an exciting future.

We hope you enjoy these special stories of nostalgia and romance, written by some of your favorite novelists. As always we welcome your comments.

Here's hoping that Century of American Romance will become part of your most cherished memories . . .

Sincerely,

Debra Matteucci
Senior Editor & Editorial Coordinator

MARGARET ST. GEORGE

1890's AMERICAN PIE

Harlequin Books

TORONTO • NEW YORK • LONDON
AMSTERDAM • PARIS • SYDNEY • HAMBURG
STOCKHOLM • ATHENS • TOKYO • MILAN

More than twelve million immigrants entered America through Ellis Island. Many of them passed through New York City's lower East Side. They lived, died, loved, despaired and labored to create a better life for themselves and for those who would follow. Their hopes and dreams helped build the America we love and cherish today.

This book is dedicated to those courageous men and women. We have not forgotten your struggle. We remember.

Published June 1990

ISBN 0-373-16345-2

Chapter One

Seen from the water the main building on Ellis Island resembled a sprawling red-brick palace replete with soaring turrets and sun-tipped domes, a formidable island fortress guarding the portals to America. Those immigrants standing at the ship's railing swallowed hard and gripped the rail in mounting anxiety. What occurred on this small island and within that intimidating, authoritative-looking building would decide whose dreams came true and who would be denied entrance to the world's depository of hope.

Lucie Kolska, pale and trembling with nerves and trepidation, followed her cousin Petor up the wide sweep of the grand staircase and finally into a cavernous hall with a ceiling so high that two trapped birds darted and swooped beneath the arches. Hundreds of people milled about in confusion until a uniformed official herded them into the famed Ellis Island pens. Like cattle, they entered a tortuous maze defined by iron pipe rails that wound toward the front of the enormous hall.

Though the din in the room was thunderous, Lucie imagined she could hear the fearful pounding of her heart. From this day forward she would never hear mention of the Tower of Babel without remembering Ellis Island. Fretful voices called and shouted questions in a dozen languages. Uniformed men yelled instructions. Hawkers from the booths near the door screamed enticements to visit the money-changing booth, the job-placement counter, the transportation center. If the noise wasn't enough to cause a headache, the odors were. The smell of nervous perspiration and closely bunched humanity overhung the packed lines like a sour miasma. As Lucie inched through the pens toward the medical examiner and the immigration authorities, she smelled urine, sweat, soiled clothing and occasionally the sharp fatty pungency of sausage.

One hour passed, then two, and still the line stretched in front of her, moving forward at a snail's pace. Heat mounted in the room and an elderly woman to Lucie's right fainted. And with each step forward, the level of anxiety increased. Lucie wet dry lips, then touched her glove to the numbered tag pinned to her coat. It would have been comforting to know what to expect. The medical examiner did not frighten her too badly; she knew she was strong and in good health. She didn't cough or limp as some did; her eyes were not red or crusted. She had no unusual growths, no skin eruptions.

But just thinking about the infamous twenty-nine questions raised a tremor of apprehension and caused Lucie's lips and hands to shake. Everyone knew the twenty-nine questions must be answered correctly but no one knew what those questions were. Everyone was terrified they would fail and be turned back.

"Stop biting your lips, it makes you look suspicious," her cousin Petor advised from directly behind her. "They'll think you're an anarchist."

"Me?" The idea was absurd but her heart lurched. Here was one more thing to worry about. Instead of chewing her lower lip, she twisted her gloves around the rope handle of her reticule.

"Number four hundred and eighty-two," a uniformed official called a moment later, screaming to be heard above the pandemonium roaring through the hall.

Lucie started violently, then stood paralyzed with fear and dread, her eyes as wide as daisies. She felt as if giant fingers squeezed her chest and she could not breathe, could not step beyond the iron pipe rails. Petor gave her a gentle push breaking her paralysis, and she stumbled forward.

The official inspected the tag pinned to her coat, requested her name, then placed a check mark on his list. "In there," he said indifferently, jerking his head toward a door behind him.

Lucie swallowed hard, pressed both hands over her thudding heart, and glanced back at Petor hoping for a nod of encouragement. But her cousin's expression indicated he felt as worried as she about being returned to Poland. *Please, God,* she prayed silently before she drew a deep breath, squared her shoulders and timidly stepped into the medical examiner's room.

"Over here," someone called. Ordinarily Lucie considered herself a capable young woman, able to contend with life's exigencies, but these were not ordinary circumstances. So much depended upon the next moments.

The examination room was larger than she had expected, partitioned into cubicles created by cloth hung over lengths of rope. While the arrangement allowed adjustment for greater or lesser numbers of cubicles, the cubicles provided scant privacy as the fronts were open for all to see into. When her summons was repeated in French and German, Lucie started and hurried forward, murmuring apologies and averting her eyes from an anxious-looking man disrobing in the far corner. A large dark growth covered the upper portion of his chest.

"Doctor John Waithe with the United States Public Health Service." After introducing himself, a balding man beckoned her forward with an impatient gesture. He matched the number on her coat to the papers he held, then ordered her to walk back and forth along the wall, watching to see if she limped. "There is nothing to fear," he said in a voice that sounded tired. He studied her closely, then made a series of rapid checks down a form. "Sit down, please."

Dr. Waithe's expressionless assurance did nothing to calm Lucie's racing heart, and her mouth was so dry she swallowed repeatedly. While he peered into her eyes, checking for trachoma, and examined her ears, throat and teeth, Lucie tried to see what was happening to the man with the growth on his chest. When the doctor instructed her to rise, she turned toward the cubicle opening and saw the man in the corner had dropped his head in his hands and was sitting in silence as his wife screamed and wrung her hands.

"You may go." Not looking up from his forms, Dr. Waithe waved toward a door she had failed to notice until now.

Clasping shaking hands against her quilted skirt, Lucie swallowed a lump the size of a biscuit. She could not speak above a whisper. "Are you turning me away?"

Now he glanced up and managed a weary smile. "No, Miss Kolska. You appear to be in excellent health."

Relief weakened her knees. Then she remembered the questions and a fresh onslaught of anxiety overwhelmed her. Inside the second room a half dozen officials directed questions at a half dozen trembling respondents. Lucie thanked heaven a stool had been provided. Her shaking legs could not have held her upright throughout the ordeal.

A man with a thick dark mustache pointed to a stool before him. "Do you speak English?"

"Yes, sir," she whispered, averting her eyes from his uniform. Petor had insisted no one in America feared uniforms, but old habits were hard to break. At home a man in uniform could conscript a brother or father into the army, could seize a wife or daughter for an hour's pleasure, could take the winter's food from the cellar. And one could do nothing but smile and bow and push the hatred deep inside.

"Can you read and write?"

"Slowly, but...yes, I can." The official murmured a word of approval and placed a check mark on his papers. Feeling bewildered Lucie's dark eyes widened. Was it possible she had already answered two of the dreaded questions? Surely not.

"What kind of work do you do?"

"Farm work. Women's work."

He wrote on his papers. "Where are you going?"

"Here. To America." She bit her lip in fright when he frowned and it appeared she had answered incorrectly. "I'm going to live in New York City of America."

He nodded. "Is someone meeting you?"

She didn't understand. The questions were so simple there had to be a trick she was too nervous to comprehend.

"Are you a polygamist?" When Lucie didn't respond, the official glanced at her over the top of his papers. "Do you believe in having two husbands or two wives?"

Her mouth dropped, then she laughed aloud, something she had not dreamed she would do during the questioning. "No!"

"Do you plan to overthrow the government of the United States of America now or in the future?"

Did anyone ever answer yes? Suddenly she understood the questions were not a trap for the unwary, not devised to turn people away. Her shoulders sagged with relief, and confidence flickered in her gaze. She identified the same expressions on the faces around her, suspicion, disbelief, then dawning elation.

Finally, it was over and the official smiled. "Welcome to America, miss. You may remove your tag now. Here is your landing card." She accepted the card with dazed pride and carefully slipped it inside her shirtwaist for safekeeping. "Collect your baggage outside, then take the number three ferry to the city."

"I'm an American!" she whispered, hardly daring to believe. Tears of elation brimmed in her eyes. Because Petor had told her people shook hands in America, she thrust out her hand, caught the official's glove and pumped his arm up and down until he smiled and protested. "Thank you," she murmured enthusiastically. Shaking his hand wasn't enough, she wanted to shout and run and dance and jump in the air. "Oh, thank you, thank you!"

Outside the main building she stopped abruptly and breathed deeply of the bright June air, joyfully filling her lungs with an American breeze. Overhead the sky was clear and bottomless, as dazzlingly blue as the harbor waters rippling between Ellis Island and the towering city of New York. This was her home now, she thought, stunned by the idea of it. She had succeeded; she was an American.

Throwing out her arms and laughing aloud, Lucie spun in a circle that sent her skirts billowing and turned her toward the city skyline. Amazingly, some of the buildings appeared to be ten or even eleven stories tall. They scraped the very sky. The vision was so stupefying that she shifted her gaze, seeking a moment of perspective in the ordinary sight of gulls swooping above the docks. Dizzy with happiness, she wrapped her arms around her short dark jacket and hugged herself, feeling the landing card safe and real against her heart.

When she could bear another burst of excitement, she rose on tiptoe to see above the throngs of people jamming the grand staircase, shouting in excitement or confusion. Yes, there it was. Lucie could glimpse the crown and torch of Lady Liberty above the turrets and domes of the main building. Moisture dampened her eyes and her heart swelled with pride. Life was going to be wonderful here.

"I've found our baggage," Petor said, appearing at her side. After dropping their knotted bundles at her feet, he wiped the sweat from his forehead and smiled. "We're Americans now, ja?"

All trace of timidity and nervousness had vanished from Lucie's expression. Her dark eyes glowed with excitement. "I can't wait to see Stefan! Have you found him? And your brother?" Rising again on tiptoe, she tried to peer above the mass of people pushing and shoving around her. Although Petor stood beside her, she had to shout in his ear to be heard. An elbow knocked against her shoulder, a swinging bundle struck her hip and she clasped Petor's arm to steady herself. "Oh dear. We'll never find Stefan in this crush!"

"I'll search for them," Petor shouted near her hat brim. "You stay with our baggage." Leaning forward, he tapped the shoulder of a man who was trying not to be pushed into the bundles at Lucie's feet. "Sir, could I impose upon you to protect my cousin while I search for our party?"

The stranger turned and his warm dark eyes settled on Lucie in a look of unabashed admiration. "I would be honored to serve your cousin, sir."

Lucie gazed into those eyes, the color of freshly turned earth, and a tiny shiver ran through her body as if lightning had struck nearby. Something tightened inside and suddenly she couldn't breathe properly. Her lips parted and her eyes widened. The handsome young man standing before her exuded a sense of confidence she had not observed today, his self-assurance stood out like an island of calm amidst the chaos surging around them.

Aware that her steady gaze was immodest, Lucie tried to look away from him, but she couldn't. She watched him remove a tweed cap to reveal a thatch of auburn hair that glowed as warmly in the sunlight as did his smile. When Lucie realized he was staring at her as intently as she stared at him, a rush of confusion heated her cheeks and she hastily ducked her head, concealing her blush beneath the brim of her straw hat.

At home in Wlad if a man stared at a woman the way this man stared at her, as if he were enchanted, the villagers said he had been struck by love's elbow. The blush deepened on Lucie's cheeks and her heart skipped a beat. No man had ever looked at her this directly, as if he were seeing something hidden from the rest of the world. The experience was thrilling and confusing, a strange, wonderful way to begin her new life in America.

"It isn't true, you know," her protector said after Petor had plunged into the shouting crowd rushing and pushing past them. Bending slightly, he peered beneath her hat brim to examine her face. "American streets are paved with mud and horse droppings just like anywhere else."

"I know," Lucie murmured, startled that he had read her mind and also feeling a twinge of disappointment. She hadn't believed the streets of America were paved with gold, not really, or that shopkeepers dined on silver platters. But it had been exciting to imagine.

She dared another look and bit her lower lip. As he was still bending near her, she inhaled the sunshiny scent of his tweed jacket and the pleasing male scents of hair oil and a faint underlying hint of clean, honest perspiration. Unsettled by her response to his attention, by the peculiar turmoil his nearness caused, Lucie pressed her hands together and ducked her head again. Never before could she recall being this intensely aware of a man. She felt as if five hundred people had faded away leaving only the two of them standing at the base of the grand staircase.

"As there's no one to introduce us...I'm Jamie Kelly, recently of Dublin, Ireland."

"Were you aboard the *Poutansia*?" Lucie inquired, peeking up at him. She did not recall any Irish on board. Certainly she had seen no man as handsome as this one.

Jamie Kelly turned the full force of his gaze on her and for an instant Lucie could not breathe. Above his waistcoat, his collar and shirtfront looked freshly starched, and his dark trousers and coat were a higher quality than any she had observed during the voyage. Moreover, he was clean shaven whereas the fashion of the day decreed mustaches and beards. His smooth jaw indicated a man who was unafraid to proclaim his individuality, a man who danced to his own music.

"I arrived last week. Oh, I see. Why am I here today?" His gaze lifted to the wide curving staircase behind her. "I hoped to find a position at the labor exchange."

The buzz and roar of people shouting just inches away made it difficult to hear. Some of the accents were familiar to Lucie, many were not. She decided none sounded as soft and melodious as Jamie Kelly's deep rolled *r*s.

His steady gaze compelled her to speak, and indeed there was much to learn, although she didn't dare raise the questions she longed to ask, questions regarding him.

"I won't bite," Jamie Kelly gently assured her, smiling as if he had again guessed her thoughts. "So, what do you think of America? Is it what you expected?" Although he had to shout, he spoke without looking away from her face.

"I—I'm so relieved about the questions. I was terribly worried about them." Because his unwavering admiration made her cheeks feel hot, Lucie dropped her gaze to the cap he turned in his hands. Surely it wasn't proper to stand this close and stare into each other's eyes. She didn't know what had come over her. Stepping back, she pretended to examine the city waiting across the sail-dotted harbor. "It's so big, isn't it? And so noisy. Did you image America would be so big?"

He grinned at seeing the excitement shining in her dark eyes. "And filled with marvels."

She could not wait to see those marvels. "Oh, please tell me about them."

Sunlight glowed like fire on his auburn hair as he tilted his head to smile down at her. "I wouldn't dream of spoiling your pleasure, though I'm tempted. You must see for yourself." Then he seemed to realize he was making her uncomfortable and he cleared his throat and shifted to scan the crowd spilling around them. "Is someone meeting you?"

"My brother, Stefan," she said, her face lighting. "I haven't seen him in two years. He's the one who paid for my passage," she confided with pride. "Our Stefan has a home of his own and a steady job. After only two years, can you imagine? In America anything is possible," she added, thinking how long it would take to acquire a home in Wlad.

When Jamie Kelly laughed, the rich rolling sound surrounded her with warmth and made Lucie smile in return. Suddenly she wondered if he thought her wool gloves and quilted skirt were too heavy for spring, wondered if he could tell she wore three blouses, two skirts and all of her petticoats. Then she realized Jamie Kelly's tweed coat and worsted trousers must be as uncomfortably warm as her quilted skirt and winter jacket.

"I'm sure you'll find work soon," Lucie assured him, overflowing with the confidence of being in America and her own natural optimism.

A frown drew Jamie Kelly's thick eyebrows together as he studied the masses of people thrusting toward the ferries. "The economy is depressed right now and more people arrive every day. Jobs aren't easy to find."

"Perhaps you aren't seeking in the right places, Mr. Kelly." Another deep blush bloomed on Lucie's cheeks. What must he think of her, who was but hours off the ship, that she would dare to offer advice? An apology hovered on her lips. It was suddenly important to her that he think well of her.

He said something but she didn't hear as Petor reappeared, shouting and tugging at her arm. "I've found them. They're waiting for us by the ferry." A thrill of excitement lifted Lucie's expression as she realized she would be seeing Stefan within minutes. Petor raised his hat to Jamie Kelly, then swung their bundles up on his shoulders.

"Wait!"

But the noise was too overwhelming, and Lucie couldn't hear what Mr. Kelly shouted as Petor impatiently nudged her forward into the crowd. There was time for one quick glance over her shoulder, time to feel the violent blush that heated her cheeks, then the throng closed over the handsome Irishman and he vanished in the crush. For an instant Lucie experienced a startling sense of loss, as if something magical had been stolen from her.

There was no time to examine her reaction as she spotted Stefan standing beside the rails in front of the ferry, leaning forward, scanning the sea of people. Joy filled her and she forgot everything except seeing her brother again. "Over here!'' she shouted, rising on tiptoe to wave, all the while knowing he couldn't hear.

Fixing her gaze on his dear face, Lucie pushed forward, dodging elbows and bundles. Stefan sported a new hat and a sturdy coat she noticed proudly, but surprisingly he still wore the same heavy trousers she had mended half a dozen times before he sailed to America.

"Stefan!'' Laughing and crying Lucie flung herself into his bearlike embrace. Stefan lifted her high, then hugged her tightly to his chest.

"Let me look at you,'' he said finally, blinking away moisture as he held her away to see her better.

"No, no, speak English,'' Lucie insisted, straightening her hat and wiping tears of happiness from her eyes. "We must speak English. We're American now!''

Holding hands they studied each other, searching for changes. After a moment Lucie happily decided Stefan was still the brother she knew. Two years older and a bit thinner perhaps, definitely in need of a haircut and a trim for his mustache, but he was still her Stefan. His brown eyes were as determined as she remembered, his jaw as stubborn as ever it had been.

Looking at him was like observing a blend of their parents. Stefan had inherited their father's imposing powerful physique, but like Lucie, his face and hands bore the more delicate mark of their mother. No one spoke of it, but everyone in Wlad knew Count Bartok had sired Marta Kolska. Lucie and Stefan had inherited their illustrious grandfather's thin nose, well-shaped mouth and aristocratic profile.

"You've grown up, Luticia,'' Stefan said softly. "How old are you now, eighteen? Nineteen? And such a beauty. I'll have to guard you from dozens of suitors.''

Lucie laughed but she thought of the attractive Irishman and love's elbow and the color in her cheeks deepened to a becoming shade of rose. "I'm almost nineteen, still three years younger than you. What else have you forgotten?'' she asked, teasing him. Then the ferry's whistle blasted above and Lucie covered her ears as Stefan accepted her bundle from Petor and guided her up the plank and onto the boat.

They were jammed too tightly aboard the ferry to talk and crowded too near the center to see much of anything. Thankfully the harbor trip was brief and within minutes a sea of people flowed down the plank and onto the wharves.

Lucie's first impression of America, once she put Jamie Kelly firmly out of her mind, was the fishy scent of oysters. Before being jostled forward, she paused to gaze at the piles of oyster shells littering the dock area, higher than a man and stretching along the waterside as far as she could see. Everywhere she looked she saw signs advertising oyster saloons or oyster bars. She wondered if Americans ate anything else. Then her attention was captured by the horse-drawn wagons racing along the street, spilling lumps of coal and, incredibly, bits of ice.

Her eyes rounded in amazement. "Ice?" she asked Stefan, who grinned at her. "In June?" Truly America was a wondrous place.

She could hardly wrench her attention from the thick traffic long enough to murmur goodbye to Petor and his brother. "Thank you for escorting me," she whispered, distracted. She shook Petor's hand and wished him well. "If Minnesota is not too far away, you must come for Sunday supper."

"Thank you," Petor agreed solemnly, gazing wide-eyed at the rush and din of the street traffic. "We will."

Laughing, Stefan swung her bundle over his shoulder and led her past the enormous mounds of oyster shells. "Minnesota is very far away," he said, but Lucie wasn't listening.

She watched the blur of galloping traffic with large astonished eyes. There were drays and beer wagons, tall swaying furniture vans and wagon beds filled with shad and mackerel. There were also vegetable wagons and butcher carts, chandler's vans and flower carts, and here and there a carriage fit for a prince. Even along the wharves the facing buildings rose five and six stories tall and here as everywhere within the city, painted advertisements sprouted over the building walls like brilliantly colored vines.

Later, Lucie couldn't recall how she and Stefan managed to cross the street, dodging spinning wheels and galloping hooves, but when next she remembered to catch her breath, Stefan was paying a horse car conductor two pennies and they were entering a stiflingly hot box, packed as tightly as the ferry. A man spit a stream of tobacco juice into the straw covering the floor then rose and offered Lucie his seat. She hesitated, not certain if she should accept until Stefan nodded.

The scene glimpsed through the dusty window caused her heart to pound with excitement and apprehension. For the most part she could not see much beyond the four lanes of traffic that sped past them so breathtakingly close that her heart lurched in fear of collision. But occasionally she caught sight of the buildings, hundreds and hundreds of buildings, pressed tightly one against the other, block after unbroken block of glass and stone and iron work. And more people than she had ever dared to imagine could inhabit a single place.

Standing above her, swaying with the motion of the ceiling strap, Stefan announced the streets as they passed, lower Broadway, then Canal Street, but the names meant nothing to her. The crush of traffic and people and noise overwhelmed Lucie's senses. She hadn't expected the city to be so busy, so large, so exciting. And nothing had prepared her for the sheer numbers.

Wistfully she recalled the handsome Irishman with the dancing eyes whom she had naively supposed she would meet again. Now she comprehended a second encounter would be akin to a miracle. Love's elbow might have struck them but they were lost to each other. Before she could experience the full weight of regret, she heard Stefan shout to the conductor and beckon her forward. Eagerly, Lucie gathered her skirts and flew down the steps to the street, her spirits lifting in fresh excitement.

She could not have described what she expected to see because she had not known what to expect. But surely this could not be where Stefan lived. Her exuberance faded to dismay as she peered into the narrow filthy street opening in front of her.

The paving stones ended where Elizabeth Street began. A haze of manure-scented dust overhung the street, which seemed even narrower due to the line of broken sagging wagons abandoned along the crumbling curb. Beneath the wagons and between them lay piles of garbage rotting in the afternoon heat, swarming with a dark covering of flies.

Pressing an uncertain hand to her breast, Lucie examined the four and five-story wooden tenements that blocked any sunlight from the street. Between lines of grayish laundry crisscrossing overhead, she glimpsed broken window panes and listless children sitting on sagging metal fire escapes that looked as if they might pull loose at any moment and crash into the street below. The people hurrying past looked exhausted and anxious, some wore disturbing expressions of bewilderment or defeat. The clothing she noticed was unlike the fashionable ensembles she had admired on Broadway. Here the attire was mended and hastily assembled, in need of a good wash and a brushing. The lowered heads and bent backs were as shockingly familiar as the despair and hopelessness she had left behind in Wlad.

"Stefan?" she whispered, swallowing with difficulty.

"This way," he said gruffly, his gaze not meeting hers.

They stepped off the paving stones into the dust and powdered manure overhanging Elizabeth Street, and immediately Lucie realized the same closely packed buildings that blocked the sunlight also trapped the heat. Before they had walked more than a few steps, a trickle of perspiration rolled down her throat, and patches of dampness spread under her arms.

The heat and the stench of raw garbage, horse manure, outhouses and too many unwashed bodies packed into too little space made her feel dizzy. Pausing, she clasped Stefan's arm, recoiling from the sympathy she read in passing glances that swept over her bundle then herself before they turned away.

"Through here," Stefan said, striding toward a dark narrow passageway leading between two buildings.

"Stefan?" she asked again, staring up at him. But Stefan stood silently, her bundle over his broad shoulder, frowning at a beer wagon that lumbered along the street, stirring dust and flies and the odors of hardship and desperation.

She caught her lower lip between her teeth, then lifted her skirts above her boots and drew a breath before she hastened through the dark tunnel that Stefan indicated. At the end of the opening lay a small shadowed courtyard of sorts, hemmed by tall buildings that trapped the stench from a row of tin-roofed latrines. Lucie halted and pressed a handkerchief to her nose, her eyes watering above the edge.

The persistent drip from a rusted pump in the center of the courtyard had created a dark puddle of slowly spreading mud. Broken cobbles littered the ground, along with heaps of refuse as fly blown and malodorous as the piles in the street. A half dozen children played in the gray dirt, three women labored over laundry tubs near the row of outhouses. A tan dog sniffed at a mound of ashes and cinders. There was not a scrap of green in the stifling courtyard, only a few yellowed lines of weeds dying in the heat.

For an instant Stefan met her gaze, then he moved past her, toward a door hanging from its hinges. Inside, a dark littered stairway stinking of urine and cooking odors led up to a hallway cast in permanent night. When Stefan opened one of the doors, Lucie stumbled inside and crossed directly to the window, leaning to inhale a long breath of hot stale air through the broken pane.

Although she was high above the street, on the third floor, higher than she had been before, the din of wheels and harness and an erupting street brawl sounded as if she were standing in their midst. Numbed by what she had seen, she straightened slowly and turned to inspect Stefan's home, now hers.

The smallness impressed her first, the sense of not having enough space to breathe. There was nothing in the bare-floored room but a scarred table, a mismatched set of chairs and a cast-iron stove, cranky from the look of it. Slowly Lucie unpinned her hat and removed her jacket, then hung them on the exposed nails driven into the wall near the door.

Darkness formed her second impression. One of the walls might have been light colored once, now it was dark with smoke and age. Brown wallpaper bubbled and peeled from the other walls, shadowed deeper in spots by oily stains.

A cramp of homesickness tightened Lucie's small shoulders. With all her heart she longed to run home to her parents' snug bright cottage and the sweet green scent of the fields. In a week her mother would clip rosemary and thyme to spread over the new straw in the loft. The cottage would smell of spring and fresh herbs and her mother's lamb stew.

Knowing Stefan watched, not wanting him to recognize her shock and homesickness, Lucie smoothed shaking hands over her quilted skirt and walked to the stove blinking rapidly as she bent to inspect the rust-crusted oven door. When she could control the moisture welling in her eyes, she straightened and focused on a tin coffeepot that had boiled over and splattered the surface of the range.

"Exactly what I was wanting," she lied, thinking of the ice wagon she had seen and the children running behind to catch the chunks that had been jostled into the street. An hour ago she had not known it was possible to have ice in June. Now she longed for a tiny piece to press over her throat and face. "A good cup of hot coffee. Do we have cups? Yes, here they are." On the wooden shelf in front of her nose.

"There's another room," Stefan said stiffly, watching her. "Many have only one room."

"Then we are fortunate," Lucie said brightly. She followed him into a second minuscule room and waited while he struck a lucifer to light the windowless blackness. Two thin mattresses were rolled and tied and pushed against the wall. When they were opened for the night, there would not be space for anything else.

"I made a private place for you." Stefan pointed to a length of faded cloth strung across one corner.

"Thank you," Lucie whispered, swallowing the lump in her throat. She pressed his hand.

They returned to the kitchen and Lucie poured coffee, noticing the grounds were not fresh and the coffee was pale as tea. She sat across the table from Stefan and lowered her eyes from his painful expression.

"I'm sorry." He ran a hand through his hair and tugged his mustache, a gesture she remembered. "It isn't what you expected."

"We all thought—" Pressing her lips together, Lucie bit off what she had been about to say. His pride suffered enough, she could see it in his dark eyes, in the wooden set of his shoulders.

"After two years I had hoped to be able to rent something better." Frowning, Stefan looked into the cup he turned between his hands. "But even a small house rents for eight hundred to a thousand dollars a year. When a man earns a dollar a day..."

"What does our home rent for?" Lucie asked, looking at the peeling walls, the broken window pane.

"Three dollars a week."

Barter was the basis of the economy in Wlad. Lucie knew to the feather how many chickens were required to buy enough cloth for skirts for her mother and herself. A half dozen eggs equaled a loaf of good black bread. A pound of autumn honey equaled a bushel of winter apples. American coins confused her.

Using her fingers she counted and figured, then raised a look of concern. "After paying the rent, you have three dollars to live on. Is everything else in America so cheap that three dollars is enough?"

Stefan's laugh was harsh. "Nothing in America is cheap."

"But you saved my passage money—"

"Until this morning I rented space to two additional men."

"I see." She could not imagine three people sharing the space around her. But it required little imagination to recognize the hardship Stefan had endured to save the twenty-seven dollars required for her passage to America. "I will make this up to you," she said softly.

He waved the promise aside then leaned forward eagerly. "Lucie, tell me about home. Are the mother and father well? Is the barley out of the ground? Did Ivan Bobich clear his forest land? And my cow—has my cow calved yet?"

After pouring more coffee, Lucie assured him their parents were well, then she spoke of the village and village gossip until darkness gathered outside the window.

"I have news, too," Stefan announced when she finished speaking. A flush of color seemed to rise from his collar and his voice softened to a tone Lucie had not heard before. "I am to be married. As soon as there is money enough."

Surprise rounded Lucie's mouth, then she clapped her hands in delight and rushed to embrace him. "Oh, Stefan! What wonderful news. Tell me everything about her!"

"Her name is Greta Laskowski," Stefan said, smiling broadly. "Her people are from a village outside Warsaw. The family immigrated to America four years ago, but things did not go well for them. The parents died. Two sisters married and returned to Poland. Her brother went west." It seemed as if a cloud passed and Stefan's expression darkened. "Greta wanted to be here to welcome you, but her health has suffered lately. Already she thinks of you as a sister."

Moisture dampened Lucie's lashes. It would be good to have a sister in this strange confusing land. Reaching across the scarred table, she clasped Stefan's hand. "It is my turn to help you. I'll find work, and in no time at all we'll save your marriage money." She owed him that much.

The softness faded from Stefan's dark eyes. "I wish it were that easy, Lucie," he said, shaking his head. "Work is hard to find; the pay is low. Every day hundreds of immigrants pour into the city, all desperate for work. Any man who demands decent wages will find someone standing behind him willing to do the same job for pennies." Frowning, he looked at the darkness pressing against the window. "It's not like we thought. Yes, there is opportunity here, but a man must look hard to find it. It isn't enough to have two hands and a strong back."

Determination firmed the lines of Lucie's mouth. "I'll find something," she said brusquely. "Tomorrow we begin saving for your marriage to my new sister."

After Stefan lit the table lamp he examined her expression, then laughed. "You sound like Greta. Both of you can find a glimmer of sunlight in the darkest shadow." He pressed Lucie's hand. "Tomorrow you must rest from your journey, then take a day or so to explore. There's so much to see."

"Right now I need to explore for our supper," she said, pushing up from the table. There was no meat in the salt box beside the scuttle, but considering the heat she hadn't really expected there would be. Nor was there much of anything else.

In the end Lucie relied on her mother's recipe for hard times and crumbled a hardening loaf of dark bread into two cracked bowls she found on the shelf. Though it added to the heat trapped in the room, she fed the stove until a pot bubbled then she poured the boiling water over the bread. After waiting a moment she poured off the excess water, added a generous amount of salt and pepper then stirred in a spoonful of the cooking grease she found in a crock on the back of the stove.

"Even when I'm rich," Stefan said with a wink, "I'll want Greta to prepare water-bread to remind me of home."

Lucie laughed and refrained from mentioning that no one in Wlad imagined people in America ate water-bread.

But she thought of it later when she was lying on her thin mattress in the tar-black second room, listening to an argument on the other side of the wall that sounded as if it were taking place at her elbow. She listened to the angry despairing voices, listened to the scrabble of mice—she hoped it was only mice—running up the walls, listened to Stefan's soft snore. A tear spilled from her eyes and dropped to the mattress.

She had not expected that she and Stefan would live in luxury or splendor. But neither had she expected squalor. As poor as they were, the villages in Wlad had fresh clean air and plentiful sunshine. And flowers on the sills. No one lived above an outhouse or piled garbage in his yard.

It was also true there was no hope for change in Wlad, no opportunity for a young man or woman to better themselves. Inheritance had carved the land into smaller and smaller plots and each year the soil seemed less fertile than the year before, the harvest less plentiful. People went to bed hungry in Wlad and shivered before empty grates when the snows came. And always there was the fear of the soldiers who might swoop through the village burning and pillaging for an evening's amusement.

Life would be better in America. But Lucie stared into the darkness and remembered the faces in Elizabeth Street. She knew those faces. Faces frozen by anxiety, faces holding fear inside. Hungry faces, ill faces, faces reflecting the uncertainty of tomorrow. Had they arrived in the land of plenty as filled with hope and excitement as she? What had happened between Ellis Island and Elizabeth Street?

Was America no more than a golden myth? No, she thought with a shudder of rejection. No soldiers would come in the night. No tax collector would appear in the morning. Her belly was full and she had two rooms to call her own. Stefan had work and so would she. They were young and strong and willing to wait for the opportunity that would surely come, as it never would in Wlad.

Lying in the darkness, listening to the sounds of Stefan's snores and the noise within and beyond the walls, Lucie finally let herself remember the Irishman whose dark eyes had made her shiver in the sunlight. Where was he tonight? Would she ever see him again? It didn't seem possible that fate had brought them together only to cast them apart.

She recalled the exhilaration she had felt when she met Jamie Kelly, followed by the shock and disappointment of seeing where she and Stefan would live. Her first day in America had been strange and bewildering—and not at all what she had expected.

In the morning she fried the last of the bread for Stefan's breakfast and sent him downstairs to empty the slop bucket and join the line waiting to pump fresh water for coffee and washing.

Shortly after Stefan departed for work, a sliver of sunlight slipped across the window's broken pane and Lucie stared at the light, mesmerized, suspecting it would be the last sunshiny brightness she would see today.

Before Stefan returned, bringing bread, cheese and sausage for their supper, she had replaced the linen on the mattresses with the sheets she brought from home, had scrubbed the rooms from floor to ceilings, had polished the lamp chimneys and had restored a semblance of respectability to the stove.

The next day, marshaling her courage, she donned her hat and gloves and timidly ventured outside determined to explore her new world. The bewildering array of streets and cross streets and back alleyways overwhelmed her but she made herself swallow the fear that lodged in her throat. The trick was to proceed slowly, memorizing her steps, progressing a bit farther each day.

By the end of the week she discovered the Hester Street market and learned the best buys could be made late in the day when the stall owners and pushcart vendors prepared to close shop for the evening. She found the station for the elevated, though she didn't dare venture inside, and made herself stand and watch and listen to the hideous shriek of hot metal until she no longer felt like running from the noise and belching cinders. She located the corners where the red horse cars stopped and examined the wares offered by the pushcarts in every street—secondhand clothing, secondhand food and scissors, eyeglasses and scraps of wood and old nails. Eventually she walked to Broadway and stood enchanted before huge glass panes that displayed items of such unimaginable luxury they took her breath away.

She discovered streets that had formed into small countries, Italians here, strange exotic Orientals there, Hebrews and Slavs and Greeks, each group claiming a section of the city for themselves. She found the dumps where the ragpickers worked and the wharves and the factories that fouled the air with soot and the sulfur smell of blast furnaces.

And always she watched for Mr. Kelly, hoping to turn the next corner and encounter him. When she did not, her disappointment was acute. As Lucie prided herself on possessing a practical nature not given to flights of fancy, her constant hope of meeting Mr. Kelly troubled her. She did not understand why she could not forget him. Or why she did not wish to.

Aware she acted foolishly and out of character, she nevertheless scanned the streets and walkway traffic, seeking a bright auburn head, a broad set of shoulders, teeth as white as bleached bone. Once she heard a man laugh and she stopped, feeling her cheeks heat with anticipation. But when she turned, it was not him and her shoulders dropped with disappointment.

She found no work, either. "Tomorrow I'll try the factories," she assured Stefan at the end of her second week in America. She considered their supper of cold potato pie and yesterday's bread and figured the cost in her mind.

"The factories have been sacking people," Stefan informed her. "Greta worries whether she'll have a job tomorrow."

Lucie still hadn't met Greta, which was a continuing disappointment, but already she admired the young woman's courage. Though ill, Greta rose each day and went to work. "Is she feeling any better?"

Stefan carried their supper plates to the tub of hot water on top of the stove. A worried frown drew his brow. "A little. She's so eager to meet you, worried what you must think that she hasn't greeted you. I hope by next week . . ."

Lucie finished her glass of warm beer and mopped her neck. It was as hot tonight as it had been last night. Heat engulfed the city, squeezing the air from every breath, turning the streets into dry choking powder. The newspapers compared this summer to the heat wave of 1896, three years ago, and the numbers of people and animals who had died of heat-related illness.

It worried her that Stefan carried his mattress up to the tenement rooftop to sleep, hoping for a breath of cooler air. At least once a week the newspapers reported the death of someone who had fallen from a rooftop.

Lucie sighed. It was imperative that she find work soon. Stefan had shown her the hiding place under the loose board in the second room where he kept his money. The small cache was steadily dwindling. Standing, thinking about it, she smoothed her hands over her apron then washed the supper dishes, saving the water for the morning.

"Tomorrow I'll bring your noonday meal to the work site," she said before Stefan departed to carry his mattress up to the roof. When he protested she turned to face him. "Please, Stefan. I need to feel useful. It will give me something to do until I find work."

After he left, she sat in the hot thick darkness wearing only her petticoat and shift, holding their remaining coins in her hand. Slowly, she counted them again, hoping she had erred.

Long after the night rustlings died in the street, Lucie continued to sit in the darkness beside the window, looking at the sagging shutters on the tenement facing her. Right now her goal of earning Stefan's marriage money seemed as far away as the handsome Irishman who continued to haunt her dreams.

A bittersweet ache settled in Lucie's small bosom. She wondered if Jamie Kelly had found a job, wondered if he remembered their brief meeting at Ellis Island, wondered if he thought about her as frequently as she found herself thinking about him.

Chapter Two

Jamie Kelly stood back from the noise and dust billowing from the street, hands thrust in his pockets, watching a mounted policeman attempt to unravel one of the ubiquitous traffic snarls that hourly paralyzed Broadway. The unrelenting heat frayed tempers and nerves, and the scene in front of him was punctuated by an eruption of shouts and curses and accusations.

Ordinarily the tangled wheels and harness would have provided an interesting diversion, but at the moment all he could think about was the tantalizing fragrance of roast pork and fried potatoes that wafted from the doorway beside him.

Counting his money by feeling the shape of the coins in his pocket, Jamie arrived at the same total he had a moment before. Sixty-two cents. The pork and potatoes, plus a slice of pie, the thought of which made his mouth water, cost twenty-five cents. He hadn't eaten since yesterday and he was tempted to step inside the hash house, out of the burning sun, and relieve the tightness cramping his stomach.

Exerting a will of their own, his fingers separated two dimes and a nickel from among his coins and curled around them. The saliva that dampened his mouth at the thought of the pie dried in the curls of dust rising from the street and he thought how good a cool pint would taste, like a wee bit of heaven.

The cost of a meal and a pint would leave him thirty-seven cents. Subtract ten cents for a bed at a lodging house, and he would start tomorrow with twenty-seven cents. If he settled for a doss house in the Bowery, he could save five cents. Even for a man brimming with optimism that cut the future too thin.

Turning aside from the hash house doorway, Jamie made himself walk away from the scents and thoughts of food. As the crush of pedestrian traffic was as thick and bad-tempered as the street traffic, he stayed near the buildings, which was better anyway as he could watch for Help Wanted signs in the windows.

And he could watch for the lovely lass he had met at Ellis Island, though he had almost abandoned hope of finding her again. A sigh lifted his shoulders and he thrust his hands deep into his pockets. Why hadn't he inquired where she was staying? Hell, he didn't even know her name. Her beautiful dark eyes had gazed into his and turned his brain to straw. Instead of asking the important questions, he had babbled like an idiot. Swearing softly, he turned a brooding expression toward the shop windows.

A week ago Jamie had begun ignoring the Irish need not apply warning added to the Help Wanted signs, hoping he could pass for an Englishman, though the thought galled him. In the end it hadn't mattered as prospective employers recognized his accent and showed him the door. He was beginning to wonder how Irishmen, Chinamen and Africans survived in New York City.

Fingering his coins, feeling the sweat that soiled his collar, he walked along Broadway, entering every door displaying a Help Wanted sign. And leaving again. It was just as well, he told himself, rejecting any thought of discouragement. A job in the establishments he had tried would only have offered a stopgap measure, something to provide the necessities until he could secure a position in construction or design.

Pausing to mop his neck and brow, Jamie looked past the edge of the pavement into a construction pit and watched a crew of laborers excavating a basement for what he guessed would eventually be another Broadway shopping emporium. The men working the shovels were bare chested, sweating profusely in the boiling noon day sun. The work was brutal and the heat in the pit would be savage, but at least the men had a job and the satisfaction of knowing they were building something wonderful.

After a moment the conversation around him focused and Jamie realized the foreman for the job site stood not three feet from him. Surely this was a sign. After dusting the tops of his shoes on the back of his trousers, he straightened his shoulders, removed his cap, and stepped forward.

"Pardon the intrusion, sir, but are you the foreman for this site?"

"The same. The name's Henry Gustoffer. Who wants to know?" Gustoffer looked him up and down, then squirted a stream of tobacco through a gap in his teeth.

"Jamie Kelly, and I'm looking for work." Before Henry Gustoffer could reject him out of hand he quickly added, "I've had two years of university and trained two years in architecture with Goblin and Greene in Dublin."

Gustoffer smiled and ran a finger between his mustache and his upper lip. "Come off your perch, son. All I got is shovel work."

"I'll take shovel work. I'll take whatever you have and gladly."

Another stream of tobacco juice splattered near Jamie's shoes, then Gustoffer lifted his head and narrowed his eyes. "I know times are hard, especially for you bastard micks. But you ain't built for shovel work. You're built lean, like a Thoroughbred, if you know what I mean, and what I want are plow horses. Hell, you wouldn't last two hours in the pit."

No one else had given him this much time and Jamie seized the opportunity, as slim as it was. Refusing to accept his dismissal, he followed Henry Gustoffer inside the shed near the rim of the pit.

"I'm wiry but I'm strong," he said to Gustoffer's broad back. "I have staying power. All I ask is a chance to prove myself."

Gustoffer turned from the table strewn with blueprints. "I'm losing patience, son. Ain't no way a tall thin drink of water like yourself has the strength for excavation."

"I have sixty-two cents in my pocket, Mr. Gustoffer," he said stiffly. Desperation trampled his pride. "I haven't eaten since yesterday. I don't know where I'll sleep tonight. If you're turning me away because I'm Irish, I'll go without apology. But if you're refusing me because you think I can't heave a shovel, I beg you to reconsider. Tell me what I can do to convince you I'm worth hiring on."

The noon whistle blew as Gustoffer eyed him up and down. He bit the corner of a plug of tobacco he took from his waistcoat pocket. "It ain't that I'm unsympathetic to your troubles—"

"I'm stronger than you think. I can work as hard as any man. All I ask is a chance."

Gustoffer walked outside to the edge of the excavation pit and watched the men drop their shovels as the sound of the noon whistle died away. "You want to prove yourself?" Turning, he grinned at Jamie. "You beat my strongest man in a one-on-one, and you got yourself a shovel job."

Jamie studied the men in the pit. Heavy sweat-slicked muscles gleamed in the sun. Every one of them looked as if they were made of cast-iron and double bolted, like evil-tempered giants.

"Worst that can happen," Gustoffer said, considering, "is my men get some entertainment with their midday chuck." He cocked an eyebrow. "You game, Mr. Kelly?"

He'd had some instruction in pugilism; he hoped to hell it would be enough. "Call out your best man," he said cheerfully. Finally he had a chance; he wasn't going to walk away. He was going to win. To do that he had to believe he could. He could not allow a single grain of fear or defeatism to enter his mind.

"I'll say this, young fella, you got sand." Gustoffer leaned over the edge of the pit. "Hey, Kolska," he shouted. "This here mick says you got a face like a cow's hole." He grinned. "Says he knows baby girls tougher'n you."

Jamie looked down at the sturdy bull Gustoffer had chosen. A furious plum color rose in the man's face, and Jamie felt his heart drop to his toes. The man outweighed Jamie by a good thirty pounds, and the muscles swelling his upper arms were work hardened and tight as rock.

"You can win," he muttered as he removed his coat and waistcoat and slowly rolled up his sleeves while Gustoffer continued to shout insults into the pit.

The man Gustoffer had chosen jabbed his shovel into the dirt and roared. The other men cheered as he ran to the side of the pit and began to pull himself up to the street.

Jamie swallowed. The bull was coming to pulverize him. This was not going to be easy. At the very moment when he most needed a sign of encouragement, the angels granted his wish. To his joy and astonishment, he spotted the young lass from Ellis Island hurrying toward him. Finding her again was a piece of luck so staggering that it had to mean he could conquer the bull.

"Wait," he called to Gustoffer, then he sprinted forward and caught her arm, hastily apologizing for startling her.

"Mr. Kelly!" Her wonderful dark eyes widened in surprise and—dare he hope?—pleasure at seeing him again.

"Please don't leave," he said, speaking rapidly. "I must speak to you. What is your name? I don't even know your name."

"Lucie," she said shyly, observing his suspenders and his state of undress.

The name was as beautiful as the woman. From the corner of his eyes he saw the bare-chested giant haul himself out of the pit and start toward him. Lucie saw the man, too, and she gasped, her hand flying to her throat.

Feeling an instinctive urge to protect her, he caught her arm as she stepped forward. "There's going to be a fight," he explained rapidly. "You'd best stay here, out of harm's way."

Wide-eyed she stared at the man rushing toward them, then darted a look of distress to Jamie. A shudder swept her small body and horror darkened her eyes. "Oh, no!"

"Don't go away. Please. I must speak to you."

There was no time to converse further. After thrusting his cap, coat and waistcoat into her hands, he turned to engage the man jumping out of the pit to beat him into pulp. Praying he wouldn't be humiliated in front of her, Jamie spit on his palms, then raised his fists and stepped forward.

Seen from a closer vantage, Jamie realized his adversary was not a giant after all, but the realization offered scant consolation. The man was an inch or two shorter but powerfully built and mad as hell.

He circled warily, measuring his opponent and formulating his strategy. Before he could decide the best approach, the man from the pit charged him. There was nothing disciplined or civilized in the bull's style of fighting, just brute strength. He rushed in low and close, fists hammering.

One of the blows split Jamie's lip. He tasted blood and heard a roar of cheers rise from the pit. Finally he saw an opening and punched the man in the gut, saw it didn't slow him down. The man was going to beat him into sausage and all he would have to show for his trouble was a broken body and no job.

Rage flooded his face with feverish heat. He hadn't come to America to die of starvation or to be humiliated in front of a very special lassie. Lucie, her name was Lucie. Thrusting forward he landed a sharp blow beside the man's eye, opening a small cut. Lucie, he chanted in his mind as he landed another blow, then another. He hadn't found her again to be mortified in front of her. Dancing and dodging he planted a blow in the man's stomach, putting his full weight behind it. He needed this job and, by God, no one was going to stop him from having it. Lucie, Lucie, Lucie.

From the corner of his eye he noticed her standing frozen in the midst of the crowd that had gathered. Her expression of mounting distress dispatched a burst of energy through his body. Her face had become as white as a chalk cliff; tears—yes, he was certain they were tears—glistened in her lovely eyes. She was trembling and her gloves fluttered anxiously about her throat and mouth. His spirit soared on wings of hope. Surely her anxiety on his behalf indicated she felt some tenderness toward him.

Then the pit man threw a punch that lifted him off his feet and sent him reeling backward. He quit talking to himself and thinking about Lucie and focused solely on living through this fight and maybe winning it.

Fifteen minutes later his eyes were swollen so badly he could hardly see, his ribs felt as if they were on fire. But, miracle of miracles, the man from the pit looked almost as bad as he did. They were both staggering, sucking for air, reeling with pain and exhaustion. Sweat rolled in waves from the bull's body, plastered Jamie's shirt to his skin. He had to finish it now, while he was still on his feet.

They stumbled toward each other in the center of the crowd, dripping sweat and drops of blood. Then, blinking at the black dots dancing in front of his vision, Jamie summoned the last of his strength. When he saw his opportunity, he drew back and struck the pit man square on the jaw below his left ear. The man's eyes rolled upward. His hands dropped to his sides and he swayed, staggered backward a step, then crashed to the ground like a fallen oak.

Unable to believe it was over and he was still standing, Jamie tottered forward and blinked down at the unconscious man at his feet. If he ever encountered Mr. Haversham again, his pugilist instructor, he would buy the man a bottle of the best champagne available.

Henry Gustoffer appeared beside him, raised his hand in the air and declared him the winner fair and square. "Pay all bets on the mick," Gustoffer shouted. He shook his head and grinned at Jamie. "Wouldn't have believed it if I ain't seen it myself. Be here at first light tomorrow. Bring your own shovel."

A minute ago he hadn't thought he could remain on his feet another second. Now elation flooded his aching body and he felt as if he could do anything, could overcome any obstacle. Blinking through his swollen and blackened eyes, he pushed into the dissipating crowd, searching for the young lass from Ellis Island. Not for a moment did he doubt she was waiting, not the way his luck was running today, but it surprised him to find her standing over the pit man, her face stricken and horrified.

"Thank you," he said through his cracked lips, taking his coat and cap from her shaking hands. She was carrying a small reticule and a tin lunch pail. And somehow she managed to look crisp and tidy though the sun blazed with brutal force. "You've dressed your hair differently," he said, blurting the observation and following it immediately with an apology for uttering an improper remark.

When he had met her on the island, she had worn her glorious chestnut hair in a knot on her neck. Today she had wrapped it fashionably higher and wore her little straw boater stylishly straight. He thought he had never seen a more beautiful woman, or one with finer skin or longer lashes.

She didn't look up from the battered pit man. The way she wrung her hands and bit her lips displayed a tender nature that he found endearing—though he wished she would direct a bit more of her anxiety in his direction rather than toward his adversary. She kept murmuring, "Oh, dear, oh, dear," and tears hung on her dark lashes.

"I've thought about you constantly," he confessed in a rush. "You don't know how many times I've berated myself for not asking your name." She dashed at the tears in her eyes, then twisted her gloves together and continued to murmur over the man beginning to stir at their feet.

"It's Lucie Kolska," she said quickly. Her blush reminded him of an Irish rose. But he didn't understand the anguish constricting her expression.

"Miss Kolska, if you feel—" He had never been good at this sort of thing. And it had never been as important before. "That is, with your permission I would very much like to call on you. May I?"

The blush intensified in her cheeks and so did her agitation. She peeked at him through that incredible sweep of lashes. Leaning toward her he tried to read her expression, hoping for a hint of encouragement. Instead, moisture welled in her eyes and she looked on the edge of weeping. Her hands laced together and rose to her breast.

"You will have to obtain my brother's permission," she murmured, biting an adorable lip. To his astonishment she knelt beside the pit man and reached a trembling finger to the bruise blossoming on his jaw.

"Of course." A terrible suspicion formed in his mind. He blinked down at the man at his feet. No. Fate would not be that cruel. "Where may I find your brother, Miss Kolska?" he asked slowly, dreading the answer.

She glanced up at his bloodied knuckles, then gently placed her hand on the pit man's cheek. "Here," she whispered. "Oh, Mr. Kelly. How could you do this?"

Jamie stared at the battered man struggling to sit up. A string of swear words sped through his mind.

"I'm sorry, sir," she said stiffly. Moisture glistened in her eyes. "But I doubt Stefan will allow you to call. And…and I could not agree to it, either."

Stunned, he stared down at her. What had he done? Suddenly everything had changed. He knew he had not imagined the pleasure softening her eyes when he first saw her again. She had been as elated to see him as he had been to see her. Even now, behind her distress, behind her loyalty to her brother, he thought he recognized a glimmer of regret.

"Miss Kolska," Jamie said, wetting his cracked lip. "There's an explanation for this. Please believe me, I did not choose to fight your brother."

Stefan Kolska was rapidly regaining his senses and he would awaken to the sight of his adversary earnestly entreating his sister's forgiveness, lost in the depths of her dark eyes.

"I think you should leave, Mr. Kelly," she said in a low voice, looking away from him.

Watching Kolska from the corner of his eye, he buttoned his waistcoat and pushed aching arms into his coat sleeves. "If you'll just allow me a moment to explain." The accusation in her gaze devastated him when she lifted her head. "I must see you again, Miss Kolska."

Her cheeks burned fiery red and he stared at her, memorizing her face, wanting to caress that gentle heat. Now that he had found her again, he couldn't bring himself to leave her.

"If I was you, Kelly," Gustoffer said from behind him. "I'd do a stamp. I wouldn't be standing here when Kolska gets up."

The look in Lucie Kolska's eyes agreed, urged him to depart. "Tell her this was your idea, Gustoffer." She had to understand he had not created the situation. "For heaven's sake, man, explain what happened," he implored Gustoffer, stepping backward, watching her bend over Kolska. Gustoffer regarded him as if he were a madman.

Before the Broadway crowds blotted her from sight, she glanced up, sorrow and anger drawing her expression.

Jamie cupped his hands around his mouth and shouted to Gustoffer. "Tell her!" If she was the woman he wanted her to be, she would forgive him once she learned the truth of the matter. He had to depend on that as it was all he had.

The man who sold him a shovel peered at him across the high sales counter. "Good Lord, man. What happened to you?"

Jamie smiled, feeling his lip crack open again. "I found a job and a girl." Gingerly, he touched his jaw. "There's a problem or two, but this is one of the best days of my life!"

The salesman inspected his slitted eyes and bleeding lip, then laughed. "That must be some girl, mister. If she did that to you on the best day of your life, I'd advise you never to make her mad."

It hurt to laugh. It hurt to move. Smiling, Jamie hefted the shovel in his hand, hoping to hell he could live up to his promise to Gustoffer. Then he counted out a nickel and a twopenny piece, lifted his cap to the salesman and strolled outside as if he were a regular brownstoner, as if he didn't have a care in the world.

What he wanted most was a bath, a bed and a plate of good Irish crubbeens. Since he had money for none of it, he washed at a horse trough, bought a penny cup of ginger pop and walked toward the bowery in search of a hammock in a doss house, swinging the shovel like a walking stick.

Come morning he knew he would feel as if he had been run over by a furniture van, but right now he felt as fit as a gold coach. He had found her again and she was as beautiful as he remembered. By all the saints, his fortunes were on the rise.

FOR TWO WEEKS Stefan had worried and fretted that Lucie might not like Greta or that Greta might not like Lucie. He need not have suffered a moment of concern. On the Sunday afternoon he brought Greta to the Elizabeth Street tenement, the two young women took one look at each other, then fell on each other with hugs and kisses and tears of happiness. What Stefan had overlooked was their need for the companionship of someone their own age and sex. Each woman was lonely for family and for someone with whom to share the small secrets of life.

He sat at the head of the table, almost forgotten, nodding, beaming and listening with pride and pleasure as the two young women established a bond that would be life-long.

Lucie refilled their glasses with lemonade she had made for the occasion. "I can't thank you enough for the geranium," she said, looking at the much needed splash of color on the window sill. "I only hope it will grow. There's isn't much direct sun."

Greta's sweet smile lit the room. "I can't grow anything where I live, so I've claimed your windowsill for my garden. It's good to see the green."

"Between us, we'll coax it to grow. But if the geranium fails, perhaps you will make us a bouquet of artificial flowers. Stefan says you make beautiful silk flowers for hats and gowns."

A modest blush of pleasure warmed Greta's rounded cheeks. "I learned at the factory." She started to reach for the glass of lemonade, then changed her mind and dropped her hand to her lap beneath the table. "I asked Mr. Church if he would consider you as a replacement for Mrs. De-Vries—Mrs. DeVries has taken ill—but the position had already been filled."

It didn't surprise Lucie that Greta had tried to help her before they even met. One had only to spend five minutes in Greta Laskowski's company to know the young woman possessed a kind and generous heart. When Lucie apologized that saving her passage money had delayed Greta's marriage, Greta placed her hand on Lucie's cheek and gently hushed her. "I long to marry our Stefan, but Stefan and I have the rest of our lives to be together," she said. "It was important that you come to America."

As the afternoon progressed they happily discovered a dozen points of compatibility. More than anything else, each yearned for a husband and hearth and fat healthy children under foot. Both enjoyed sewing, wished there were more time for it, and each missed working with the soil.

"In good years the turnips were this big," Lucie said, making a circle with her hands and winking.

Greta laughed, the sound reminding Lucie of tiny chiming bells. "No, no, this big." Forgetting herself she raised her hands to make a circle and Lucie saw the angry red rash she had tried to conceal. When Greta noticed the direction of Lucie's gaze, a flush of embarrassment tinted her cheeks. "It's so ugly, isn't it?" she murmured, dropping her hands to her lap.

"What causes it?" Lucie asked, moving around the table to take Greta's hand in her own.

"Several women at the factory have similar rashes. Mrs. Klepke believes something in the paper and silk causes it. Miss Iverson believes it's not the materials but the dyes. Mrs. Ryan blames the dust that comes off the dyes." She raised her gaze to Lucie. "Mr. Church complains that too many of us are ill too often, but he says it has nothing to do with the factory."

"I'm not sure I believe that." The worried frown above Stefan's blackened eyes made him look as fierce as a cossack. He rubbed a hand over the bruise on his jaw. "You weren't sick before you started working at the factory."

"I don't understand it," Greta admitted, rubbing the rash on her hand and wrist. "But I can't think that paper or silk or dust could hurt anyone. That's bunkum." She laughed at Lucie's raised eyebrows. "Bunkum is American for nonsense."

"I make a cream that might soothe the roughness," Lucie said, rising. "It's my own recipe." She fetched a twist of newspaper from her shelf in the sleeping room, opened it, and gently rubbed the emollient over Greta's rash.

"It feels better already," Greta assured her. "And the scent is lovely." The two women smiled at each other.

Later they worked together to singe and pluck the two hens Lucie had purchased for the occasion. While they worked Lucie told Greta about her lessons at the nearby settlement house and Greta told her about the people she lived with. They discussed hairstyles and fashions and which markets were cheapest and how best to travel from here to there.

"You shouldn't have gone to this expense," Greta said when the hens were prepared for roasting.

"It isn't everyday that I meet Stefan's betrothed and discover a new sister."

"Dearest Lucie, I'm so glad I found you." Greta's eyes filled with tears. "With no family and . . ." She lowered her eyes. "Sometimes it's been so lonely." Distress filled her eyes. "I don't mean that Stefan has not been wonderful, I assure you he has. Stefan is the most wonderful man in the world! It's just that—"

"Sometimes we need a sister."

"Yes! That is it exactly." She took Lucie's hands. "Now I have you and everything is perfect!"

Lucie decided if she had chosen Stefan's bride herself, she could not have chosen better than Greta Laskowski. Greta's gentle temperament would soften Stefan's impatience. Her utter belief in him would sustain her brother when dreams seemed far away. Instinctively Lucie knew Greta would keep a good house and be a fine mother to Stefan's children.

Plus, she was lovely. Greta had hair as golden as sunshine and eyes of a deeper, purer blue than any Lucie had observed. Her mouth was small but full and constantly smiling. She was the same height as Lucie but fuller figured, which Lucie admired. If it hadn't been for the slight puffiness left from her recent illness, Greta Laskowski would have been breathtakingly beautiful. It was no wonder Stefan gazed at her with such pride and adoration.

Because roasting the hens transformed the kitchen into an oven, Stefan carried their chairs to the rooftop and they took their plates upstairs into the air to eat. The rooftop was crowded and noisy, but they had the pleasure of watching a brilliant sunset as the dying sun slipped behind the taller buildings to the west.

"You see, Stefan," Greta said softly, touching his hand, "we don't have to spend money to have beauty in our lives. A geranium on the windowsill and a lovely sunset—"

"You deserve more," Stefan said gruffly. "I promise, someday you will have a home of your own, and you won't make flowers for other people, you'll wear them yourself!"

"On silk gowns?" Greta teased.

"And satin, too! We'll dine out once a week and attend the theater. We'll look back on these days of waiting and doing without and we'll laugh."

"My dear Stefan, I don't care about silks or satins or dining out. If I can have you and Lucie and a beautiful sunset—and my geraniums—I'll be content." Concealing the action beneath the folds of her dark skirt, she reached for Stefan's hand and they sat in silence, enjoying the cooler air and the nearness of each other, watching the glow from the factories tint the night sky like a second sunset.

Smiling, Lucie sat quietly, watching her brother and her new sister, observing the small touches, the loving exchange of glances and murmured words. She sensed their joy in each other and thanked heaven for the miracle that had allowed them to find each other in this city teeming with strangers.

Although she dreaded returning to the heat inside the rooms below, she understood Stefan and Greta wished to be alone. After rising to her feet, she bent to kiss Greta's cheek. "You hardly ate a thing," she murmured near Greta's ear. "Are you certain you're feeling well?"

"The supper was wonderful, it's only that my appetite seems to rise and fall." A hint of apology rose in her large blue eyes. "Dearest Lucie, I can't bear the thought of offending you. I would have eaten every bite if—"

"No, no, don't apologize. I was merely concerned for your health." She winked at Stefan. "Our Stefan will be pleased by the leftovers in his lunch pail tomorrow." And she could hardly wait for the opportunity to see Jamie Kelly again even though she knew Stefan would explode in anger if he knew.

Greta started to rise, offering to help with the dishes. "I won't hear of it," Lucie insisted, pressing her back into her chair. "I enjoy straightening the kitchen, really I do." When both Stefan and Greta laughed, she smiled. "You'll come again next Sunday, won't you?"

"Thank you." Understanding and gratitude lay in Greta's smile for the small degree of privacy Lucie offered them, such privacy as could be found on the crowded rooftop.

Once below Lucie stripped off her cotton skirt and high-necked shirtwaist and hung them on the pegs between her work clothes and the ensemble she saved for best. With a sigh she unhooked her corset and folded it on the shelf, then tied a light wrapper around her waist.

Even half-naked she found the heat intolerable. Wetting the sash of the wrapper in the basin of wash water, she ran the wet strip over her neck and breasts. Everyone suffered. Yesterday the city had dispatched trucks to spray the tenement streets with carbolic acid, hoping to settle the dust and the spread of disease.

After washing the supper dishes and tidying the stove, she placed the leftover chicken in the salt box, extinguished the light and sat beside the window Stefan had forced open for her, hoping for an elusive breath of cool air. Already the leaves of Greta's geranium had begun to droop in the heat. How Stefan and Jamie Kelly and others at the excavation site endured heavy labor beneath the scorching sun mystified her. But they did. According to Stefan only one man at the site had fallen from heat prostration. To Stefan's regret and her relief, the man had not been Jamie Kelly.

She saw him every day when she delivered Stefan's lunch pail but she didn't dare speak to him, of course, knowing her brother despised him. By now Stefan had learned the true cause behind the fight last week; Henry Gustoffer had attempted to make peace between the two men by relating the entire story as soon as Stefan regained consciousness.

Lucie believed she detected a hint of admiration beneath Stefan's grudging admission that Jamie Kelly had displayed ingenuity and courage in accepting Gustoffer's challenge. But he had not relaxed his hatred toward the Irishman. Stefan's pride had suffered for being bested before his companions.

Lucie waved listlessly at a fly, then tucked a heavy strand of damp hair off her neck. It would be so nice to have someone of her own to sit with in the hot summer darkness. Unfortunately she had settled her heart on a man whom destiny did not seem inclined to grant her.

LUCIE'S HEARTBEAT accelerated as she approached the construction site to deliver Stefan's lunch pail. As it did every day, her mouth went dry when she sensed Jamie Kelly's intent gaze, and she experienced an agonizing conflict of loyalty. Stefan would rightly consider it betrayal if she uttered a single word to Jamie Kelly. But, oh, how she longed to.

Waiting for Stefan, holding the lunch pail tightly in her gloved hand, she guiltily anticipated the moment when she could safely look into the pit. Each day she wondered if Jamie would still be there. Each day her heart soared to discover him leaning on his shovel, watching her, and Lucie felt a secret pride grow that Jamie was proving himself and making his way.

When she was certain Stefan would not see, she darted a swift glance toward Jamie's wheelbarrow. As if he had been waiting, too, he stood looking up at her, his dark eyes moving intently over her trim figure, pausing mischievously at a glimpse of ankle revealed by the hot breeze.

Lucie's breath caught in her throat. Sweat oiled his naked upper body, and the mat of auburn hair tangling across his chest glistened. When he saw her, tension swelled the muscles on his shoulders and upper arms and his sunburned hands tightened on the handle of his shovel. He gazed at her as eagerly as a drowning man might gaze at sky and air.

Lucie wet her lips and swallowed, aware her pulse beat thundered in her ear, smothering the traffic noises behind her. Before Stefan pulled himself out of the pit and came toward her, she met Jamie's eyes and silently assured him that she understood about the fight, that she forgave him. Then Stefan was bending to the lunch pail, and she didn't dare glance at Jamie Kelly again.

But she felt him watching her, sensed when he moved away from the wheelbarrow to sit against the dirt wall of the pit where he could see her as he ate his noonday meal. If proof was needed that she responded to his half-naked body and the intensity of his stare, she saw it in the tremble of fingers as she removed Stefan's lunch items from the pail.

Afterward, as she returned to the tenement, stopping to call wherever she spotted a Help Wanted sign in a shop window, thoughts of Jamie Kelly whirled through her mind. She saw again the sunlight glowing in his hair, the line of his strong jaw, the way his tensing shoulders tapered to a lean waist. Blushing, she recalled the glistening sweat that drew her attention to his naked chest. And she thought about the strange heated flutter in her stomach when she met his gaze. She would have given anything to speak to him even for a few minutes.

She absently tucked a heat-damp tendril beneath the brim of her straw boater. Practical Lucie, she thought with a rueful smile. Was it possible she had been wrong all these years and actually she was a romantic at heart—thinking immodest thoughts and pining for a man she could not have? Stefan would never agree to Jamie Kelly, not in a hundred years.

Sighing, she tried to banish Jamie from her thoughts and concentrated on crossing the jammed street, holding her hem away from horse droppings, tobacco splats and the ever present summer dust. But Jamie Kelly would not be banished so easily. Already her practical mind counted the hours until noon tomorrow. And the romantic leaning that had gone unsuspected until now wished for a fresh blossom to pin to her breast. Something pretty and bright to make her desirable in one man's eyes.

"I DIDN'T THINK you'd still be here, boyo," Gustoffer said with a grin as he counted a dollar into Jamie's blistered palm. "The Broadway book's been losing a bundle betting each day is your last."

"And I've been making a bundle," Jamie said with a tired smile, "betting that it's not."

"Shrewd one, aren't you?" Gustoffer laughed. He winked. "Last four days I been betting on you myself, hoping to recoup my losses." He started to clap Jamie on the shoulder, saw the sun-scorched redness and changed his mind. After waiting for Jamie to hang up his shovel, Gustoffer followed him outside and locked the shed for the night. The rest of the men had gone. "Finding it a bit unfriendly, son?"

"A bit," Jamie said, easing his shirt over his sunburned skin. He slicked back sweat-damp hair and settled his cap at a jaunty angle.

"Give it time." They stood beside the pit for a moment, studying the deepening excavation, then walked toward lower Broadway, idly examining the lavish displays behind the windows they passed. "It ain't none of my business . . ."

"But?" Jamie asked, smiling.

"But there's trouble coming. Every horse on the site knows you're lollygagging after Kolska's sister. Except Kolska. And that ain't gonna last, boyo. If Kolska don't see soon what's right under his whiskers, some buck is going to tell him. You get my meaning?"

Jamie thrust his hands into his pockets and kicked a stone along the pavement. "I mean to court her."

Gustoffer made a sound of disgust. "Only a bastard mick could be so gol-damned stupid! You was lucky once, you ain't gonna be again. Next time Kolska is going to kill your arse.''

He suspected Gustoffer was right. "As long as you're in an advice-giving frame of mind, how do I persuade Kolska to allow me to call?''

"Son, you got to be the most stubborn set of coattails this mother's son ever seen." Gustoffer spit a stream of brown juice toward a passing carriage, then stopped to stare at Jamie. "Believe me, this ain't the girl for you.''

Jamie's chin firmed. "Yes, she is. I knew it the minute I saw her.''

"Well, you ain't gonna get her. Not while Stefan Kolska is alive. You ain't never going to be on borrowing terms with Stefan and that's regrettable, but that's a pure fact.''

"There was a time, Mr. Gustoffer, when no one thought I could get to America. And here I am. A time when it didn't look as if I could find work. But I did." He reached in his pocket. "I've got two dollars that says Kolska will eventually allow me to see his sister. I won't give up until it happens.''

"Two dollars?" Gustoffer's eyebrows soared. "How much have you been betting on yourself with the books?''

"Are you willing to wager two dollars?''

"Hell no, son. It don't take no wall to fall on Henry T. Gustoffer. I lost enough money betting against you, I ain't gonna lose no more." He grinned, waved, then turned into a side street.

Jamie continued along Broadway for another block, then cut toward his new lodging house. It wasn't fancy, he hadn't won that much money. For three dollars a week he received breakfast and a cold supper, and shared a room with only one other man who worked the night shift at the Chatham Street El station. That's where Jamie slept; he lived for the moments he saw Lucie.

The next day when he realized he was listening for the noon whistle and waiting for his first glimpse of her, he remembered what Gustoffer had said about everyone on the site being aware of the long silent looks he exchanged with Lucie Kolska. He warned himself to be more discreet, but when he saw her pert straw hat appear over the rim of the pit, his mouth dried and his spirits soared. Just the sight of her was balm to his aching back and blistered hands. She refreshed him in a way nothing else could.

At some point before she departed each day, she managed to send him a secret smile and today was no different. He stared up at her and read volumes into that single wonderful smile. He believed she was telling him that he was never further from her thoughts than she was from his. Yesterday her smile had spoken of pride in his staying power and he had returned to his shovel with renewed vigor. The day before her smile had turned tender with sympathy for his raw sun-burn. Always her smile gave him hope for the future. He could not see that lovely sweet smile and doubt that someday they would be together.

Today after Lucie departed and Gustoffer shouted them back to the shovels, he crossed the pit and forced a place for himself beside Stefan Kolska. Matching the heavier man scoop for shovel scoop, he worked in silence for several minutes, rehearsing his approach. It was pointless to request permission to call on Lucie until they settled the bad blood between them.

Stopping work, Jamie straightened and looked at Kolska. "Gustoffer made the choice, Kolska. I didn't."

Stefan dug his shovel into the dirt with savage force, refusing to acknowledge he was being addressed.

"It was luck and desperation, that's all. In any other circumstance, you would have won." He was flattered that Kolska did not seem to believe him, but he knew it was the truth. "It's over. There's no reason you and I can't be friends."

Finally Kolska straightened and glared at him. His dark eyes glittered with loathing. Beads of sweat clung to his heavy mustache and eyebrows. "Ordinarily I'm not a fighting man, Kelly, but anytime you want a rematch, you just say the word. I'm ready."

Jamie stared at him, seeing Lucie in Stefan's thin nose and beautiful dark eyes. "I have no quarrel with you. No wish to fight again."

The muscles in Kolska's jaw knotted. His knuckles turned white on the shovel's handle. "Get out of my sight, Kelly, before I take you on right now and cost both of us our jobs."

Someone nearby laughed and Jamie swore he heard Lucie's name mentioned. He didn't have much time to put things right. As it seemed he would end in another fist fight no matter what, he decided to force the issue. And he had to do it soon.

Chapter Three

By the end of June, the New York *Morning Journal* announced the heat wave had diminished but it didn't seem so to Lucie.

Fatigued by the heat, her feet sore from walking, she returned from a day of seeking work and paused in the courtyard to wet her hands and face at the rusty pump.

"Any luck today?" Maria Brovnic asked as she bent over the pump to fill a cooking pot, but only a dribble emerged.

Unpinning her hat, Lucie waved it before her flushed face. She looked toward the tenement door, thinking how hot it would be inside. "I'm sure something will turn up tomorrow," she said. Because Maria did not speak English, they spoke in a mixture of Polish and Russian. "Is your husband feeling better?"

Shortly before Lucie's arrival Woicheck Brovnic had suffered a serious accident. The oyster wagon he drove collided with a heavy chandler's van and overturned. The iron wheels of the chandler's van had crushed Woicheck Brovnic's hands. Now he was unable to find work, and worse, he had given up trying.

Maria balanced the cook pot on her hip and pushed back the kerchief covering her dark hair. "I don't know what to do," she said in a low voice, frowning at the row of reeking latrines everyone called "school sinks." After drawing a breath, she shouted at her two oldest children to play farther away from the stench. "If it wasn't for them, I'd go home." Bitterness hardened her voice. "There's nothing for us here."

"Oh, Mrs. Brovnic!" Lucie turned to her in distress. "You've suffered a terrible misfortune, but surely you remember what it was like at home?"

"I remember we took care of each other," Maria said, closing her eyes. "I remember shade at the edge of the plots."

Lucie took her hand and peered into her eyes. "Do you remember what it was like to bend over all day in the fields? Do you remember when the rains didn't come and the harvest burned in the sun? Do you remember the cossacks?" She shuddered.

"Miss Kolska, I know you're trying to offer encouragement, but there is none. Soon the money will run out. Then what difference does it make if my children starve here or at home?"

"Here there is a chance for something better! At home nothing changes except each year life gets harder."

Maria gazed at the twilight sky. "We were saving to bring Woicheck's brother and his wife to America." She drew a breath. "We could use the money ourselves. We could go home."

"But you have work, Mrs. Brovnic. And money to carry you through this difficult time. For the sake of your children, I beg you not to give up. In time Mr. Brovnic will—"

"Time has healed his hands, but time cannot heal the sickness in his soul. Only home can do that."

Lucie stared at her. The country they had fled was dismal, oppressive, and life there was desperately hard. But it was home. Before she could shake it off, a wave of intense homesickness overwhelmed her and she understood Maria Brovnic.

Maria occupied Lucie's mind while she prepared supper. The Brovnics would leave as others had left. A steady flux and flow of families moved in and out of the tenements. Some moved north to better addresses and occasionally, if good fortune prevailed, to a home outside the city. Others moved from one room on Elizabeth Street to two rooms on Ludlow or Baxter or Mulberry streets, hoping the change would improve their luck. Others, defeated, took whatever money they managed to save and fled home to conditions as dismal as they found in America but where misfortune was shared by family and familiar faces.

When Stefan came in the door, Lucie shook her head quickly before he hung his hat and coat on the nail. "Not today, but surely I'll find work tomorrow." She sounded more cheerful and optimistic than she felt.

He patted her arm and gave her his day's pay to place beneath the loose board in the sleeping room. "Water-bread again?" he asked when she placed their bowls on the table and sat across from him.

"I thought you liked water-bread."

"I do, but not so often." When he saw her stricken expression, he apologized. "I'm sorry, Lucie. I know you're saving money, but can't we afford a bit of meat on occasion?"

"If we cut a few corners, I can put aside a little for you and Greta." By shopping carefully and by serving water-bread twice a week she had stopped the steady drainage of their coins and had managed to add a few pennies.

He drew a breath. "Dear Lucie, it is not your responsibility to provide my marriage money."

But that was her goal. She was determined to repay the debt she owed him. It was a matter of personal honor.

Raising a hand, he halted her protest. "Greta is able to save a little, and as soon as you find work, so will I." He smiled at her. "If you don't spend all your earnings on ribbons and silks, we'll be rich."

She laughed as he wanted her to, but nothing he said could change her mind.

"I have a surprise for you. Sunday there is a free band concert in Battery Park. If you and Greta promise to stop talking to each other long enough to pay some attention to me, I could be persuaded to take you to the concert," he said with twinkling eyes, watching as Lucie clapped her hands. "And if you could be persuaded to relinquish a dime for flavored ice."

"Flavored ice! And a concert! Oh, Stefan, could we?"

"We could." Smiling, he carried their bowls to the wash tub on top of the stove. "This doesn't make sense to me but Greta said it would to you. She said to tell you she's wearing the striped shirtwaist with the mutton sleeves. She thinks the cotton stripe and solid tie would be nice for you." He frowned. "Or was it the striped waist and the cotton puffs?" When Lucie laughed, he shrugged. "Anyway, she's bringing a paper geranium for your hat. I was especially instructed to tell you."

"Every time I see Greta, I love her more, Stefan."

"Yes," he said softly.

"But you must tell her to stop bringing me geraniums." The latest specimen wilted over the window sill, dying as the others had done. "Flowers don't like it here." The words hung between them for a long moment, evoking thoughts of home. Home.

Worrying about the Brovnics had opened a flood of memories that confused Lucie with their intensity and selectivity. She didn't remember the hardships that had brought her to America. She remembered the closeness of the villagers, the harvest fairs, the sweet smell of the fields on a summer evening. She remembered her mother telling stories beside the fire, the shape of her father's sunburned hands. Thoughts of her friend, Magda, rose in her mind and many memories of snowy nights and whispered laughter, shared secrets, the warmth of a cottage made snug for winter.

Tears sprang to her eyes and she swallowed hard. She had made her decision; there was no turning back. Memories of home ate at the foundation of her strength and resolve. She told herself she could not afford such weakness or she was lost.

Lucie bit her lip and smoothed her hands over her apron and rose on tiptoe to blink at the shelf over the stove. "Where did I put my scissors? If we're going to attend a concert, we must trim your whiskers." She didn't dare permit a single discouraging thought.

"Do hurry, Lucie," Greta called into the sleeping room, her voice sounding eager with excitement. "Are you certain we have enough money for a horse car? It would be a long walk, but—"

Lucie laughed. "Much too long a walk. Yes, we have money for the horse car, and yes, I'm hurrying." Ducking back behind the curtain she raised a sliver of mirror and inspected the red paper geranium pinned to her hat. "I hope it doesn't rain and spoil my flower."

"Everyone in the city is praying it will rain," Stefan called.

"Don't tease her, Stefan. If it rains, I'll make you another flower." Greta drew on a pair of mended summer gloves, covering the persistent rash. "Dear Lucie, it isn't too late to change your mind about Mr. Pachecko. We could stop by the bend and invite him to join us."

"Pachecko asked again for permission to call on you," Stefan said as Lucie emerged from the sleeping room. "I can't understand your objection. He has a steady butcher's job at Fulton's Market, has two rooms all to himself. Which is almost unheard of! He would make a good match for you."

"Thank you, but I'm not interested," Lucie said, aware that Greta watched her with a puzzled expression. "My, don't we look grand," she enthused, changing the subject. "Stefan you look so handsome in your best waistcoat and bowler. And, Greta, the blue stripe matches your eyes."

"I wish my waist was as slim and narrow as yours," Greta said admiringly. "But if I lace another inch I won't be able to breathe." She smoothed her gloves over the striped shirtwaist and her golden eyebrows met as she frowned. "I don't understand why I've gained weight, I don't have much appetite at all."

It puzzled all of them. In Lucie's opinion, Greta didn't eat enough to keep a kitten alive. Sometimes the very sight of food made her feel ill. Then, in a startling about-face, she would experience a brief period of ravening hunger during which she ate as if she were starving. These episodes did not last long and were followed by spells of nausea; certainly they were not enough to account for a weight gain.

And in fact the gain was not substantial, but it was becoming noticeable. Greta's porcelain cheeks were a little fuller, her shoulders more rounded, her bosom more prominent.

Stefan slipped his arm around her waist and gave her a quick embrace. "I like a woman with meat on her bones," he said with a smile that didn't quite erase the worry that clouded his eyes whenever he looked at her. "Greta—"

But Greta laughed and straightened her hat, turning aside any discussion of health problems as she always did. "So do I. As long as I don't gain any more."

Laughing and teasing they left the rooms, descended the dark staircase and walked out into the noon shadows covering the courtyard square. They had progressed only a few steps when Lucie stopped abruptly and gasped, her hands flying to her mouth.

Greta turned with concern. "Lucie, what is it?"

But she could not answer, her mouth had dried to dust and she trembled.

Jamie Kelly had emerged from the opening leading between the two buildings to Elizabeth Street. One glance and Lucie knew why he had come. He wore his best clothes, the heavy clothing he had worn the day she met him at Ellis Island. The coat had been meticulously brushed until the nap stood up just so. His collar, cuffs and shirtfront were dazzlingly white and stiffly starched, his dark tie perfectly knotted. He had never looked more handsome. When he saw them he removed his cap, and Lucie noticed his hair was parted down the middle and brushed to a high auburn sheen. He carried a bouquet of July roses in his gloved hand. For an instant their eyes met and held, and Lucie saw her own longing reflected in his gaze.

Immediately Stefan stiffened and his shoulders squared with anger.

"Please, Stefan," Lucie whispered, placing her fingertips on his sleeve. "Please agree for my sake."

A puzzled expression drew Stefan's brows together then a dawning look of comprehension. "You know him?" he demanded. Rage contorted Stefan's face as he swung toward Jamie. "You bastard mick! How do you know my sister?"

Lucie drew a sharp breath, pride mixing with fear, as Jamie strode toward Stefan wearing a look of determination. Stefan shook off her hand and stepped forward, then she felt Greta's arm slip around her waist.

"I would have a word with you, Mr. Kolska."

"You have nothing to say to me, Kelly."

"You and I stepped off to a bad start and I apologize for that. There are no hard feelings on my side. I hope there are none on yours." Looking over Stefan's shoulder, he gave Lucie a quick look. "Mr. Kolska, I respectfully request permission to call upon your sister."

Stefan followed Jamie's glance, read the silent plea in Lucie's eyes. Then he thrust his face inches from Jamie's and spoke through teeth as tightly clenched as his fists. "Never," he growled, the word coming from deep in his throat. "I would rather put my sister on a ship returning to Poland!"

Lucie gasped and turned her face into Greta's shoulder. Nose to nose, the two men stared into each other's eyes.

"I care for your sister, and I believe she cares for me. If you ask her, I believe she will—"

Stefan's hand shot forward and he slapped the roses from Jamie's hand. "I am the head of this family," he roared. "I will decide who calls on my sister and who does not! And she can do a damned sight better than some arrogant Irish son of a—"

"Stefan!" Greta's anxious voice reminded him that ladies were present.

"Get out!" Stefan said between his teeth. With an obvious exercise of willpower, he lowered his arms to his sides but his hands remained clenched in fists.

"I shall return, Mr. Kolska," Jamie promised, speaking firmly. "I will continue to return until I receive your permission." Without glancing at the roses scattered in the dry gray dust, he inclined his head to Lucie and Greta holding Lucie's stricken gaze, then he walked out of the courtyard and turned into the opening leading to Elizabeth Street.

"Oh, Stefan," Lucie whispered, blinking at the roses. Tears glistened in her eyes. "I beg you to reconsider."

"Never!" His scowl swung to her. "No," he said sharply when she would have bent to retrieve the roses. "How do you know Jamie Kelly?" Stepping forward he deliberately ground one of the blossoms under the heel of his boot.

Slowly, Lucie raised her head. "I met Mr. Kelly at Ellis Island. Petor asked him to watch over me while he looked for you. He was kind to me, Stefan." Angry that she was not permitted to have the roses, she straightened her shoulders and matched his dark scowl. "Please, Stefan, I would like permission to see him."

"I won't hear of it! We shall speak no more of this."

Astonished by a rebelliousness she had not suspected she possessed, Lucie faced him with flaming cheeks and trembling hands. "I thought you cared for me, Stefan. Don't you love me enough to care for my happiness?"

It was his turn to be astonished. "Of course I care about you. I love you enough to spare you a painful mistake."

Deeply distressed, Greta looked anxiously from one hurt and angry face to the other. Then she cast a quick glance toward the people listening in the courtyard and those gazing with interest from the sagging fire escapes above.

Stepping between Stefan and Lucie, she linked arms with each and pressed their arms to her side. "Please don't quarrel," she begged, her beautiful eyes pleading with them to make peace. "We have a lovely outing planned. Please, let's not spoil it."

For the first time since Lucie's arrival, Stefan glared at Greta. "This has to be finished."

Gently, Greta touched his cheek. "An angry word cannot be recalled. Perhaps the subject would benefit by resting a little?"

Although Lucie conceded the wisdom of Greta's advice, she too wished an immediate resolution. But she did not wish to continue the confrontation before the interested eyes and listening ears of their neighbors. Indecision clouded her expression and the sharpness faded from her eyes. But high color burned on her cheeks and she remained tight-lipped, defiant.

"We'll discuss this later," Stefan snapped.

Only the thought of Jamie Kelly gave her the courage not to quail before Stefan's angry glare. "Indeed we shall!"

The pressure Greta exerted on their arms propelled them forward toward Elizabeth Street. "I haven't had flavored ice since last summer," she said brightly, smiling up at Stefan. "Won't it be lovely?" To Lucie she added enthusiastically, "The cherry flavor is my favorite, though blueberry is also nice."

If it hadn't been for Greta's determined conversation, not a word would have been uttered during the stifling ride in the horse car. Stefan clasped the ceiling strap and stared fixedly out the window above their hats. Lucie kept her gaze trained steadfastly on the dirty tobacco-stained straw at their feet.

Before they left the horse car to enter Battery Park, Lucie lifted an irritated frown to Greta. "Why are you nudging me?" she asked. Immediately she apologized for her tone. "I'm sorry, Greta. It's crowded, and I'm hot and out of sorts." And she kept thinking of Jamie, of how achingly handsome he had looked. And the courage he had displayed in seeking out Stefan. And she thought sadly of the roses scattered and wilting in the courtyard dust. Tears rose in her eyes and she blinked them back with difficulty.

"Was I nudging you?" Greta inquired with exaggerated innocence. She met Lucie's gaze with a meaningful look, suggesting a message that could not be stated aloud. When Lucie raised her eyebrows, too distracted to comprehend, Greta darted a glance at Stefan, then lifted her glove to straighten her hat. Still watching Lucie, she tilted the brim in a definite nod toward the end of the car.

Puzzled, Lucie turned toward the back windows. Immediately her heart leaped against her rib cage. Jamie Kelly was one of the men riding outside, hanging on to the bumper handles. For an instant his twinkling gaze met hers, then the crowd shifted inside the car and he was lost from view. Feeling the sudden heat in her cheeks and tremor in her fingertips, Lucie shot a glance of gratitude toward Greta. Truly Greta was her sister.

Greta winked. "Are we almost there? It's so dreadfully hot in here. Though better than walking," she added quickly. Walking made her legs ache.

When they alighted from the horse car, Greta took one of Stefan's arms and Lucie accepted the other. It was all she could do not to peer at the crowd around them in hope of catching a glimpse of Jamie. Guilt intensified the sun's warmth on her cheeks. It was wrong to defy Stefan but heaven help her, she could not prevent herself from searching for Jamie Kelly. A pang of disappointment drove the color from her face when she did not find him. Perhaps he had remained with the horse car as it swung around and started back uptown.

Stefan located a shaded bench within sight of the band-stand, draped in red, white and blue bunting, then he departed with a minimum of words to purchase flavored ices from the pushcart vendors working the crowds strolling along the boulevard. When he had gone Greta turned on the bench to take Lucie's hand.

"It's so romantic! No wonder you've refused our efforts to find you a suitor. But you didn't say a word. My dearest sister, you must tell me everything!"

"Oh, Greta," she whispered, turning her eyes to watch the bright sails cutting through the harbor waters. "I've longed to tell you." An inner glow lit her eyes as she confided how she had met Jamie Kelly. She confessed their secret smiles and yearning glances when she delivered Stefan's lunch pail to the construction site. "He makes me feel, I can't explain it." A frown appeared on her face. "All fluttery and warm inside." Now a blush fired her cheeks. "Am I foolish to feel so strongly about someone I know so little?"

Greta regarded her with a soft expression. "But you know quite a lot about your Jamie Kelly. You know he's determined, and a bit stubborn." She smiled. "He certainly showed courage to fight our Stefan. He's a hard worker. And a man of honor. And he's very handsome." Taking Lucie's hand in hers, she smiled again and murmured, "Besides, who can resist when love's elbow strikes?" When she saw Stefan returning, Greta pressed Lucie's fingers and leaned to her ear. "I'll do what I can to help."

"Thank you," Lucie said gratefully. "If Stefan will listen to anyone, it will be you." Then she experienced the amazement of flavored ice, her exclamations bringing smiles to Greta and Stefan's lips.

Stefan winked at Greta, his good humor restored. "Quick, eat yours before Lucie snatches it from your hand."

But shaved ice on a hot July day was to be savored and they nibbled slowly, observing the parade of summer fashion strolling along the boulevard while the city band tuned their instruments and arranged their music. Men in white muslin and jaunty boaters spread checkered cloths over the grass for ladies wearing straw hats, gaily colored ribbons and shirtwaists. The scent of peanuts and hot popcorn drifted on the breeze floating from the harbor. Young mothers called to darting children, and blushing young men performed feats of derring-do on their bicycles before rosy cheeked young ladies who pretended not to see.

The holiday atmosphere was enhanced by the band's first selection, an enthusiastic rendition of "Ta-ra-ra-boom-de-ay," which brought cheers from those seated on the grass beneath the trees and smiles to every face.

It was during the performance of a new song called "Hello Ma Baby" that Lucie spotted Jamie Kelly leaning against a tree. He was watching her as if there were no one in the leafy park but Lucie Kolska, no one inhabiting his world but her. His countenance expressed a longing that stopped her heart in her breast. He looked at her with naked yearning as if his survival depended upon a smile from her lips.

For one heartaching moment their eyes met and held and Lucie knew her yearning was as painfully exposed as his. How glorious the day would have been if she could have sat next to him as Greta sat next to Stefan. If she could know the joy of being near him, of hearing his melodious voice whisper in her ear.

Looking at him, meeting his dark eyes in secret communion, the day no longer seemed too hot. It was perfect. A splendid summer afternoon adrift with bright sails on the water and music in the air. Knowing her eyes sparkled with guilty pleasure, Lucie self-consciously turned to stare at the bandstand. And her heart soared when she turned again to peek at him and discovered he had not looked away from her. Not another man in Battery Park could hold a candle to him, he was that handsome. And joy of joys, it was she who had captivated his interest. The knowledge made her dizzy with happiness.

JAMIE WATCHED THE COLOR rise in Lucie's cheeks and would have given a day's pay to know what she was thinking. She was so lovely today he could not look away from her. The striped shirtwaist with the high starched collar and pretty dark bow was not expensive but it fit her well, molding a figure that caused his stomach to tighten.

Her silky mass of chestnut hair was wrapped high beneath her straw hat; her lips were cherry red from the flavored ice. He knew his stare made her nervous, but he could not turn his gaze away. He longed to hold her in his arms and gently pull the pins from her glorious hair and feel its glossy weight in his hands.

Too soon the concert ended. As the music faded he watched with regret as Stefan, Lucie and the beautiful blond lass rose to their feet. The temptation to follow, to prolong his nearness to her, was great. But he understood he had pushed his luck as it was. Under no circumstances did he wish to provoke Stefan Kolska into another fight. To do so would injure his cause.

After Jamie watched them board a horse car, he caught the next. Exiting at the Bowery, the poor man's Broadway, he strolled along the wide street dodging the cinders that floated down from the elevated trains whizzing past on the tracks above.

Because today was a special occasion, his first approach to Kolska, Jamie treated himself to an expensive fifteen cent glass of wine in an oyster bar. And because wine elicited the philosopher within each man, and because today he felt the loneliness of being in a strange country, a strange city, and not having anyone with whom to share the experience, his thoughts turned to the mysterious force that drew one man to one woman.

His life would be much simpler if he could only put Lucie Kolska out of his mind. There were thousands of good

Irish colleens in New York City; surely there was one among them with whom he could be compatible.

But would the mere sight of her send his spirits soaring? Would she have a smile that touched a man's soul? Would she possess that particular look of determination? That faintly stubborn set of the chin? Would laughter sit waiting on her lips? Would he want her as he had wanted no other woman?

Shrugging, Jamie wished he were standing in Patrick's pub in Dublin with Johnny Ryan playing melancholy love ballads on his mouth harp. It was that kind of bittersweet day.

WHEN STEFAN RETURNED from seeing Greta home, Lucie stood and faced him across the kitchen table. "If you truly care for me, Stefan, then I beg you to permit me to see Mr. Kelly."

"I'm sorry, Lucie. No." He hung his hat and coat on the nails, then poured two cups of beer from the growler he had purchased on his way home.

Lucie did not touch hers. "I've tried to think of a tactful way to state this, but I can think of none." She drew a breath and clasped her shaking hands behind her back. "I think you're letting injured pride stand in the way of my happiness."

Stefan sat heavily at the table and stared up at her. "I'm sorry you think that," he said stiffly. "The truth is you can do better than an Irishman, especially that particular Irishman."

At home this quarrel would have been unthinkable and they both knew it. Stefan's refusal would have ended the matter. But, they were not at home.

Lucie inhaled slowly, then said very quietly, "Stefan, how would you feel if someone refused you permission to court Greta?"

"It's not the same thing."

"Isn't it? You promised you would not force me into a match unless I agreed. I assumed you meant I would have freedom of choice."

Frowning, he spread his hands. "I've given you freedom of choice. Haven't I respected your wishes regarding Mr. Pachecko?"

Lucie shook her head and grasped the top rung of the chair. "That is freedom of refusal, not freedom of choice. It's not the same." She bit her lip and her eyes pleaded with him. "All I ask is the right to choose as you have chosen. I ask you to be fair."

Stefan's fist struck the table. "It is not how things are done. And for good reason. You ask to make your own choice, then prove a lack of wisdom in these matters by choosing the Irishman." Lifting his hands, he delivered an exaggerated shrug. "Listen to what you are saying, Lucie. Can you hear the lack of logic?"

"I'm sorry if it seems so to you. It doesn't to me."

She could see his effort to restrain his temper and remain patient with her. "Women do not choose suitors or husbands. It's not how things are done," he repeated stubbornly.

"Have we brought our limitations with us, then?" she asked. "Have we changed nothing but our geography?"

"Lucie—"

"No, please. Let me finish, Stefan." The confrontation was painful because it went against her instincts, against habit and background. To help, she summoned Jamie's face in her memory and held it before her. "I wish I could welcome Mr. Pachecko or the others you have suggested. But I can't. I wish I did not care for Mr. Kelly. But I do." She lifted a hand before he exploded. "I don't want to end on the shelf, but rather that than agree to a loveless match. Freedom for you, Stefan, is the freedom of opportunity. The freedom to prosper and better yourself if you can. Freedom for me is the freedom to chart my own life. Which, for a woman, means choosing her own husband. That is what I seek in America. That is the freedom I believe you promised me."

"Then I owe you an apology," he said, staring at her. "I never promised to stand aside and permit you to throw yourself away on a bastard mick. I regret whatever I said that gave you that impression. As long as you are my responsibility, I won't agree to a match that can only cause you unhappiness."

"I'm not seeking your consent to wed, Stefan. All I ask is permission to walk out with Mr. Kelly. If we were truly speaking of a match, perhaps I could understand your objection." It was a politic concession, one she secretly disavowed. "But we're not speaking of a match." Her knuckles turned pale on the chair rung. "In any case," she added stubbornly, lifting her chin, "I should be the judge of my happiness or unhappiness."

He lowered his head and thrust his hand through his hair and then tugged violently on his mustache. "This is how it begins. The assimilation process we hear so much about. Is this what they teach you at the settlement house? To defy the head of your household? To chase after men of your own choosing?"

"They teach us history, counsel us on customs and—"

"I don't want you going there anymore. Those people are filling your head with strange new ideas, with dangerous nonsense."

"Stefan—"

"No!" he roared up at her. "I'll have no more discussion! You will not see the Irishman and that is final!"

For a moment she stood as still as stone, gazing into his blazing eyes. Then her head dropped. Her acquiescence was the result of generations of cultural conditioning. But her heart had not accepted the lesson. Her heart did not surrender.

Turning away from him, she moved on unsteady legs to the stove. "I'm taking this bread downstairs to Maria

Brovnic," she murmured, not looking at him. "I'll return soon."

He didn't respond, did not look up from his beer until she reached the door. "I'm doing what I think is best for you."

"I know," she whispered, her hand on the latch. "But you're wrong, Stefan."

"You're not to come to the construction site again. I'll take my lunch pail with me in the morning."

So she was to be denied even the sight of Jamie Kelly. Closing the door behind her, Lucie stepped into the tenement hall and leaned against the decaying wall, closing her eyes and touching shaking fingertips to her forehead.

She did not want to quarrel with Stefan or cause any distress between them. She would have given anything to have it otherwise. But she could not help being drawn to Jamie Kelly. She hadn't chosen the situation; it had simply happened. Could she help it that she looked at him and her heart quickened? Could she halt the tide of thoughts that caused her to imagine his fingertips on her cheek? His lips brushing hers? Helplessly, she shook her head. "Oh, Jamie," she whispered to the dark hallway.

The attraction between herself and Jamie Kelly must end. And it would, of course. She had no choice. But oh how it hurt. More than she had expected.

She did not descend the staircase to call on the Brovnics until she had forced the ache into a manageable corner of her mind, then she lifted her skirts above the filth littering the steps and continued downstairs.

The smile she forced to her lips before she rapped on Maria Brovnic's door felt as wooden and artificial as it was. "I brought you some bread," she explained when Maria peeked through a crack in the door.

"I thought you might be the rent collector," Maria said. She opened the door. "Come inside."

The windowless room was stiflingly hot and smelled of the smoke rising from a kerosene lamp on a small table. Other odors assailed Lucie's nostrils. The smells of the chamber pot, stale beer, cooked cabbage and old clothing. The smell of sickness and despair.

"Where are the children?" she inquired.

"On the rooftop. Mrs. Blassing is keeping an eye on them. I thought the air might do Jon good." Maria waved toward one of two chairs. "Would you like a glass of water?"

To refuse would have been an insult. "Thank you."

"Don't drink the milk," said a voice from the shadows near the floor.

Lucie jumped. She had forgotten Mr. Brovnic. "Good evening, Mr. Brovnic. How are you feeling?"

"Don't drink the milk at Mosha's market," he said again, not looking at her. He lay on a floor mattress, as still as death, his twisted hands folded on top of a light blanket. He stared at the ceiling. "Mosha improves his profit by cutting his milk with chalk and water."

Such adulterations were common. Last week Lucie had paid an exorbitant price for a lump of butter only to discover it had been laced with mashed potatoes to increase the bulk. And it wasn't unusual to discover ground dried peas mixed with coffee for the same purpose.

"We're going home," Maria said quietly. A dreamy light entered her eyes. "Home."

Lucie wasn't sure what to say. "If that's what you want, then I'm glad for you." She glanced toward Woicheck Brovnic lying motionless in the shadows. "When will you leave?"

"At the end of the week. Think of it—we're going home!" She lifted glowing eyes to Lucie. "I'm glad you came tonight. I would have come to you if you hadn't. You should apply for my laundry job." When Lucie caught a quick breath, Maria smiled. "I've already told Mrs. Greene about you." She waved a hand. "At least I tried. My English is not so good. But Mrs. Greene said you could come by."

"Oh, Maria! How can I thank you?"

"I don't promise you will be hired, but I hope you will be. You must go tomorrow and speak to the butler, Mr. Grist." Leaning forward, she gave Lucie directions to the Roper mansion on Madison Avenue.

"I don't know what to say. Thank you!" At the door the two women embraced. "I wish you a safe journey and no regrets."

"Miss Kolska?" A timid look came into Maria Brovnic's eyes. "After you and your brother and Miss Laskowski left this afternoon, I found this in the courtyard." Reaching into her apron pocket she carefully removed a drooping rose. "I thought you might like to have it."

Too moved to speak, Lucie cupped the blossom in her palms and blinked down at it. "Thank you," she whispered finally.

"He is very handsome, your Irishman," Maria said softly. "I hope your brother reconsiders." Maria looked over her shoulder at the man lying in the floor shadows. "Sometimes love is all we have. Without it a home is just a place to sleep." She touched Lucie's warm cheek. "I wish you had known Woicheck before the accident." Memory made her eyes glisten. "People said they could hear his laugh for a mile." She passed a hand over her eyes. "He will be as he used to be once as we get home."

"I hope so." Lucie pressed her cheek to Maria's and looked into the shadows over Maria's shoulder. She did not think Woicheck Brovnic would ever again be as he had been.

Outside Maria's door she raised the rose to her cheek and stroked the petals across her skin, imagining Jamie's fingertips in their place. Then she inhaled the delicate sweet scent, wondering if he had inhaled the fragrance of this very blossom. "Please," she whispered, the word a formless plea.

Chapter Four

The Bowery Street station was decorated with ornamental iron painted a delicate green. Between five and seven in the morning, the hours of reduced fares, the station was jammed with those who hurried north to jobs that would have been unmanageable without the speed and convenience of the elevated trains.

Swept along by the crush Lucie was carried inside the station where she paid for her ticket, then deposited it in the chop box and moved with the flow to the platform outside. A whistle screamed as the train appeared, hissing and breathing hot cinders like a long brown dragon. Lucie would have fled in terror except the crowd forced her forward and inside. Before she could catch her breath the train swept out of the station, the lurch toppling her into an upholstered seat.

She sat rigidly, clasping her reticule in both gloved hands, her eyes wide, her heart pounding wildly. When she dared, she glanced out the windows. Second story windows flashed past on both sides. Someone in the station had mentioned the trains averaged twelve miles per hour, a speed so dizzying Lucie forced the frightening thought out of her mind. Instead she focused on the conductor's brass-and-blue flannel uniform, waiting for Forty-second Street, terrified she might not hear him call out.

When the shout came, she popped to her feet and ran to solid ground. Once her heart resumed a normal cadence, she stared up at the tracks and felt a burst of elated pride. Having triumphed over the dragon, how could she fail at the Roper mansion? Surely the laundry job was as good as hers.

But her confidence dimmed when she located and stood in front of Theodore Roper's Madison Avenue mansion. Three stories of brick and iron work towered above and sprawled to both sides. It was a palace. While Lucie stood gaping, a sound behind her caused her to turn toward the street. Immediately, she gasped and flattened herself against the iron gate.

A horseless box, belching smoke and steam, rolled to the curbside and stopped in front of her. After a moment of terrified astonishment, Lucie caught hold of herself enough to guess this was one of the automobiles she had read and heard about. But she had never expected to actually see one. Wide-eyed, she examined the polished black lacquer and shiny brass fittings as the coachman stepped outside, pushed up a pair of smoked goggles, then helped a princess descend to the pavement.

The princess paused and fixed Lucie with a cool look until, flustered, Lucie mumbled an apology and stepped aside so the princess could pass through the gate. Lucie stared after her, awed by the richness of dress and coiffure before she turned back to the amazing contraption at the curb.

"What's your business here, miss?" The coachman eyed her up and down. His expression told her plainly that she did not belong on this street standing before this palace.

"I've come to see about work," she whispered, clasping and unclasping her reticule. "I'm expected."

The coachman jerked his head in the direction she had come, indicating a smaller gate Lucie had failed to notice. "Go 'round back." A smile of pride touched his mouth as he ran a glove over the machine's fender. "It's a Stanley Steamer," he said when he saw she couldn't look away from the vehicle. "Someday everyone will own an automobile. You won't see a horse on the street."

Lucie did not believe this for a minute but she nodded politely, backing along the pavement toward the smaller gate.

Feeling more comfortable than she would have at the front door, Lucie followed a stone path that led around to the kitchen door. Before she lifted a glove to knock, she inhaled deeply with a sigh of pleasure. It didn't smell of garbage here, nor was it dry and barren. Shrubs and flowers framed the door; a spreading elm shaded the stoop. She could smell roses and delphinium and forget-me-nots. The cooking odors escaping from the open windows made her mouth water.

It would be so good to work here. After drawing a deep breath to quell her nerves, she touched the spot where Jamie's rose was pinned to her chemise, then she straightened her shoulders and rapped at the kitchen door.

Following a long pause a man dressed in a gray morning coat and dark trousers opened the door and looked at her expectantly.

"Mr. Roper?" she stammered.

"Mr. Grist, the butler. How may we assist you?"

Lucie wet her lips and felt the heat of embarrassment flare on her cheeks. Viewing the automobile had rattled her so badly she had mistaken the butler for the master of the house. "I've come about the laundry job. Mrs. Brovnic sent me."

"Yes, indeed." The door opened wider, which she interpreted as permission to step inside. "Follow me, please."

The kitchen was enormous, larger than her parent's entire cottage in Wlad. She would have loved to inspect the range and ovens, the shining unfamiliar appliances. Instead she followed Mr. Grist through a bewildering maze of back hallways and finally into a beautifully furnished room that Mr. Grist obligingly identified as his office.

Dozens of questions followed, eliciting her background, how long she had resided in New York City, whom she lived with, what Stefan did for a living.

"Do you have laundry experience, Miss Kolska?"

This question puzzled her. Was there a woman alive who had never done a wash? When Mr. Grist noticed her confusion, a thin smile touched his equally thin lips. "Have you cleaned velvet? Lace? Muslin or gauze? Have you worked with bleach? With a crimping iron?"

She touched her breast above Jamie's rose. "I'm quick witted and eager to learn, sir. I don't require coddling. What I don't know, I can learn quickly, sir." His steady appraisal unnerved her. "I'm strong. I'll give a day's work for a day's pay."

"Come along, then."

She followed behind half believing he was showing her the gate until he opened a door to a huge room fitted for laundry. A range for boiling water sat on the far wall surrounded by large metal tubs. A smaller stove was covered with pressing irons and faced by a half dozen different sized boards. There were tubs for washing, rinsing, bluing and starching. Tables for ironing, folding and stacking. Dozens of drying racks. A wall of shelves holding boxes and bottles of supplies.

But what caught Lucie's attention was a young woman standing before the back tub. She turned a tap and instantly water gushed into the tub. The idea of water inside a house was so wonderful and so utterly sensible that Lucie wondered why no one had thought of it before.

While she stared at this new marvel Mr. Grist called, "Mrs. Greene," and a large boned woman appeared out of the steam boiling up in front of the range.

Mrs. Greene shoved at limp strands of graying dark hair that leaked from her white cap. She narrowed one eye and inspected Lucie in critical silence. "Does she speak English?" she asked Mr. Grist. "Well, thank God for that!" Stepping forward she pinched Lucie's arm below the shoulder. "Strong. That's good. Let me see your hands." Lucie peeled off her gloves and extended her palms. "Clean, that's good, too." Mrs. Greene's eyebrows came together with a snap that Lucie imagined she could hear. "No calluses. That's bad."

"I cream my hands every night—"

"How do you wash bed sheets? And don't give me no poppycock about spreading sheep manure on 'em and putting 'em in the sun for three days. We don't do them kind of things here in America."

Her mind raced trying to remember the procedure Maria had described. "I would use soap, soda and quicklime."

"Good." Mrs. Green fired a series of questions. "How do you know if the lime is quick and fresh?" she demanded.

"Fresh lime will bubble when boiling water hits it."

"After you pour off the lime water, then what?"

"Wring out the sheets, which have been soaking overnight. Boil them at least half an hour. A bit longer is better."

"How many rinses?"

"Two. And add bluing to the last." When she saw Mrs. Greene's expression, she thanked heaven she had listened to Maria or she would not have known about the lime or the bluing.

Mrs. Greene's red face relaxed. "If she can do sheets and linens, I can teach her the rest." A water-wrinkled hand clapped Lucie on the back. "You start at six and finish at six. You get eighty cents a day and your midday chuck. Your first two days' wage goes for your uniform." She indicated the white apron she wore over a dark cotton dress and pointed to her cap.

Having won Mrs. Greene's approval, and feeling slightly overwhelmed, Lucie followed Mr. Grist out of the steam.

"Mrs. Roper prefers to meet her employees, Miss Kolska. If you will follow me." As she was now one of them,

Mr. Grist hastily assured her, "The interview will be brief. Stand straight and do not stammer."

Later, when she tried to describe the Roper mansion to Stefan, she found herself speechless, unable to recall specific details. The splendor of the crowded rooms lay so far outside Lucie's experience or expectation that her mind failed to register everything she saw. She passed through room after luxurious room, awed by porcelain and brass and silver and polished wood. By damask table dressings and velvet draperies and richly upholstered furnishings. By patterned carpets so richly woven and dyed she loathed to tread upon them.

When they reached the first landing of a wide curving staircase, she heard music and her mouth fell open. "Do the Ropers employ their own symphony?" she whispered.

Mr. Grist smiled. "What you hear is Miss Delfi's Gramophone." Her lack of comprehension caused his thin smile to broaden. "It's a windup box that plays music."

The thought of having music whenever one wanted enchanted her. Such a possibility had never entered her mind.

Eventually she was led into Mrs. Roper's morning room, a small jewel box composed of air and light and overflowing with yellow daisies. The walls and furnishings were a rich blend of cream and yellow, awash with morning sunlight.

Even the woman sitting behind the delicate carved desk wore cream and yellow. And she bore a distinct resemblance to the princess whom Lucie had observed alighting from the Stanley Steamer. Her iron-colored hair was caught up in the Gibson style, softening an angular face that sunlight did not flatter. Friends referred to Mrs. Axa Roper as handsome. Those less kind claimed nature had carved lines of vanity and ambition across a face already less than blessed.

"Well, Miss Kolska." Mrs. Roper's all-seeing glance moved from Lucie's mended gloves to her plain straw hat. "Do you think you will enjoy working in Mr. Roper's household?"

"Oh, yes, ma'am."

"What lovely skin you have." The faintest trace of envy entered Mrs. Roper's carefully articulated speech.

"Thank you, ma'am." A blush of pleasure tinted her cheeks. "I use a special cream. It's my own recipe."

"Have you worked in a large household before?"

"No, ma'am."

"I'm confident Mr. Grist and Mrs. Greene will take you in hand." Mrs. Roper darted a glance to Mr. Grist who stepped forward and touched Lucie's elbow. The interview had ended.

Dazed, she followed Mr. Grist back to the kitchen door. There was a moment to notice the kitchen also had a water tap, then she was standing outside on the stoop. And she was employed.

Restraining a cry of joy she pressed both hands to the rose beneath her shirtwaist, then she hurried around the path to stare with proprietary pleasure at the front of the magical mansion. She belonged here. The realization amazed and overwhelmed her. She wished so much that she could have shared the glad news with Jamie. She was convinced his rose had turned the tide.

Jamie. The jubilation faded from her expression, replaced by an aching sense of loss. Would she ever see him again?

THE ROPER HOUSEHOLD employed thirty-two servants. Within a week Lucie could identify many of them from the smell and state of their uniforms. Until she proved herself, she was not allowed to wash or iron the Ropers' clothing but was relegated to the servant's laundry and washing household linens.

By the end of her second week she knew that Mrs. Greene and Mr. Grist despised Monsieur Duffoux, the excitable chef; knew that Miss Clements, Mrs. Roper's personal maid, considered herself head and shoulders above everyone else and was roundly loathed for this but was tolerated as she provided an excellent source of family gossip. The coachman and the gardener both vied for the attentions of the parlor maid and one of the chars was suspected of stealing Miss Augusta's silver thimble.

Those who served the household were small satellites orbiting the brilliance of the Ropers, depending upon them for sustenance and stimulation. The details of the Ropers' lives occupied every thought, motivated every action, formed the basis for endless conversation and speculation at work and at home.

"Everyone says Miss Delfi is a handful. She's fifteen and has taken to painting her lips," Lucie told Greta with a scandalized roll of her eyes. "We found rouge on her riding jacket and again on the tea dress she wore last Wednesday."

"No!" Greta poured a pail of water into the tub on top of the stove. "Does Miss Augusta wear rouge, too?"

Lucie fed the fire with lumps of coal and wiped her forehead. "If you ask me, she should. She's so pale from all the weeping. You see, Mrs. Roper wants Miss Augusta to marry a European title but Miss Augusta has her eye set on Mr. Whitcomb, who Mrs. Roper doesn't consider suitable."

"But maybe she loves him," Greta suggested.

"We all think she does," Lucie agreed sadly. "But Mrs. Roper has her sights set on a count or a baron." Miss Augusta's tale of family interference cut too close to Lucie's own situation to discuss with comfort. Bending over the stove, she stirred the laundry stick through the boiling sheets and towels.

Today, as on the last Sunday of each month, Lucie and Greta did laundry together, lightening the drudgery with the pleasure of each other's company. Greta updated Lucie regarding the ongoing feuds among the members of the family with whom she boarded and Lucie confided the fairy-tale existence of the Roper family.

"Tell again about the flowers," Greta begged after they had strung the laundry to dry on the line stretching from

Lucie's window to the window of the tenement across the courtyard.

"I only saw the main rooms once," Lucie said, beginning the story as she always did. "But there was one room—a side parlor, I think it was—where I saw a bay window and the window was filled to bursting with geraniums."

"Oh, I do love geraniums!" Greta said, her eyes glowing. She glanced at the poor specimen on Lucie's windowsill. "Tell about the colors."

Lucie smiled at her eagerness. "The window was filled with crimson and rose and cream-colored whites." When Greta sighed deeply, she patted her hand. "Someday you'll have a window garden filled with geraniums."

"I know. Stefan has promised." Absently, Greta scratched the rash on the back of her hands.

"Remind me to give you some more cream," Lucie commented, thinking it was time she mixed a new batch. A frown of concern troubled her gaze. It seemed that Greta's rash had spread. "Does it itch all the time?"

"Lately it seems to," Greta admitted, tucking her hands under her apron. "I know it's silly to be so vain," she apologized with a blush. Then she smiled. "I'd love to have more of your cream. I think it helps and it makes my skin feel soft."

Lucie leaned to look at her. "You look tired today. Are you sleeping well?"

"It's been so hot," Greta answered vaguely. She touched Lucie's flushed face. "Do you still think of Mr. Kelly?" she asked gently, changing the subject. Sympathy filled her eyes.

"All of the time," Lucie said simply. She dropped her gaze to the mending in her lap, concealing her look of pain.

"I've spoken to Stefan a dozen times," Greta confided in a low voice. Distress tugged her lips. "I'm sorry, Lucie."

"Dear Greta, please don't quarrel with Stefan about my troubles. There's nothing anyone can do."

"Usually Stefan is so kind and understanding." Greta frowned and lowered her mending. "I do swear, I believe the eye of this needle has shrunk! I can't see it at all.'' She rubbed her eyes and blinked hard at the thread she jabbed toward the needle. When Lucie smiled and took it from her, she made a sound of exasperation and lifted both hands. Then her expression softened. ''Stefan can't forget being humiliated in front of his friends.''

''I know.'' Lucie's shoulders drooped. ''I know.''

For a time she prayed she would encounter Jamie accidentally. Finally she conceded that was unlikely. The city was enormous and crowded with masses of people. Her path and Jamie's had diverged. The likelihood of meeting again was depressingly minuscule. She couldn't bear to think about it.

When the laundry and mending was finished and a pot of cabbage soup bubbled on the stove for supper, Lucie and Greta carried the dirty wash water down to the courtyard, emptied the tub, then washed their hands and faces at the pump.

''I hope Maria Brovnic found what she was seeking.'' Lucie fanned her face with the hem of her apron, stirring the scent of heat-rotted garbage from the piles fringing the courtyard. ''Greta, do you ever think about returning? About going home?''

''Stefan is here,'' Greta answered simply.

''They sell cat meat in the carts,'' Lucie said quietly. ''Did you know that people eat cat meat?'' Tilting her head, she looked up at the purple sky. ''I like my work,'' she said slowly. ''But going to Madison Avenue everyday, where it's clean and where it smells fresh, somehow it makes all this—'' she waved a hand at the piles of cinders and garbage, at the tin roof latrines and the layers of laundry flapping overhead ''—seem worse.''

''We won't always live in the tenements,'' Greta reminded her in a quiet voice.

''Every day the pot boy puts the Ropers' garbage on the street and the white-wings come and take it away in a big wagon. The ashes and garbage are whisked away like magic.

And every night the lamplighter comes and lights the street lamps. No one walks in darkness on Madison Avenue. There are no abandoned wagons at the curb. No brawling in the street. Flowers bloom in the window boxes and every house has a backyard with trees.''

She fell silent looking at the tenements with the broken window panes and sagging metal fire escapes. ''I'm not saying I envy the Ropers or that I envy what they have. I know who I am and I know my place. I don't want a lot more, just a little. Just fresh air and sunshine, no bad smells.'' And Jamie Kelly.

Greta placed her hand on Lucie's arm. ''Someday you and I and Stefan will have a small house of our own,'' she promised earnestly. ''With many windows and a tree outside the door. We'll have water inside our kitchen and geraniums on every window ledge. And so much sunshine we won't light the lamps until after dark. Lucie, I believe this and you must, too.''

Lucie blinked and gave herself a shake. ''Forgive me, dearest Greta. Of course you're right. Someday...'' But someday seemed very far away to one whose soul yearned for sunlight now. And one special man.

''If we abandon our dreams,'' Greta said softly, ''then we're defeated. We have to hold our dreams close and believe.''

Lucie thought about that as she and Greta prepared supper. Stefan dreamed of one day owning a small prosperous business. Greta dreamed of a sunny kitchen with geraniums on the sill and children to hug and tell stories to. But aside from providing Stefan and Greta's marriage money, what was Lucie's dream? A wistful expression came into her eyes and she sighed, thinking about Jamie Kelly.

ALTHOUGH STEFAN had forbidden her to continue her lessons at the settlement house, Lucie quietly ignored his wishes and continued to attend the Tuesday night lectures. She understood Stefan knew of her small rebellion because he called on Greta on Tuesday evenings and didn't return until thirty minutes after the settlement house closed. Pride prohibited him from admitting he had spoken in anger and haste, but his love for her allowed him to pretend he didn't know she went out on Tuesday nights.

This Tuesday, however, she would miss the lecture. Mrs. Greene had been teaching her to clean lace collars and neither had noticed the hour. Consequently, Lucie had missed her train.

When she finally arrived at the Bowery Street station and descended to the street, there was no longer any reason to rush. Enjoying an idle moment, she gazed down the wide street watching the glow of gaslight as lamps came on behind the windows of the beer halls and the entertainment establishments. And she smiled at the people strolling toward the sounds of laughter and music, taking their pleasure in the warm summer night.

Buoyed by the sight of people enjoying themselves, she turned her steps toward Elizabeth Street, away from the light and sounds of the Bowery. Stefan worried about her walking alone from the station to Elizabeth Street but no one bothered her. Already she recognized a few faces along the route and occasionally someone tipped his cap to her, or one of the women smiled.

"Miss Kolska?"

Her heart jumped as a man stood away from a shadowed doorway. When she recognized who it was the color drained from her cheeks, her breath stopped in her chest. "Mr. Kelly!"

For a long moment they stood facing each other, lost in each other as the pedestrian traffic broke around them. Lucie noticed his sunburn had deepened to a healthy bronze, imparting a golden tone to the eyes that moved eagerly over her face. He seemed taller than she recalled and had his shoulders always been so broad? His teeth so white? Longing overcame her as she forced herself to step backward, her mouth suddenly dry.

"What a nice surprise to run into you," he said in a deep voice that dispatched tiny shivers down her spine, that made her think of music and honey.

Lucie couldn't have spoken a word if the world depended on it. Her reticule trembled in her fingers, and a peculiar tightness spread through her body. Hastily she lowered her eyes from his wide mouth.

"Should you be walking alone at night? May I walk with you?"

Lucie clasped her gloved hands tightly in front of her skirts. "Stefan would be very angry," she whispered, the words scarcely audible.

"I know." He smiled down at her. "Every Saturday night as we lock our tools in the shed, I request your brother's permission to call on you."

"You do?" She hadn't known. As Stefan had said nothing she had assumed Jamie Kelly had accepted her brother's decision.

"And every Saturday night he refuses and threatens to pulverize me if I ask again."

His grin teased a shy smile from her lips. "You don't look pulverized," she commented in a low voice. Because being with him made her nervous, she edged backward a step. "I don't think . . ."

He fell into step beside her. "Stubbornness aside, I truly don't believe Stefan seeks another fight. Although if that's what it takes, I'm willing to have another round."

Lucie darted a blushing look at him from beneath the brim of her straw boater. He was so handsome he took her breath away. "Please don't fight again, Mr. Kelly." She didn't think Stefan would suddenly appear but the possibility worried her. "You must know Stefan would be very angry if he knew we were walking together." Guilt attacked her pleasure in seeing him and actually speaking to him.

Stopping, Jamie touched her shoulders, forcing her to look at him directly. A shock of warmth burned under his fingertips, scalding through her sleeves and into the skin beneath. Her heart lurched and pounded wildly.

"Lucie—may I call you Lucie?—the truth is, running into you was no accident." He drew a long breath. "I know I shouldn't seek you out, and I deeply regret any distress my presence may cause you." His dark eyes peered into hers. "I also know it isn't proper to say this, but...I can't forget you. I think of you constantly and I'd like to know you. If my interest is objectionable, if you find me offensive, you have only to nod and I won't bother you or your brother again." She stared into his eyes as the lovely rolled *r*s caressed her ear. "Lucie?" he inquired softly. "Shall I leave you?"

She closed her eyes and swallowed, scarcely able to think past the thrilling touch of his hands framing her shoulders. The warmth of his fingertips radiated through her body and erupted in an inner earthquake. "No," she answered in a strangled whisper, staring at his mouth and wondering how it was possible for such a light touch to cause such turmoil. It was almost a relief when he dropped his arms. Almost.

"Praise the saints! I was so afraid you would send me away, or that you didn't feel..."

"I feel terrible about defying Stefan," she said, guilt and distress darkening her eyes. "I hate deceiving him. But..."

The trailing sentences spoke volumes to them both. "When you stopped coming to the site, I was so worried," Jamie confessed, his gaze shamelessly caressing her lips, her eyes, the heavy coil of chestnut hair. "I wondered where you were and what you were doing, and if you ever spared a small thought for me."

"I do think about you," she confessed in a voice so low he had to lean forward to hear. His nearness increased the pleasant barbershop smell of bay rum and Madagascar hair oil. A tiny shiver traced down Lucie's spine and she hastily resumed walking, resisting the urge to press her gloves to the fiery heat in her cheeks. She drew a deep breath and summoned a cheerful tone. "But even if Stefan had not forbidden me to return to the site, I couldn't go anymore. I have a job now.''

''That's wonderful!'' But his enthusiasm waned as she told him about the laundry room at the Roper mansion. At the entrance to Elizabeth Street Jamie gazed up toward the voices murmuring on the rooftops and scowled. ''I hate the thought of you washing other people's dirty laundry.''

Lucie laughed. ''I'm not a countess, Mr. Kelly. I'm not afraid to dirty my hands. And I don't shrink from hard work. Truly, I don't mind. Laundry is something I can do and do well. There's no shame in it.''

''I didn't mean to imply there was,'' he apologized hastily, bending to peer beneath her hat brim. ''I just wish it wasn't necessary for you to work at all.''

It was a lovely idea but not very practical. When she expressed the thought, Jamie smiled. ''I suppose not,'' he admitted. ''But no man likes to see a woman going off to work. It's job enough to care for a home.'' A thoughtful expression creased his brow. ''But you do that, too, don't you?'' Then he laughed. ''Actually, I think women are the stronger of the sexes. You do whatever is necessary and without complaint.'' He grinned and his eyes twinkled. ''Tell me, do you really enjoy washing other people's laundry? Or are you making the best of it?''

Lucie returned his smile, thinking how much she liked him. ''The truth?'' she pretended to consider. ''There are things I'd rather do. But since I have a laundry job, it's best to put a bright face on it.''

''What would you rather do?''

Her steps slowed as they turned into Elizabeth Street and passed beneath a broken street lamp. She didn't want these enchanted minutes to end. ''It would be nice to work in one of the emporiums and sell lovely things. But I don't have the training for that. Or teaching would be lovely. Perhaps at the Settlement House.'' She slid a teasing look in his direction, amazed by how easy it was to talk to him. ''Or maybe

I'd enjoy business.'' This last was pure invention, created out of the turmoil of being near him.

He feigned a horrified look. ''No, not business! Are you one of those—what do they call them?—suffergettes?''

Lucie laughed. ''And if I were, Mr. Kelly? Would you still wish to walk out with me?''

His grin flashed a row of even white teeth. ''You astound me, lass. Hardly have you placed your feet on American soil before you're speaking of business. It's enough to rattle the poor brain of a conventional man.''

Although she enjoyed his teasing enormously, and his intense interest in everything she said made her feel warm all over, she wanted to know more about him and their time together was slipping through the glass. ''Actually I can't imagine myself conducting business,'' she admitted, smiling. She didn't tell him she still figured her market money on her fingers. ''How are you faring, Mr. Kelly?''

''Jamie.''

''Jamie,'' she repeated, tasting his name on her lips and feeling another rush of heat flare across her cheeks.

''I'm treading water, I fear, not progressing an inch. But a man has to begin somewhere.'' He shrugged and followed her between the buildings into the darkened courtyard. They lingered beside the dripping pump as lamps went on behind the windows.

''Do you have a dream?'' Lucie asked shyly. He stood near enough that she could smell the scent of his bay rum. The realization that they leaned toward each other, heads almost touching, brought another blush to her throat. Then she smiled. ''Of course you do. Everyone in America has a dream.''

Jamie returned her smile and drew a line in the dirt with the toe of his boot. ''Someday I want to build buildings so wonderful no one will knock them down and put others in their place.'' Raising his head, he looked at the tenement. ''And I want to build houses affordable to people like you and me, clean houses with adequate ventilation and airy sunny rooms."

Lucie stared at him with admiration, restraining an urge to touch his sleeve. "That's a wonderful dream!"

"All that's needed is a wee bit of Irish luck." Another smile curved his lips. "And a lot of money."

It was difficult to look away from his mouth; he had a beautiful firm mouth and she decided the sensuality in the curve suggested a poetic bent that fit nicely with his dream. But gazing at his lips made Lucie feel hot and strange inside. She swallowed and turned her face aside, hoping he could not read her mind, or hear the pounding of her heart.

"I must go inside, Mr.—Jamie." The words emerged with reluctance, but she cast an anxious glance toward the dark opening between the buildings. "Stefan could return at any moment..."

"I like you, Lucie Kolska," Jamie said softly. The deepening night blurred his features, but she could feel the intensity of his eyes on her face, responded to the unsettling sense of urgency drawing them together. "I'd like to see you again."

Uncertainty darkened her gaze. It was wrong to defy Stefan's wishes. So alien to her nature.

"Please."

She looked into Jamie Kelly's warm eyes and her heart constricted. How could something so utterly right be wrong? But she knew she should refuse, and when she thought of Stefan she experienced a scalding rush of guilt. But...she also felt the magnetic heat of Jamie Kelly's nearness and heard the thumping of her racing heart. She saw the admiration in his eyes, felt a tingle when he looked at her. Something larger than logic overwhelmed her senses.

She ducked her head and studied her hands twisting across the front of her skirts. "I...if I should accidentally encounter you again next Tuesday evening..."

A joyful shout broke from his lips, then he hastily looked over his shoulder and gave her an apologetic grin. "Until then,'' he said, backing toward the exit between the buildings.

Reason urged him along lest he bump into Stefan. But her rebellious heart wanted him to linger.

"Until then," she whispered, feeling the weight of guilt pressing against her conscience.

She stood beside the pump, placing her fingertips on the handle still warm from his hand and she watched him back away from her. At the opening he paused, and they looked at each other across the dirt floor of the courtyard.

When she realized he would not leave until she did, Lucie made herself turn away and lifted her skirts. Almost floating, her feet scarcely touching the stairs, she hurried up the staircase and into her rooms. Without pausing to remove her hat or light the lamp, she hastened to the window overlooking the street and leaned out for a last glimpse of him.

She saw him immediately, but he didn't know she watched. He tossed his cap in the air with a shout, then caught the pole of the street lamp in one hand and swung around it.

His exuberance brought a smile to Lucie's lips and she watched with laughing eyes as he retrieved his cap, settled it at a cocky angle, then, whistling, he pushed his hands in his pockets and walked toward Canal Street.

Then, because she could not bear to face Stefan knowing she intended to deceive him, she swiftly washed and dressed for bed, then rolled into her mattress and pretended to be asleep when she heard the door open, hoping Stefan couldn't hear the jubilant pounding of her heart.

Chapter Five

"It's hotter'n a ride in Hades!" Mrs. Greene's booming complaint stirred the steam in front of the shirts boiling on the laundry room range top. Fanning her face with her apron, she emerged from a cloud of white haze and surveyed her domain with a critical eye. "Hilda, how many times I got to tell you?" she bawled. "*One* part oxalic acid and *two* parts Prussian blue! Lucie, from now on you mix the bluing."

Lucie adjusted the sleeve of a maid's uniform on the small bosom board and cast Hilda a sympathetic smile. Then she wet her finger, touched the surface of the iron to check if it was still hot, and applied herself to pressing the sleeve.

Mrs. Greene loomed over her with a scowl. "Where's your mind, Lucie Kolska? That ain't the proper iron. For sleeves you want a polishing iron, not a coarse iron." She spread chapped red hands and rolled her eyes toward heaven. "Why, Lord? Why is it you seen fit to burden me with a room full of pumblechooks?"

"Good heavens." Lucie raised the iron and blinked at it. "I'm sorry, Mrs. Greene, I don't know that I was thinking."

"It's Tuesday."

"Beg pardon?" Lucie asked with a start.

"Every Tuesday you get all dreamy airy like you was thinking about lollygagging. You got a young man, Lucie

Kolska?'' Mrs. Greene demanded. She studied Lucie's flaming cheeks and heaved a sigh. "Lord help us. Ain't nothing worse than trying to coax a day's work out of a love-struck biddy." She fisted her large hands on massive hips. "Well, when you going to marry that young man? That'll take care of any love problems."

"I . . . my brother objects." Not looking up, Lucie exchanged the coarse iron for one with rounded ends.

"Is that a fact?" An interested gleam appeared in Mrs. Greene's eyes. "As if it ain't enough having Miss Augusta moping about, now we got you to worry about." Dipping her fist in a basin of water, she began sprinkling a pile of maid's aprons and rolling them into damp balls.

Lucie hadn't realized her Tuesday euphoria was so obvious, but it didn't surprise her. She lived for Tuesdays and her time with Jamie. Whatever happened during the week— scalded hands, an aching back, missed trains—became insignificant when she thought forward to Tuesday night. To seeing his eager smile when she stepped out of the Bowery Street station. That smile put the world right and sent her spirits soaring.

Tonight when she saw him she forgot the weight of the hot irons and her aching shoulder. Her face lit when she spotted him waiting on the platform and she flew out of the train, made breathless by the joy warming his eyes as she hurried toward him.

For a moment neither of them could speak. Jamie clasped her hands and examined her upturned smile. Finally he spoke in a gruff voice. "Each Tuesday, I'm afraid you've changed your mind. That you'll send me away."

"How could you think that?" Lucie whispered. But she understood. Every Tuesday as the train approached the station her heart beat faster and she wondered if he would be waiting. Then, when she saw him, her happiness was so overpowering she wondered that she could endure it.

After settling his gray summer bowler, Jamie tucked her hand around his arm and led her down the steps and across the street to the small Bowery Street pub they had claimed as their own. The moment they entered the beer-jugger brought a pail of Marva stout and two glass mugs to their table.

"You'll tell us when it's nine o'clock?" Jamie asked the beer-jugger as he always did. Then, to make doubly sure, he placed his pocket watch on the table beside Lucie's reticule. Neither of them wholly trusted the pocket watch. It seemed to run fast on Tuesday nights. "So," Jamie said softly. His wonderful dark eyes lingered on her face. "What kind of week has it been?"

"I learned about iron rust this week," she said, trying to memorize the angle of his jaw, noticing the way his lips parted when he leaned forward. Each Tuesday they rediscovered the thrill of each other. A laugh bubbled up from her breast. "You don't care about rust stains!"

"I care about everything that's important to you. Tell me if Miss Delfi received the two-wheeler she's been badgering Mr. Roper to have."

The spicy scent of bay rum reached her across the tabletop and she inhaled deeply, wondering if he could smell the lilac toilet water she splashed on her wrists before she departed the Roper mansion. "I'd rather talk about you. Tell me what you did this week."

The exchange of news helped them learn about each other and what was important in their lives and Lucie devoured each word. She also loved the Tuesday evenings when Jamie showed her parts of the city she might not have seen otherwise. They visited construction sites and Jamie explained what she was seeing; they toured the locomotive museum, the harbor, an automotive display. They shared a pint in the popular music halls and attended lectures at Cooper Institute.

Cooper Institute seated an enormous number of people, and, on the next Tuesday, Lucie found her mind wandering from the governor's speech in favor of examining the people around her. Only when she had satisfied herself that none of the men were as handsome as the man seated beside her did she happily return her attention to Theodore Roosevelt. He strutted and marched across the stage, waving his arms and expending so much energy it wearied Lucie just to watch. The only thing she remembered him saying was: "I wish to preach, not the doctrine of ignoble ease, but the doctrine of the strenuous life."

"I wonder who he was speaking to," Lucie murmured as they ducked out early. They couldn't remain for the conclusion of the speech as she had to be at the tenement before Stefan returned. "Most of the audience looked to be working people like us. But I hardly consider that we're living a life of 'ignoble ease,' as the governor phrased it."

Jamie grinned and pulled her forward to catch the horse car. Lucie tried to read the advertising posters on the side of the car before Jamie urged her inside. One showed the new Klinger stove, gleaming black and nickel-plated, featuring a hot water reservoir and a drawer for pots and pans.

"Some say Roosevelt should run for president. You don't agree?"

She took a seat next to the window and looked up at him as he clasped the overhead strap when the car lurched forward. A lot of men, most men in fact, would not have taken a woman to a political speech. Certainly they would not have inquired as to a woman's opinion regarding a political topic. Although she did not require further persuasion that Jamie Kelly was a special man, his apparent assumption that her opinion was valid impressed her and she liked him for it. She liked him a great deal.

They discussed the speech all the way to the entrance of Elizabeth Street, delighted to discover their opinions were of one accord. "Though it hardly matters as I can't vote," Lucie admitted.

"Would you like to?" Jamie teased her.

"Maybe I would," she said with a toss of her head. But the face she made stated otherwise. Actually, she hadn't made up her mind if she agreed with those who pressed for woman's suffrage. Voting was a tremendous responsibility. She loved the idea but didn't feel she was informed enough to make a responsible choice. Maybe someday women would possess the education to vote wisely, but she doubted that day would arrive anytime soon.

She said as much and Jamie agreed. They discussed the subject again the next week as they strolled along Broadway, peering into darkened shop windows, choosing which objects they would buy if money were no concern, laughing at each other's choices.

Raising her head abruptly at something Jamie said, Lucie turned to him and discovered her mouth inches from his. An explosion of butterflies fluttered in her stomach confusing her thoughts as she asked a daft question, requesting his opinion about belts replacing suspenders. But it didn't matter. She wanted to know everything about him, the silly small things, as well as more important ones.

She learned about his family the night they inspected the newly constructed New York Yacht Club building, having gone there to admire the galleonlike windows. And she told him about her own family and childhood the evening he took her to a soda fountain and insisted she try a Coca-Cola, which made her laugh with surprise when it fizzed under her nose.

Among her favorite outings were their visits to the library where Jamie helped her obtain cards for fiction and nonfiction. It astonished her to discover she was trusted to return the books she checked out. She had never heard of such a thing.

"I read part of *The Gentleman from Indiana* to Greta last Sunday," she told Jamie eagerly. They were seated in their favorite Bowery Street pub, watching the dial of Jamie's pocket watch speed across the clock face. "It's a first novel by Booth Tarkington. Both Greta and I think the book is lovely!"

Jamie's warm chocolate eyes met hers across the table top and sent a tiny shiver down her spine. "When you've finished Mr. Tarkington's book, you must read *War of the Worlds* by a chap named Wells. You'll be amazed.''

The back of his hand brushed hers and an eruption of heat ignited throughout her body. She felt the resultant tingle down to her toes and whatever they had been discussing fled her mind. Just to look at Jamie was enough to raise strange pleasant sensations that she couldn't fully explain. Although the feeling was pleasurable, it was uncomfortable, too. More and more often, she found herself stealing small looks at his mouth, wondering if he would ever kiss her and what she would do if he did.

When the beer-jugger arrived to inform them it was almost nine they looked up in amazement as if it were impossible. Together they dropped their heads to stare at Jamie's pocket-watch, convinced it must be in error.

Leaving the pub with reluctance, they walked slowly through the warm August night toward the entrance to Elizabeth Street. This was the best and the worst of each Tuesday evening. The best because Jamie held her arm tightly against his side and the touch of him thrilled her and left her light-headed. During the weeks of clandestine meetings, Lucie had felt the slow building of an interior pressure that seemed to wind another notch tighter whenever Jamie looked at her or pressed her arm to his side. This was also the worst moment of the evening because it meant it would be seven long days before she saw him again.

They stopped on the street beside the dark tunnel leading into the courtyard and faced each other. People hurried home along the broken pavement behind them. Two ragged children played in the derelict wagon abandoned at the curb. A group of twelve-year-old boot blacks sat on their boxes, pitching pennies in a circle. Overhead, the evening sky formed a canopy of deep lavender and gold.

''Each Tuesday when I leave you,'' Jamie said in a soft voice that recognized nothing but her, ''I wonder how I find the strength to walk away from you.''

"I know," she whispered, feeling the ache and tension of farewell. Her gaze was intense as she etched his features in her mind to carry her through the next seven days. She wanted to stroke his strong clean-shaven face, to feel his warm skin under her fingertips. She longed to explore the determined line of his jaw, to place her palms flat against the solid strength of his chest and feel his heartbeat beneath her hands.

His gaze caressed her brow, the curve of her cheek, then settled on her mouth and her chest constricted and she stopped breathing. "Goodbye, dear Lucie. Until next Tuesday."

"Until next Tuesday," she whispered, her throat so tight she could hardly speak.

As was their habit she reluctantly stepped into the dark opening between the buildings, feeling his eyes on her hips, her ankles, on the nape of her neck, then at the courtyard she turned and lifted her glove in a farewell wave. After he returned the gesture, she raised her skirts and ran pell-mell toward the tenement door, up the stairs and into her rooms where she went directly to the window. He waited, looking up. When she appeared he waved again. Tonight he touched his fingertips to his lips and blew her the kiss he didn't dare deliver in person. Lucie gasped, and her hands fluttered to her throat then moved to her trembling mouth.

Then he was gone, swallowed up by the deepening twilight shadows and the night became gray again. For a time Lucie remained at the window, exhilarated by his fanciful kiss, imagining the taste and pressure on her lips, wishing with all her immodest woman's heart that his kiss had been real.

By the time Stefan returned she had recovered enough to light the lamp, don her apron, and warm the supper she had prepared this morning before she left for work. And she had achieved an uneasy mastery over the ever present guilt, though it was difficult to meet Stefan's eyes.

"How is Greta feeling tonight?" she inquired as she placed his bread and stew on the table.

"Her eyes are bothering her." Stefan sat down slowly and stared at his plate. Even if Lucie had not seen him tug his mustache, she would have known he was disturbed by the scowl in his dark eyes. "The oldest Poppalov boy told me he thought he saw the Irishman here tonight."

Lucie's heart stopped. "Oh?" she said faintly, turning back to the stove. "I didn't know you had a spy, Stefan."

She sensed discomfort in his silence, as acute as her own. "The Irishman still asks to call on you," he said at length. "Every week, regular as clockwork, he persists in asking."

"You've conceded he's a good worker. You've said he carries his own weight and works as hard as any man. Sometimes I think you respect him if you would only admit it."

"Perhaps," he admitted grudgingly. "But there's more to it than that."

Lucie gripped the handle of the oven door, not looking at him. "Please, Stefan. Grant us your permission." Sometimes she did not think she could bear the anguish of deceiving him one more instant.

"I can't do that." The harshness of his voice bowed Lucie's head. "I'd look like a fool. The decision has been made." When she made no reply, he reached for the bread and broke off a chunk, turning it in his hand. "If I discovered he was coming around here I would have to fight him again. You know that."

She closed her eyes and nodded.

"There is another man at work—Stanislas Sarnoff. I would like to invite him to Sunday supper."

"No," Lucie said quietly, staring down at the range top.

"Damn it, Lucie!" She heard his fist strike the table. "Greta is correct. It isn't right for a beautiful young woman not to have a man of her own. You should be thinking about your own marriage, thinking about your own children. But you're both wrong about the Irishman. Can't you understand? I don't want you to make a mistake. All I want is for you to be happy!''

She turned and looked at him with glistening eyes. "Then permit me to make my own choice. Allow me to decide where my happiness lies."

He stared at her, then he swore again and angrily smeared a spoonful of melting butter across his bread.

STEFAN TOOK GRETA AND LUCIE to the Hester Street market on Sunday afternoon to do the week's shopping. As usual the stalls and pushcarts encroached on the street and the crowds were so thick the street had been closed to horses and vehicles. People shouted and haggled for bargains in half a dozen languages. One couldn't walk three steps without being jostled by throngs of people or accosted by a vendor.

"Fifteen cents a pound for a scrawny chicken who died of starvation," Greta lamented in tones of resignation. Her shining blond hair was a rarity among the dark heads in Hester Street and she attracted much attention, though she seemed unaware of it.

"I can't decide," Lucie said, beckoning Greta toward the bins in the stall next to the meat. "Shall I spend fourteen cents for a dozen eggs or buy oranges instead?" The oranges would be an extravagance, but they smelled so tantalizing and good. Removing her glove, she reached toward an orange and touched the rough pebbled surface with her fingertips and inhaled the scent. Surely heaven smelled like oranges.

Greta's chiming laughter caused the vendor to sigh and he gazed at her with a besotted smile. "Oh, no, heaven smells like geraniums."

"You and your geraniums." Lucie smiled. "Oh, look over there. Eyeglasses." She tugged Greta through the crush of dark coats and flaring hems to a cart filled with wire-rimmed spectacles. "We're not leaving until you find exactly the right pair."

Leaning, Greta read the sign on the side of the cart. "Thirty-five cents? I don't know, that seems an awful price."

"Not if the glasses will stop your eyes from hurting. And you'll be able to see your beloved geraniums better. Here. Try these." Under the watchful eye of the vendor, Lucie selected a pair of spectacles and handed them to Greta who tilted her head to one side.

"I don't know... good heavens! Who is this handsome man!" Greta said, laughing up at Stefan. "Give us your opinion, sir. Do I look like a scholar?"

"You look beautiful," Stefan said softly, gazing down into her face. "To me you will always be beautiful."

A rush of pink brightened Greta's pale cheeks. Her eyes shone behind the wire-rimmed glass. "Dearest Stefan."

Lucie recognized the longing in their gaze as they stood close together looking into each other's eyes, the crowds around them forgotten. Seeing them together reminded her of her goal and how little she had progressed toward achieving it.

When they returned to the Elizabeth Street courtyard, the Poppalov children and Mrs. Cransky's daughter spotted Greta immediately and ran forward to clasp her hands and hang on her skirts. "Tell us a story, Miss Laskowski. Please? Just one?"

Greta's protesting laughter rang on the air like tiny bells. "Not today, I promised to help Miss Kolska prepare supper."

"I can manage," Lucie insisted, smiling. "You go on." When Greta lifted her eyebrows in a gesture of indecision, Lucie made a shooing motion with her hands. "Stefan promised to mend our boots today. He can join you on the roof and do it there." She lowered a mock scowl to the children. "And he'll make sure these tyrants don't tire you."

She and Stefan watched the children pull Greta toward the door and the stairs. "She should have children of her own," Lucie observed quietly.

"I know." Stefan's jawline tightened.

"I've been thinking. Greta and I love each other. We get on well together." After shifting the net bag of oranges on her arm, Lucie looked up at him. "We could all live together, Stefan."

"Thank you, Lucie. But Greta and I have talked about it, and it wouldn't work." Frustration darkened his eyes as he watched Greta and the children disappear inside the tenement.

"We'd be crowded, but—"

"If Greta and I married and she came to us, Lucie, the babies would soon follow. She couldn't work for a while, at least not until the babe was weaned." He removed his bowler and raked a hand through his hair. "You remember how it was before you found work. We had barely enough money for rent and food. When it turns cold we'll need extra coal for the stove. And what about winter coats and boots? Or, God forbid, if we needed a doctor or medicine?" Worry constricted his expression.

"I can help—"

He cut her off with a chopping motion of his hand. "Lucie, I can't ask you to support my family. I appreciate your suggestion and I wish it were possible. But it isn't right now."

"Stefan, how is Greta feeling, really?" Slowly, they walked around a ragpicker's bundle and approached the tenement door. "When I ask, she smiles and always says 'better,' but it seems as if she's gained a little more weight. I don't see how, she only picks at her food. And she's mentioned vomiting . . ."

Stefan stopped at the door and looked at Lucie but he was seeing something in a private distance. "I bought Greta some medicine for her cough and for the vomiting. The druggist in Mercer Street said she's probably suffering from the summer complaint. But that doesn't sound right. Sometimes she can't sleep. Other times she sleeps like a drugged person and worries she won't wake in time for work. Her appetite comes and goes. She doesn't seem to be getting better. In fact..." He clenched his jaw. "I know she's worried about her health, but she refuses to talk about it. When I ask, she just waves it off and says it's nothing."

"She doesn't want to trouble you."

"But I am troubled. I worry all the time." Stefan met Lucie's eyes and said simply, "If anything happened to Greta, life wouldn't be worth living. I love her."

"I know," Lucie said softly.

After sending Stefan up to the roof she put away the shopping items, then cut the chicken into the pot and set aside the carrots and turnips to be added later. With luck the stewed chicken would stretch over the next three days.

While she worked she occasionally glanced at the geranium on the windowsill. It was a poor straggly thing, starved for sunlight. Every Sunday Greta fussed over it, adding water and pulling off the brown leaves, murmuring endearments in an effort to coax forth a small blossom.

"Grow," Lucie commanded, staring at the heat-limp stalk.

"I feel terrible that I've abandoned you all afternoon," Greta called, coming in the door. Her cheeks were flushed by the rooftop sun and wisps of golden hair floated around her face. The new eyeglasses had become smudged by the inspection of small fingers.

"Let me have those," Lucie said, smiling. "I was about to polish the lamp chimney, I'll do your glasses, too."

"May I borrow your hairbrush? I forgot to bring mine. The wind on the roof was determined to have my pins."

"A brush and extra pins are on my shelf."

She cleaned the fingerprints from Greta's eyeglasses and took them into the sleeping room. Greta stood beside the curtain, examining the blond hair in Lucie's brush with an expression of dismay. Slowly she combed the hair out of the bristles.

"It's the oddest thing," she murmured as she replaced the brush on Lucie's shelf. "My hair seems to be getting thinner." Troubled blue eyes turned to Lucie. "Does it seem to you that I'm losing a lot of hair?"

Lucie led her into the kitchen where the light was better and inspected her head. They both wore their hair in the fashionable Gibson style, full around the face and caught up in a loose knot at the crown.

"Your hair seems as thick as it's always been," Lucie insisted. But she wasn't as certain as she sounded. Now that she thought of it she recalled the luxuriant heavy mass of honey-colored hair that she had admired so profusely the day she first met Greta. In truth, it didn't seem that Greta's hair was quite as fulsome today. "Are you taking the medicine Stefan gave you?"

When Greta's coughing spell ended, she sat down to catch her breath. "You would think at fifty cents a bottle, Doctor Sage's Catarrh Remedy would melt this silly congestion."

"And you're hiding your hands again. Is the rash worse?"

Greta shrugged and tucked her hands beneath the folds of her skirt. "I'm falling apart, aren't I? It's the silliest thing." She turned her head to gaze at the geranium wilting on the sill, then she looked up at Lucie and smiled. "What can I do to help with supper?"

"You can make coffee while I peel the potatoes. The grounds are almost new. Greta, don't let me forget to give you more cream for your hands. I made up a new batch not long ago."

"That reminds me, dear Lucie. Three of the women at the factory would like to try your cream if you have any to spare."

The compliment pleased her. "I'm flattered you thought to mention it to them." Pride flushed her cheeks and she paused in her work to look at Greta. "I know you don't like to talk about this, and I apologize for belaboring the point, but, Greta, are you all right?"

For an instant their eyes met and held and Lucie's chest tightened in alarm. Fear and anxiety flared behind Greta's new spectacles. Then Greta smiled and her gaze was again as gentle and steady as always. "Of course I am. I'll be as right as a raindrop as soon as cooler weather comes."

FROM THE FERRY the city reminded Lucie of a cluster of stars fallen to earth. Lights flickered in distant windows, and a glow radiated above Broadway. She stood at the ferry railing, her shoulder touching Jamie's, her small gloved hand beneath his on the rail. Weeks ago she had believed if she could just see him, if she could just spend an hour a week in his company, that would be enough. But it wasn't.

In many ways the brief hours they spent together each Tuesday made their situation worse. Her curiosity had become a yearning that approached a physical ache. The moment she stepped off the train and found Jamie waiting, an acute awareness blossomed into being. Suddenly she could think of nothing but his wide smiling mouth, his lips, the pull of his trousers across his thighs, the warm intensity of dark Irish eyes that spoke a mute language of the heart.

This strange sharp focus extended to herself, as well. In Jamie's company she became intensely aware of herself as a woman. Usually she didn't think about such immodest things as the feel of her own skin, or the sway of her hips when she walked, or the curve of her shirtwaist over her chemise.

But when she recognized the desire in Jamie's gaze, she blushed with pleasure and thought about her small firm breasts and how they would feel beneath his rough palms. Such shameless thoughts brought a rush of pink to her cheeks, but she could no more have halted her awakening than she could have halted the currents that returned them to the landing dock.

"Jamie?" she asked softly, wetting her lips and banishing these unsettling thoughts. "Is something troubling you tonight?" The gay mood they had established earlier at the outdoor concert in Brooklyn had moved toward something more somber.

When he turned to gaze at her the look in his eyes stopped the breath in her lungs.

"The same thing that's troubled us from the beginning, Lucie." The jaw she longed to stroke hardened into a tight line. "I hate deceiving Stefan as much as you do. I hate knowing how guilty I've made you feel. When you told me about the Poppalov boy seeing us together..." His voice trailed off and he gripped the rail so hard that his hands turned pale at the knuckles. "It's not enough that we must sneak about like criminals, or that we're denied any hope of privacy, now I can't even accompany you home."

Her heart shifted in her chest and her breath stopped. "What are you saying Jamie? That we shouldn't meet again?"

"Lord no, lass!" Forgetting they were surrounded by people, he lifted a quick hand to her cheek. "I couldn't bear not seeing you! You are the one bright spot in my week, in my life. Without you, there would be no reason to start a new day. I'm saying I loathe our situation. I know you do, too. I despise acting in a dishonorable manner and what that does to you."

"I chose our Tuesday nights. You didn't force them on me."

"Is there anything I can do or say to change Stefan's mind?"

"I don't think so," Lucie said in a low voice.

Jamie gripped her hands so tightly she winced. "Somehow, some way, I swear I will convince Stefan Kolska that I'm good enough for you. And someday I will be, Lucie, that I promise."

"Oh, Jamie. You're good enough."

His dark eyes blazed with conviction as he turned back to the dark water and stared at the approaching city. "I'm going to be successful. I'm going to have my slice of the pie. In America a man can go as far as his talents and his ambition will take him. Someday everyone in this city will know of Kelly's Design and Construction Company. That is going to happen, dearest Lucie, just as we've discussed it. Not as soon as I would like it to, but it *is* going to happen.''

"I believe you," she said softly. How could she doubt? When he spoke of his dreams and ambitions, his eyes glowed with determination. Surely no one could want success that badly and fail to achieve it. His opportunity would come.

"And when I'm rich, I'll buy you wonderful presents," he said, smiling at her. "I'll buy all those wonderful things we've seen in the emporium windows along Ladies Mile."

She laughed aloud, enjoying his vision, thrilled by the strength of his hands pressing hers. When Jamie spoke like this, hinting of a wonderful future together, her heart soared. At least until they parted. Then she couldn't help wondering if Jamie's vision, and hers, would really happen or if it would remain in the misty realm of dreams. But it was lovely to think about.

After disembarking from the ferry they fell silent in dread of parting, resenting that they could no longer walk together to the opening between the buildings. They would have to part sooner to avoid the risk of being observed.

When they approached Elizabeth Street, Jamie stopped and guided her toward a doorway out of the flow of pedestrian traffic. Gently, he turned her toward him, taking both her hands and frowning down into her face.

"I just realized...I've assumed a hell of a lot. I apologize, dear Lucie. Here I am talking about buying you presents...and I don't know if you..."

All she could think about was his large hands holding hers. Making an effort she raised a smile against the tremble in her lips. "Jamie Kelly, don't tell me there's a streak of uncertainty in you. Are you saying now that I have a choice?"

His grin made her knees go weak. "As a matter of fact, lass, you don't. If I wish to shower you with gifts you'll simply have to accept them, proper or not."

Lucie's laugh momentarily relaxed the tension coiling her stomach. But immediately it returned. For a moment she forgot the people hurrying around them, forgot they were not alone. All she wanted was to wrap her arms around him and assure him that he had assumed nothing.

His hands tightened painfully around hers and corded muscles rose on his neck. "When you look at me like that I would give ten years of my life to have three minutes alone with you," he murmured in a husky voice. His warm breath flowed over her mouth and cheeks. "I've never wanted anything so much in my life!"

"I know," she murmured helplessly.

What they were doing was madness. Someone she knew could pass and discover them standing close together, absorbed in each other, and inform Stefan. But she was powerless to step away and deny what she was feeling. She wanted Jamie Kelly's arms around her, longed to know his kiss, his touch.

"Lucie." His voice was hoarse, his gaze fastened to her parted lips. "I must leave at once before I dishonor you."

"Nothing you do could ever dishonor me, Jamie Kelly," she whispered.

Lost in the moment and in each other, they stood so close they could feel each other's magnetic heat. And suddenly Lucie knew he would kiss her. She felt as if she were drowning in the chocolate melt of his eyes. Her lips parted and her breath quickened. The sound of passing voices and street traffic faded from her ears, replaced by the accelerated pulse of her thudding heart. Slowly he leaned to her, looked deeply into her eyes, then his warm mouth brushed her lips as tenderly as the whisper of a butterfly's wing.

Her response was electric. Her scalp tingled and an explosive heat raced downward to her shaking limbs. For a moment she thought her knees would collapse and was grateful for his steadying hands.

"Forgive me, Lucie," he murmured, his voice shaken. "I've claimed a liberty I had no right to—"

"I wanted you to," she admitted, still tasting him on her lips. And she wanted him to kiss her again. The kiss they had shared had been gentle, exploratory, the passion they felt held in check. But passion had flamed to life. She saw it in his fevered eyes, felt it coursing through her own blood and bone.

His fingertips trembled as he raised her chin. "You've become very important to me, Lucie Kolska. I love the look of you, and the sound of your laughter. I love it that you believe in me and I love your loyalty to those you care about. You never complain, you make everyone around you feel a little better."

She stared into his steady gaze, her heart pounding, waiting for him to say the three words she longed to hear. But, of course he could not. No honorable man would, not in their present circumstances. "Oh, Jamie. Stefan will never change his mind," she murmured. Sadness filled her eyes with sudden moisture.

"Neither will I," he said, smiling. His thumb caressed the line of her cheek. Then, controlling the emotion she read in his expression, he moved away from her with obvious reluctance.

She lingered at the entrance to Elizabeth Street and watched him walk away from her. Later, she lay on her mattress and relived his kiss, imagining the pressure of his lips on hers, the sweet taste of his mouth. A tingling rush of heat spread over her body as she remembered his hands on her waist, the feel of his hard thighs against her skirts. Restlessly she turned on her bed and her cheeks burned in the darkness.

Chapter Six

The sky was gray and overcast the day the last of the dirt and debris was removed from the construction pit and Mr. Gustoffer assigned his crews to make forms and mix concrete to build the load-bearing walls. By the time the noon whistle blew several of the forms were built, set in place and poured.

As the sound of the whistle died away Jamie climbed to street level, pushed his hammer through the loop on his nail apron, and stood on the edge of the foundation frowning down at the forms. The perspective was better here; his suspicion was confirmed. When he was positive of what he was seeing he strode toward the shed and leaned inside.

"We've got a problem," he announced when Gustoffer looked up from his lunch pail. "The main bearing wall is out of position."

"What?" Gustoffer stared, then set down his lunch pail and rose to his feet. "What the hell are you talking about?"

"Come have a look." Gustoffer followed him to the edge of the pit. "This building will be twelve stories tall. The major stress and weight should be evenly distributed, but in fact the center support accepts the primary strain." Frowning, Jamie looked at Gustoffer. "But the center support is misaligned. If you pour the form where it's sitting now, eventually the upper stories will crash into the basement."

A silence had fallen over the site. Several of the men unabashedly eavesdropped on the conversation.

Without a word Gustoffer turned on his heel and hurried back into the shed where he bent over the blueprints scattered across his worktable. When he raised his head he was scowling.

"You're crazier than a bedbug, Kelly. That wall is going up just where the plans say it should. Have a look for yourself."

Jamie bent over the table and studied the plans. "Good Lord," he said softly. "The architect made a serious error."

"Well, I'll be gol-damned." Gustoffer's thick eyebrows soared. He made a disgusted sound and spit a stream of tobacco juice toward the corner. "If you ain't the most arrogant mick I ever seen. You're telling me that you—a shovel and hammer man—know more than one of the best architects in this city?"

"No," Jamie said slowly. "But I am saying everyone makes an error now and again. And I'm saying that center support is misaligned. You know it, too, Gustoffer."

"Unlike you, Kelly, I don't claim to know more than the architect." He tapped a blunt finger on the set of plans. "This here wall might be some newfangled way of doing things."

Jamie looked out the shed door at the tangle of Broadway traffic. "No," he said finally, shaking his head. "It's a mistake, and it's dangerous. You have to inform Mr. Tucker that his architect made an error."

"He's right, Gustoffer," Stefan Kolska said, appearing in the doorway. Jamie turned in surprise but Stefan didn't look at him. He stepped up to the worktable and fixed a troubled expression on Gustoffer. "I never thought I'd agree with Kelly on anything. But I overheard what he said, and he's right."

"You, too?" Gustoffer blinked at him. "You're both crazy!"

Now Stefan looked at Jamie, a frown drawing his heavy eyebrows together. "Kelly's also right about informing the owner and the architect. You have to stop work and you have to tell them."

"I ain't gonna do no such thing! I'm gonna do my job and build this building just like the plans say I should build it."

"Henry, you can't do that." After casting a look of gratitude toward Stefan, Jamie turned back to Gustoffer. "If you erect a building over those support walls, the building will be unsafe. Maybe it will stand for a month, maybe it will stand for six months or longer. But it *will* come down, and people will be hurt or killed. You must inform Mr. Tucker."

"*You* say!"

"I say so, too," Stefan repeated.

"You two go eat your chuck and forget about this."

"I can't do that," Jamie said finally. "If you won't tell Mr. Tucker—" he hesitated "—then, I will." Reaching behind he untied his nail apron and hung it on one of the pegs.

Stefan and Henry Gustoffer followed him to the street and watched in silence as he washed his face and hands at the horse trough, then pulled his coat over his arms.

"If you walk off the job site, son, I got to fire you. There ain't no choice. If you go now, no point in you coming back."

"I know that." He also knew there were situations that appeared to offer choices, but in which there was actually no decision to make. A man had to do what he knew was right. Even if the cost came high. To his surprise, it appeared Stefan agreed. Stefan unhooked his apron and prepared to accompany him.

"Wait," he said, raising a hand. "I appreciate your show of support, Kolska." More than he could say. "But there's no point in both of us losing our jobs. I started this. I'll finish it."

"I agree with you. I'm willing to go with you and say so."

It must have pained Stefan Kolska to set aside his pride and support Jamie Kelly. An hour earlier Jamie would not have believed Kolska's integrity would win over his personal hatred. He had seriously misjudged the man.

"You can't afford to lose this job, you have a family," Jamie said quietly. The allusion to Lucie blunted both their expressions. "If I go home tonight without a pay packet, the only person who suffers is me. I'll go to Mr. Tucker alone." After a moment's hesitation Jamie thrust out his hand and Gustoffer clasped it. "I'm sorry, Henry. I have to do this."

Gustoffer shrugged and spit out a brown stream. "All's that's gonna happen is you're gonna get your ears clipped and find yourself out of work. And that's a gol-damned pity 'cause you're a good worker, Jamie Kelly. Never thought I'd say that about no Thoroughbred, but it's the God's honest truth."

"If I don't bring this to Mr. Tucker's attention, and this building falls in, I'll feel responsible."

"Next to you, son, a mule is the very soul of compliance. You get some crack-brained idea in your head and nothing on God's green earth is gonna dislodge it! Do you really think there's so many jobs in this town that you can afford to throw yours away?"

Jamie's jaw settled in a line. "Whatever happens, Henry Gustoffer, I thank you for hiring me and giving me a chance."

"Which you are throwing away." Gustoffer released Jamie's grip and threw his hands in the air. "Ain't no figuring a bastard mick! So go do what you got to do. But don't be telling Mr. Tucker that Henry T. Gustoffer agrees with any of this bunkum."

"If it makes a difference, you can tell Mr. Tucker that Stefan Kolska does agree with you." For one fleeting instant, it appeared Stefan would shake his hand. Then Stefan thrust his thumbs under his suspenders and turned to scowl at the pit workers who had listened to the exchange with great interest.

Before Jamie walked down Broadway to seek a Wall Street horse car, he saw the triumphant satisfaction spreading across the faces of several of the pit workers. For an instant he wavered, knowing he was walking away from whatever small security he possessed. Then he glanced at the grudging respect he read in Stefan Kolska's eyes, and he looked into the pit at the wooden forms waiting to be poured. His shoulders squared.

As the delicate fabrics of the small clothes were too fragile for a washboard, they were agitated with a plunger in a tub of warm sudsy water before being wrung out by hand, then placed in an empty tub and the first rinse poured over them.

Everyone in the laundry gathered around the rinse tub to have a peek at the Neena bust improver Mrs. Roper had purchased for Miss Augusta at Wanamaker's. Hilda knelt over the tub and poked the padding with a fingertip, then collapsed in giggles, earning a glare from Mrs. Greene.

"Stop that right now! This might look like fuss and feathers to you, Hilda Horshack, but Miss Augusta could use a bit to go on! If fashion says a woman's got to look like an S from the side, then that's how the pippins have to look. Our Miss Augusta has the lower part of the S, but she needs a bit of deceiver to help along the top half."

"Our Miss Augusta isn't a pippin," Hilda muttered sulkily.

Mrs. Greene's face turned a deeper shade of red. "She is so popular!"

"She's not so popular with the beaux and that's a fact."

Lucie smiled with affection as Mrs. Greene exploded, loudly and loyally defending Miss Augusta's virtues.

At that moment the object of the discussion burst into the laundry room, followed by an overwrought Mrs. Roper. As no one could remember any of the Ropers visiting the laundry, mouths fell open and an astonished silence dropped over the room. Mrs. Greene halted midstride. Lucie paused with the polishing iron hovering in her hand.

Neither Miss Augusta nor Mrs. Roper glanced at anyone. Red eyed and wringing her hands, Miss Augusta stormed past the ironing tables, her flounced hem dragging the damp floor.

"Augusta, this is outrageous behavior!" Mrs. Roper held her skirts away from a puddle of bluing and followed in pursuit of her daughter. Every eye in the room watched in amazement. "You will return to the parlor at once! Do you hear? At once!"

Miss Augusta raised her hands to cover her ears and shook her dark curls. "Is there nowhere I can escape? No, Mama, I won't talk about it any more! No, no, no. I will not marry Baron Grieple! He's old and fat and he spits when he talks."

Mrs. Roper cast a furious scowl at the figures standing frozen in the laundry room. "We will not discuss these matters in front of the servants," she hissed through her teeth.

"Excellent! We shall say no more." Swatting at the steam swirling in front of her, Miss Augusta wound between the wash tubs scattered across the floor. "If being here will give me a moment's respite, I'll never leave the laundry."

"You foolish chit!" Mrs. Roper followed into the gauntlet of tubs. Forgetting her own dictum, she raised her voice to her daughter's back. "Don't you realize you could be a baroness?"

"I don't want to be a baroness!" Miss Augusta pressed her hands over her ears. "I want to marry Mr. Charles Whitcomb!"

A look of distaste twisted Axa Roper's sharp features. "Whitcomb! That coal oil Johnny!"

"He's not, Mama. If only you would give him a chance, he—"

"We shall never agree to such a misalliance. You must stop behaving so foolishly. You are going to marry the baron!"

Tears spilled down Miss Augusta's cheeks as she rounded the drying racks. Distraught, she threw out her hands, toppling one of the racks. "Do you plan to lock me in my room and keep me prisoner? Like Mrs. Vanderbilt did to poor Consuélo?"

"Poor Consuélo? Consuélo Vanderbilt is now the Duchess of Marlborough!" Envy raised a greenish cast to Mrs. Roper's skin. "Poor Consuélo, indeed!"

Miss Augusta stopped in front of Lucie, not seeing her. Her head dropped into her hands and her lace-clad shoulders convulsed in sobs of despair.

"I'm so sorry," Lucie whispered, not realizing she spoke aloud until Miss Augusta raised her tearstained face and fastened on the sympathy filling Lucie's eyes. A strangled sound tore from her throat, then she whirled on her heel and ran from the laundry, slamming the door behind her.

Everyone swiveled to look at Mrs. Roper. In the sudden silence they could hear the water bubbling on the range top, the popping of the irons as they heated.

Aside from twin circles of crimson flaming on Mrs. Roper's cheeks there was nothing in her manner to indicate an unseemly scene had transpired. She drew herself upright and stepped forward with practiced dignity as if she had deliberately chosen to visit the laundry to inspect the proceedings.

"We'll be into woolens soon," she informed Mrs. Greene. None of the strain thinning her voice appeared in her imperial manner. "Do we have ether on hand for spots?"

"I've laid in a good supply, ma'am." Mrs. Greene's eyes were as wide as the bluing tub.

Moving toward the door, Mrs. Roper paused to inspect the box of starch frozen in Hilda's hand. "Kingsford's Pure? We don't use economy brands in this household, if you please. From now on, you will use Silver Gloss.'' Hilda nodded, too dumbfounded to speak.

As was Lucie. She forgot to bob her head as Mrs. Roper approached. Mrs. Roper glanced at the chemise draped over the bosom board, then at the iron in Lucie's hand.

''Well? Why are you standing there like a statue? Is that what we pay you for?''

''I . . . no, ma'am.'' Lowering the iron, she pressed it carefully along Miss Delfi's ribbons, feeling Mrs. Roper's stare.

''You're the one with the lovely skin,'' Mrs. Roper observed, her voice still sharp. She watched Lucie's hands pushing the iron down the string of ribbons. The barest suggestion of a sigh escaped her lips as she transferred her gaze to her own hands. ''I don't know how you manage. I should expect your hands to be red and chapped from the soap and hot water.''

''I make a cream, ma'am. It seems to help.''

''Oh?'' Mrs. Roper turned her gaze to the door so recently slammed by her daughter. ''You must bring me a sample one day.''

Lucie couldn't believe her ears. Mrs. Roper asking for a sample of her cream. ''I would be honored!''

''What?'' Distracted, Mrs. Roper turned from the door wearing a look of annoyance.

''To bring you a sample of my cream.''

''Oh, yes. Yes, you do that.'' She opened the door and glanced into the empty hallway and lifted a hand in an absent motion. ''You may carry on, Mrs. Greene.''

''Thank you for stopping in, ma'am.'' Finally able to move, Mrs. Greene hurried toward the mistress of the house bobbing her cap up and down in a belated gesture of respect.

Mrs. Roper raised her chin to a regal posture. ''One must keep abreast of one's household.'' With a final nodding glance around the room she lifted her skirts, then hurried down the corridor. ''Augusta! Where have you gotten to?''

When Mrs. Roper's voice died away, Lucie exchanged her cool iron for one that was heated. In five minutes they would go to the kitchen for the midday meal and spend the next half hour discussing every tiny detail of this morning's extraordinary events. None the least of which was Mrs. Roper's astonishing request for a sample of Lucie's cream.

Her mind jumped ahead. The minute she completed her Sunday chores, she would ask Stefan to accompany her to the chemist in Mercer Street to purchase the ingredients. Imagining a grand lady like Axa Roper using her cream sent Lucie's spirits soaring. Such a thing could happen only in America.

Moreover she felt a sudden rush of appreciation for Stefan. Although he refused her permission to follow her heart, he did offer her the right of refusal. In some ways, she was richer than Augusta Roper.

THE RAIN BEGAN shortly after Jamie boarded the Wall Street horse car. By the time he stepped out of the car in front of Trinity Church and turned up his collar, Wall Street had been churned into a stew of offal, mud and debris. The torrents of muddy water running down the pavement had driven the curb-side brokers indoors and the street appeared deserted.

Feeling the water seeping through the soles of his shoes, Jamie pulled down his cap and dashed through the downpour toward the building where Mr. Jonas Tucker kept his office.

Once inside he shook the rain from his cap and brushed at the dampness on his shoulders. His shoes and pant cuffs were a muddy disgrace, but there was no help for it. On the bright side, the rain would prevent Gustoffer from pouring the load wall.

After rapping at Mr. Tucker's office door he boldly stepped inside and presented himself before a stern-looking man seated behind a large desk. Behind the gentleman two neatly dressed typewriters glanced at him, then continued tapping their fingers across the keys. Jamie would like to have examined the printing machines at closer quarters and question the typewriters about them. But that was not why he had come.

He swept his cap from his dripping hair. "Mr. Tucker?"

The grim-mouthed man looked up from his desk and inspected Jamie with obvious distaste. "I am Mr. Haversham, Mr. Tucker's personal secretary. Do you have an appointment?"

Jamie leaned over the desk and looked Mr. Haversham square in the eyes. "I assure you Mr. Tucker will want to receive me. I've come on a matter of great urgency."

"I'm afraid Mr. Tucker is too busy to receive someone without an appointment."

Jamie leaned farther over the desk. His eyes narrowed and he spoke through his teeth. "I didn't throw away my job and ruin my shoes to be turned aside." Now he saw the second door. "You inform Mr. Tucker that Mr. Jamie Kelly is here from Mr. Tucker's building site on Broadway. And I mean to see him today."

Mr. Haversham's nostrils pinched in a sniff. "I doubt Mr. Tucker will welcome being ordered about by a common laborer."

"I may be a laborer, Mr. Haversham, but I assure you I am not common." One of the typewriters smiled and sent him a sidelong glance. "Now you announce me to Mr. Tucker, or I'll do the job myself," he said, eyeing the door.

Mr. Haversham looked appalled. His face clamped into a disapproving mask as he slowly rose to his feet.

While he waited for Mr. Haversham to emerge from Mr. Tucker's office, Jamie considered what he would do if Mr. Tucker refused to admit him, a possibility that had not previously occurred. What did occur was the dawning impact of realizing he no longer had a job. Some of the ardor cooled from his gaze as his prospects dimmed. Worse, his future with Lucie moved toward an impossibly distant horizon.

"You may step inside," Mr. Haversham announced in a stiff, disapproving tone.

As Jamie entered an office with a stunning view of the harbor, Mr. Tucker rose behind his desk. Anger flickered in his narrowed gaze.

"You had better have a damned good reason for bullying your way into my office, Mr. Kelly."

"I do, sir." Aware he was dripping mud and water on Mr. Tucker's carpet, he moved to stand before a massive polished desk. "I've come about the main bearing wall."

"What in hell are you talking about?" Mr. Tucker sat down behind his desk, but he did not invite Jamie to sit. Leaning back in his chair, he brushed back his lapels and hooked his thumbs beneath his suspenders. His thick steel-colored eyebrows knit in a line across his brow as Jamie explained the problem.

Mr. Tucker stared at him when he finished speaking. "Are you the foreman on the site?" Jamie admitted he was not. "I see. Does my foreman believe the bearing wall is positioned incorrectly?"

"Mr. Gustoffer disagrees with me. He's building the wall where the plan says it should be built."

Mr. Tucker's eyes narrowed. "So who the hell are you?"

"I work at the site."

"A laborer?" Mr. Tucker jumped to his feet and pointed angrily to the door. "Get out of my office. If Gustoffer hasn't fired you for wasting his time, I'm firing you for wasting mine!"

Jamie didn't budge. "Mr. Tucker, if you proceed without correction, the building will eventually crash." Mr. Tucker started around the desk, his face reddening in anger. Then Jamie spoke the magic words. "You will lose a lot of money."

The statement halted Mr. Tucker's progress. He stared at Jamie, trying to evaluate his expression. "What makes you think you're right about this and my architect is wrong?"

"I studied architecture with Goblin and Greene in Dublin. I've worked construction sites since I was wee. Mistakes can happen, Mr. Tucker, expensive mistakes. The question is, can you afford to take the risk that I'm wrong?"

Jonas Tucker turned on his heel and moved to the window. He stroked his jaw. Finally he rang the brass bell next to an expensive crystal ink well.

"If you're wrong about this, Kelly, I'll have your hide for a lamp shade." When Mr. Haversham appeared in response to the bell, Tucker glared at him. "Send a message to Clem Whitesall. Tell him to meet me at the Broadway site at once."

"Shall I use the telephone, sir? I believe his firm has one." Having received permission, Haversham exited quietly.

"Thank you, Mr. Tucker." In spite of himself, Jamie was impressed that Jonas Tucker possessed a telephone. "You won't regret this."

"I regret it already," Tucker grumbled, reaching for his hat and umbrella. "No, you don't," he snapped when Jamie turned to leave. "You're coming, too. I want to hear you explain to Clem Whitesall how a hammer man knows more than the city's celebrated architect. The only reason I'm agreeing to this tomfoolery is the remote possibility that you may be right."

"I am." The conviction Jamie felt allowed him to meet Jonas Tucker's glare without a waver.

They didn't exchange further words inside Tucker's brougham during the ride to the site. The wheels of the brougham slipped and slid and once it appeared they would collide with a wagon, but Tucker's coachman was a skilled whip and managed to guide a matched set of blacks through the muddy streets without incident.

Still without speaking they stepped to the pavement in front of the site, and Mr. Tucker unfurled his umbrella and moved to scowl into the muddy pit. Jamie stood in the rain, aware that Gustoffer, Stefan and the others sheltering beneath the shed's overhang watched with silent interest, most of them anticipating his forthcoming comeuppance.

Gustoffer shot Jamie an irritated glance, then slogged through the diminishing rain to greet Mr. Tucker. When Stefan started to follow, Gustoffer waved him back to the shed with an angry gesture.

Tucker nodded his bowler toward the dripping forms at the bottom of the pit. "Well?"

"Those forms are spaced exactly as the plans show they ought. Mr. Kelly is dead wrong, sir."

They all turned toward the street as a hansom slid up on the curb and Mr. Clem Whitesall emerged, swearing and kicking at the carriage wheels. He was younger than Jonas Tucker but equally well dressed and equally furious at being called out on a fool's errand.

He charged forward, jabbing his umbrella at the sky. "What's this poppycock about a bearing wall being misaligned?" Advancing with long strides to the edge of the pit, he halted two steps in front of Jamie. "This is an outrage! How dare you question my plans!" He stared at the rain running down Jamie's face, plastering his hair to his skull and his clothing to his body.

In answer Jamie silently turned to face the pit and waved a hand to encompass the view below.

While everyone watched, Clem Whitesall directed his angry glare into the pit and onto the wet forms. His body jerked and his mouth fell open. Then his mouth closed. He stared, blinked, ran a shaking hand over his eyes and stared again. "Good God."

Jonas Tucker's eyebrows arched toward his hat brim. "What? Are you saying the Irishman is right?"

Whitesall rounded on Gustoffer. "You didn't follow my plans!"

"But I did, sir. I followed your plans to the letter!"

"That's not possible." Grim faced, Clem Whitesall stepped off the boards laid over the mud and strode toward the shed, oblivious of his boots and cuffs. The others followed and the pit crews moved backward to allow them inside the shed.

Whitesall went directly to the worktable and flipped through the prints until he found the one he sought. For a long silent moment he stared down at the page.

When he lifted his head his face was ashen. No one in the shed needed to be told what he had discovered on the plans. "I owe you an apology, Mr. Kelly," Clem Whitesall said in a strained voice. "I don't know how this happened. I would not have believed it possible. But if you had not noticed and if you had not insisted on this review, a terrible disaster would surely have occurred. I am in your debt, sir."

The shouting and cursing rising from the street outside sounded overloud within the silence of the shed.

Mr. Tucker was first to recover from the collective contemplation of the averted disaster. And the money that would have been lost. He aimed the tip of his umbrella at Gustoffer. "You are fired." The umbrella swung toward Jamie. "And you are hired as foreman of this site. Mr. Gustoffer will turn over the keys to the shed and the safe. Should further problems develop on this site," he added with a dark glance at Clem Whitesall, "I shall expect to find you in my office at once, Mr. Kelly."

"Yes, sir," Jamie said as Jonas Tucker ducked through the door of the shed and picked his way across the muddy boards toward his waiting brougham. There was opportunity here. Jamie could sense it, could smell it on the damp air. The question was, could he seize it? Stepping up to Clem Whitesall, he cleared his throat. "While I'm pleased by the position Mr. Tucker has granted me, my true interest is design. I trained with Goblin and—"

"Not now, for God's sake," Whitesall hissed, keeping an eye on Tucker's retreat as he hastily rolled the erroneous print into a tube and stuffed it inside his coat. "New prints will be waiting when you arrive tomorrow morning." Before he dashed out the door, he gave Jamie a long stare.

"You needn't fear that I shall forget Jamie Kelly. I'll remember you, all right."

But Whitesall's tone didn't encourage Jamie to think the remembrance would be pleasant. As he stood in the doorway watching Clem Whitesall dash through the drizzle to catch Jonas Tucker, he knew he was watching opportunity fly away.

When he turned back into the shed, Henry Gustoffer was standing beside the table, hands thrust deep in his pockets, his eyes on the floor.

"I'm sorry, Henry," he said in a low voice.

"Not your fault, son. These things happen. I should have known better than to bet against you." They stood in silence, aware the men outside had overheard everything. Then Gustoffer withdrew his hand from his pocket and placed his keys on the work table.

"Henry, if there's anything I can—"

"Don't make this no worse than it is, boyo." Gustoffer reached for his cap and dropped it on his head. He thrust out a callused palm and shook Jamie's hand. "I'll just be on my way."

"There may be work at the new University Club."

Gustoffer managed a grin before he ducked out of the shed door. "I started thinking about it the minute that architect looked into the pit." He waved, then hunched his shoulders against the drizzle and walked past the silent crew.

Jamie picked up the keys and held them in his palm. The opportunity he wanted had eluded him, but his situation had improved markedly since morning. He had received a promotion and, he assumed, the raise in pay that accompanied it. Things could be a whole lot worse. An hour ago he hadn't had a job. Now he was foreman of a major site. His future was his again.

Stepping to the door, he watched Henry Gustoffer march through the drizzle toward Broadway and regretted that his good fortune had come at Henry's expense. Henry had only done what he believed was right.

After a moment he sighed, then cleared his throat. "Martin?" Wilbur Martin stepped away from the overhang. "The drizzle doesn't appear to be letting up. Close down the site for today. The rest of you men line up for half pay."

He sat behind the worktable, opened the safety box and paid out wages without looking up at the men behind the outstretched palms. Already his mind leaped ahead, planning tomorrow and the changes he would make.

It wasn't until he was walking home, unaware the drizzle had stopped and a brilliant sunset had broken past the clouds, that he realized it was possible opportunity had not bypassed him after all. He was doing what he loved best, building a wonderful building. And he had moved a step up in the world.

His regret for Henry Gustoffer's altered fortunes had not allowed him to fully appreciate the change in his own. But as he gradually accepted there was nothing he could do to correct the injustices of the world, the realization of his altered circumstances brought an abrupt lift of his spirits. He couldn't wait to tell Lucie about this astonishing day.

LUCIE PUMPED A PAIL of water and carried it upstairs, then changed out of her wet clothing while the water heated on the stove. Since her hair was already wet from the drizzle, this was a good time to wash it. Bending over the pan she dipped her head into the water, then worked a bar of Castilian soap into a lather and rubbed it into her hair. Then she leaned over the slop bucket and poured the water over her head, hoping all the soap rinsed out. It seldom did, but she always hoped.

After toweling and combing the waist-length strands, she placed a chair in front of the stove and sat with her back to the heat, her long hair falling over the rungs of the chair.

While she waited for her hair to dry, she composed a list of ingredients she would need to make her cream. Ointment of rose water, oil of sweet almonds, glycerine, boric acid, solution of soda and rose oil for the scent. The only item she worried about finding was the quince seed mucilage, and that was the only item she absolutely could not do without. Mucilage was the gummy adhesive that prevented the cream from separating over time. In her opinion, quince seed mucilage served the purpose best.

When Stefan came in the door and hung his cap and coat on the nails, she looked up with sparkling eyes. "You'll never guess what happened! Mrs. Roper requested a sample of my cream! Can you imagine? Mrs. Roper could buy any cream in the world, but she asked—" The words died in her throat when Stefan turned and she saw his pale face. Her pencil and paper fell to the floor as she stood. "Stefan! What's wrong? What's happened?"

He dropped heavily onto a chair, then placed half a day's wage on the tabletop before he gave her a bleak expression.

"Gustoffer was fired today." He passed a hand over his eyes. "As sure as I'm sitting here, I'm next. Tomorrow I'll be out of a job." He told her what had occurred.

"But you supported Jamie Kelly," Lucie said, sitting across from him at the table. "He wouldn't fire you."

"Kelly knows I despise the very sight of him. I supported him because he was right in what he was saying. But that doesn't change how I feel, and he knows it. First thing tomorrow he'll tell me to take my shovel and hammer and go."

Lucie lowered her head and blinked at the coins on the table. A battle erupted in her heart. Pride in Jamie's success warred with fear for Stefan's future. Once again her loyalties were tugged from two sides. Heart aching, she realized there was nothing she could say.

Chapter Seven

For the all important occasion of delivering the cream to Mrs. Roper, Lucie dressed her hair with extra attention, taking care that no errant strands would escape the edges of her cap. Before she approached Mr. Grist, she ironed a freshly starched apron and replaced the damp apron she had worn all morning.

"I would prefer to deliver the cream myself, sir."

The barest hint of a smile appeared on Mr. Grist's thin lips. "I'll discover if Mrs. Roper will receive you."

Lucie hoped Mrs. Roper would exclaim over the cream, her best batch ever. Also, she wanted another peek at the family's rooms. She and Greta had exhausted the recollections of her first visit. As she followed Mr. Grist upstairs she wished Greta could view the profusion of blooms in every room.

"Don't touch the bannister, miss. It's just been polished."

She could smell the waxy lemon scent. One of the wonderful things about the Roper mansion was the abundance of good smells. The kitchen and garden always smelled wonderful, of course. But there was also the heavy sweet fragrance of fresh flowers in every room, the citrus scent of furniture polish. The faintly herbal drift that rose from the carpets as they passed, and traces of holly from the tall candles in silver brackets.

Inhaling deeply, Lucie wondered what it must be like to always breathe sweet air. Never to gasp and turn aside from the odor of rotting garbage or overflowing latrines. To open a window and breathe deeply instead of recoiling.

And the music. Pausing on the landing, she closed her eyes and smiled with pleasure at the sound of Miss Delfi's Gramophone. Today Miss Delfi was playing the new raggety-time music. Lucie recognized the piece "The Maple Leaf Rag." She had fallen in love with it last week when Stefan took her and Greta to the Bowery Street Music Hall. Standing on the landing, tapping her foot to Scott Joplin, Lucie decided it would be a fine, fine thing to have music anytime one wished.

When she stepped into Mrs. Roper's sitting room, taking a moment to dart a glance at the bric-a-brac and table scarves, Mrs. Roper glanced up from her embroidery frame and regarded her without a flicker of recognition. "Yes? What is it?"

"I . . ." Lucie smoothed a hand over her apron. "It's the cream, ma'am," she explained in a rush.

Annoyed, Mrs. Roper looked at Mr. Grist before returning her gaze to Lucie. "Whatever are you talking about?"

"The day you . . . visited the laundry, ma'am. You mentioned you would welcome a sample of my hand and face cream."

"I did? How extraordinary."

Lucie thrust out the twist of newspaper she had prepared. "I didn't know how much to bring. This should last a week or two."

Mrs. Roper shuddered as she inspected the greasy twist of newspaper. "Place it there, in the silver dish."

Lucie did as she was bid, then gave Mrs. Roper a shy smile. "I think you'll find the cream soothing and refreshing, ma'am."

"Indeed," Mrs. Roper said faintly. This time when she directed a glance at Mr. Grist, he stepped forward.

After bobbing her head, Lucie followed Mr. Grist into the hallway. "Imagine," she breathed, her cheeks glowing. "Mrs. Roper and my cream. This must be the proudest moment of my life!"

Mr. Grist touched a meticulously knotted cravat and released a sound resembling a sigh. "As you say, miss."

Dazed and smiling happily, she returned to the laundry room. It was only later that she remembered Miss Augusta standing red-eyed beside the parlor archway, peering at Lucie as if she wished to speak to her. Lucie had actually halted in expectation, but Miss Augusta turned away from Mr. Grist and waved them on. Lucie decided she and Mr. Grist had misinterpreted Miss Augusta's intention. Still, the moment had been peculiar and puzzling.

But not significant enough to diminish her happiness. Jamie had been promoted, Greta was doing well and finally Lucie had something wonderful to share. She almost danced back to the laundry room.

"I'M TELLING YOU no the same as I told you last Saturday and the Saturday before and the Saturday before that." Stefan spread his hands and glared at Jamie before he hung his tool belt on the shed wall. "I will never permit you to call on my sister."

"May I inquire why not?"

"You know why not." Stefan strode to the door, then halted abruptly. On impulse he turned back into the shed. "There's a matter to clear between us and I don't want to do it here." He flicked a glanced toward Wilbur Martin.

Jamie's eyebrows rose. "The Bag and Boodle is nearby. Give me a moment to finish here, then I'll buy your thirst."

"I'll pay for my own beer," Stefan replied sharply.

After he finished locking the shed for the night, Jamie found Stefan waiting on the curb beside the horse trough. Without speaking they walked along Broadway to Canal Street, then turned into the Bag and Boodle and ordered a pail of German ale.

As Stefan still did not speak, Jamie accepted the free sausage and pickled eggs for them both, then glanced into the mirror above the back bar. "What's on your mind?"

"There's something I have to know." Frowning, Stefan studied Jamie's image in the glass. "Why didn't you fire me along with the others you sacked? Did you keep me on and give me a promotion because you thought I'd agree to let you call on Lucie?"

"No." After draining his glass, Jamie tipped the pail and poured another. "I'd never jeopardize the site for personal reasons." Stefan's gaslit image was fierce and defensive. "You thought I'd give you the sack, too?"

"Of course I did."

"Then you did me an injustice. I kept you because no one works harder or better. As for the promotion, you should have been promoted a long time ago. You manage people well, you show initiative, you're smart and you get the job done right the first time. Moreover, you were the only person besides myself to recognize the bearing wall was misaligned. At least the only person who had the courage to say so."

Stefan's narrowed gaze did not waver. "I didn't expect you to recognize or admit any of that."

Jamie smiled. "Believe me, I wish you weren't the man you are. Every time I look at you, I see an obstacle standing in my way. But firing you was never a consideration. Whether I like it or not, you're needed on the site and you're the best man to manage the concrete crew."

Stefan's chin jutted. "The answer is still no."

"I'm not going to give up, Kolska. I'll continue requesting your permission to call on your sister."

"The answer will always be no." When Jamie smiled and shrugged, Stefan frowned at his mug, moving it around so that it left damp circles on the counter. "There's something else," he said finally. "It wasn't right for you to fire those other men. They had families."

"They were slackers." Jamie shifted on his stool and looked at Stefan directly. "We can't afford to carry men who aren't giving a day's work for a day's pay. It wouldn't be fair to those of you who do earn your packet. But I agree to this extent—a man who loses his job should have some recourse. He should be protected from personal animosity. He should be entitled to know why he was terminated. And he shouldn't be sacked on impulse the way Henry Gustoffer was."

Surprised, Stefan said, "That sounds like union talk. Are you a sympathizer?"

Jamie didn't answer immediately. "In some ways I guess I am. I've been following the coal miner's efforts in the newspaper reports. As a man who hopes to own a business one day, I understand a business owner's desire to control his operation and make a profit. I also understand the working man's need to earn a decent wage for his labor and not feel he's being exploited to service another man's greed. At present a large gap exists between those two positions. Maybe the answer is to unite."

Stefan's nod was emphatic. "Right now only three and a half percent of all workers are organized. But the unions are coming, and we need them. Even with a promotion and a raise, I can't support a wife and family. Damn it, a man who works ten hours a day six days a week ought to be able to support a family."

"I agree. Everyone in this country is watching what happens with the new United Mine Workers. Those fourteen miners who died and those who were wounded in the Mount Olive massacre in Illinois last year deserved better. All they asked was fair working conditions. Now that the bituminous workers have joined the anthracite workers, maybe their next strike will make a difference. If the United Mine Workers can be successful, other industries will follow."

"But that's the question: Can they succeed? The iron and steel workers struck in 1892 and didn't win a damned thing. All they got was no pay for five months. And the AF of L seems more interested in signing up members than in doing anything for them. I believe unions are the fist of the future and the only way we're going to change things. But so far the unions' record is dismal."

They discussed the miners' ongoing struggle and rumblings of unionization within the garment industry, then Stefan gave him a curious look. "You said you hope to own a business of your own. What kind of business?" When Jamie finished explaining his love for design and construction, Stefan hesitated, then confided he too hoped to own a business one day. "But I'm not as fortunate as you. I don't know yet what I want to get into. I just know I don't want to spend the rest of my life working for someone else. That isn't why I came to America."

Later Jamie could not recall if he ordered the second growler or if Stefan did. Regardless, a full pail appeared before them and neither was willing to waste his money by leaving it behind. Over another pail of ale the conversation drifted to the hurricane that had recently devastated Puerto Rico and the rebuilding that would be necessary. Then they rehashed the Jeffries/Fitzsimmons heavyweight title fight thrashed out in June at Coney Island.

"I wish I'd seen it," Stefan said. "No one can beat Jeffries."

They talked about the new catch phrase, "conspicuous consumption," and what it meant. They talked about F. F. Stanley driving his steamer to the top of Mount Washington and they argued the future of the automobile and the need for improved roads and what would happen to horses and related businesses such as carriage makers, stables and feed stores.

Two hours later, slightly foxed, they clapped each other on the back and shook hands, preparing to part company. Misjudging the hours of pleasant companionship Jamie gripped Stefan's hand and asked, "Stefan, may I call on Lucie?"

Stefan's eyebrows knitted together. "No."

IT'S FUN! IT'S FREE!
AND IT COULD MAKE YOU A
MILLIONAIRE

If you've ever played scratch-off lottery tickets, you should be familiar with how our games work. On each of the first four tickets (numbered 1 to 4 in the upper right)—there are PINK METALLIC STRIPS to scratch off.

Using a coin, do just that—carefully scratch the PINK STRIPS to reveal how much each ticket could be worth if it is a winning ticket. Tickets could be worth from $5.00 to $1,000,000.00 in lifetime money.

Note, also, that each of your 4 tickets has a unique sweepstakes Lucky Number...and that's 4 chances for a **BIG WIN!**

FREE BOOKS!

At the same time you play your tickets for big cash prizes, you are invited to play ticket #5 for the chance to get one or more free book(s) from Harlequin. We give away free book(s) to introduce readers to the benefits of the *Harlequin Reader Service®*.

Accepting the free book(s) places you under no obligation to buy anything! You may keep your free book(s) and return the accompanying statement marked "cancel". But if we don't hear from you, then every month we'll deliver 4 of the newest Harlequin American Romance® novels right to your door. You'll pay the low members-only discount price of just $2.74* each—a savings of 21¢ apiece off the cover price. And there's no charge for shipping and handling!

Of course, you may play "THE BIG WIN" without requesting any free book(s) by scratching tickets #1 through #4 only. But remember, the first shipment of one or more books is FREE!

PLUS A FREE GIFT!

One more thing, when you accept the free book(s) on ticket #5 you are also entitled to play ticket #6 which is GOOD FOR A VALUABLE GIFT! Like the book(s) this gift is totally free and yours to keep as thanks for giving our Reader Service a try!

So scratch off the PINK STRIPS on all your BIG WIN tickets and send for everything today! You've got nothing to lose and everything to gain!

Here are your BIG WIN Game Tickets, worth from $5.00 to $1,000,000.00 each. Scratch off the PINK METALLIC STRIP on each of your sweepstakes tickets to see what you could win and mail your entry right away. (See official rules in back of book for details!)

This could be your lucky day – GOOD LUCK!

THE FOLLOWING SATURDAY, Jamie discovered Stefan waiting beside the horse trough when he finished locking the shed. They studied each other for a moment, then fell into step and returned to the Bag and Boodle.

"Will you be wanting sausage and pickled eggs?" Jamie asked, eyeing the platter the barkeep slid to their end of the counter.

"Lucie and Greta are waiting supper for me."

"Who is Greta?" Jamie inquired, as if he were hearing the name for the first time. After Stefan's explanation he murmured, "Your fiancée sounds like a lovely young lass. I'm sorry her health isn't all it should be." Lifting his head, he met Stefan's eyes in the back-bar mirror and smiled. "I'm interested in a lovely young lass, too. Shall I tell you about her?"

Stefan raised his eyes to the tin ceiling and spread his hands. "What's wrong with you, Kelly, that you can't recognize 'no' when you hear it?"

"A man doesn't get what he wants by hearing no. You know that, Kolska. Every person who comes through Ellis Island knows that. The way to succeed is to keep trying. Isn't that why you came to America?"

"I came to America because Russian cossacks were raiding the border villages conscripting men of my age into the army. I didn't want to give the czar twenty-five years of my life."

"You wanted to succeed in a life of your own choosing. And you will if you keep your eye on the prize." Jamie sliced one of the pickled eggs with his pocket knife. "You and I aren't so different, Stefan. We want to make our own mistakes and our own successes. We want a loving wife, a family and a business to build for our sons."

"The answer is no."

"JAMIE, STEFAN HAS NOT spoken a word to explain why he returns late on Saturday nights." Lucie raised a puzzled expression and looked at him across the table. She couldn't keep her mind on the comedian performing on stage and was glad when the gaslights dimmed and intermission arrived. "I don't understand."

"I'm not sure I do, either," Jamie admitted. They had arrived too late to obtain a seat near the stage and sat at the back of the hall beside a window fronting the street. A flake of snow tumbled past the panes and floated toward the pavement.

"What do the two of you talk about?"

"Last Saturday we discussed electric elevators. Without them, multistory buildings would be impossible. We argue about the Giants, discuss politics. We talk about the site, about advances in reinforced concrete and better steel." He raked his fingers through his auburn hair. "We talk about everything but you. Before Stefan leaves, I request permission to call on you, and he refuses."

Lucie lowered her head and bit her lip. "How long can we go on like this?" she whispered, returning the pressure of his fingers when he squeezed her hand across the table. "I hate deceiving Stefan. He's so good to me." She touched her fingertips to her forehead. "If it wasn't for Stefan, I would still be in Wlad. He's a good man, Jamie."

"Aye. I know. These last few weeks I've come to know and like Stefan as well as respect him."

Not even the comic's broad jests and pratfalls elevated her mood, nor did the music, which she usually loved. Turning her face to the window Lucie watched the snowflakes floating out of the darkness past the street lamps. When she first met Jamie, it was spring. Now winter was almost upon them and they were no closer to budging Stefan.

"I care for you, Jamie Kelly," she said softly, turning back to him. She couldn't be the first to mention love, but weeks ago she had admitted the truth to herself. She loved Jamie Kelly with a fierce possessiveness that extended beyond reason and family loyalty. "And I care for Stefan. Sometimes I feel as if I'm being torn in pieces, pulled between the two of you."

"I'm sorry, Lucie. I should never have placed you in this position." He studied her face in the gaslight. "But I love you, lass."

Lucie's head snapped up and her mouth formed a circle. A soft sound issued from her throat, and she couldn't breathe. Tears sprang into her soft eyes. "Oh, Jamie," she whispered. "You must know I love you, too."

The words had finally been spoken and her heart leapt with joy, hammering against the front of her striped shirt-waist. She wanted to caress his face, his hair, his shoulders, his eyelids. She wanted his kiss and his touch and the warmth of his arms around her. She wanted the thrill of his kisses and most of all in this stunning moment, she wanted privacy and deep lingering kisses that weren't rushed or hidden in doorways. She looked at him and her heart glowed in her eyes.

"Let's get out of here," Jamie said gruffly. "Unless you want to stay for the next act . . . ?"

Lucie laughed out loud. Her joy was so intense she would not have heard a word of what happened on stage. After gathering her gloves, reticule and winter coat, she accepted his arm with shyly possessive pride. He loved her! He had spoken the words aloud. He loved her, he loved her. It seemed she had waited forever to hear those words from him and to say them aloud herself.

They stepped outside into a world that had been magically transformed. Snow spread over the city like a clean white shawl, concealing the trash heaps and ash piles, the street offal and debris. The cold night air smelled wonderfully fresh and sharp; snowflakes settled like feathers on her cheeks.

Lucie lifted her face in delight. "It's like heaven did this for us! At home we bake a special bread to celebrate the first snow," she said, her dark eyes sparkling. "And sometimes we exchange small gifts." She pressed his arm close to her side and smiled up at him. "You gave me a wonderful gift tonight."

Because it was dark and the snowy street nearly deserted, he slipped an arm around her waist and held her close, smiling down into her eyes. "Ah, lass, you make loving so easy. I've loved you for so long, but I didn't feel I had a right to say so." A frown chased his smile. "I still don't have that right, but—"

Before he could say anything to diminish this jubilant moment, Lucie caught his hand and tugged him beneath the tracks of the elevated. "Aye, lass," he murmured. When Jamie recognized the side street leading to the deserted doorway they claimed as their own, they hurried toward it.

When Jamie reached for her, Lucie went eagerly into his arms. He opened his coat and she snuggled inside the folds, drawing his warmth into herself, loving the rough feel of tweed against her cheek, inhaling the scent of bay rum and Madagascar oil, starch and wool and all the scents that she knew as Jamie.

"Please say it again," she whispered.

"Lucie, Lucie," he murmured hoarsely. "Ah, lass, God, I love you so much."

A thrilling shock of heat shot through her body as his warm lips met her snowy mouth and his hands tightened on her waist. Her arms circled his neck and she pressed against the hard need of his growing passion, wanting to absorb him, to become him, to meld and blend and unite as one single being.

When his lips released hers he held her so tightly she smiled against his starched collar and breathlessly protested he was crushing her heart and her bones.

His ragged breath melted the snowflakes on her cheek. "The hardest thing about being poor is having no privacy, no place of one's own."

The dark snowy night was their privacy and their place. Smiling, Lucie traced the contour of his lips with her fingertip. "The hardest thing about being poor is having no money."

She loved the sound of his laughter. He grinned down at her and kissed the tip of her nose. "My practical lassie. And what would you do with a barrel of money?"

Leaning back in his arms she gazed up at him with a serious expression, though it was hard to think past his declaration of love. "I would give Stefan and Greta enough money to marry. I owe them that. My goal is to repay my passage fare."

"I doubt Stefan would agree," Jamie said. "Things have reached a pretty pass when a woman must provide a man's marriage money." His lips nuzzled her throat, then moved to her temples, her forehead, her eyelids.

When his lips burned against her skin, she could think of nothing else. For an instant she pressed against him and forgot everything but the lean hard length of his body molded against hers. She could feel the strength of his thighs through her skirts, the muscles swelling on his arms. Her breath quickened in her breast and to calm herself she tried to remember what they were discussing.

"A woman isn't allowed to give the future a little nudge?" she murmured, her eyes closing as she raised her mouth.

His kiss drew the strength from her limbs and left her feeling shaken and helpless. This then was passion, this feverish yearning for something more than stolen kisses in a dark doorway. This longing to fulfill an emptiness hitherto unrecognized. The depth of her need frightened her.

"Dearest Lucie," he murmured against her mouth. "The future is not your responsibility." That he could continue their conversation indicated he too struggled for control.

As he spoke his hands tightened on her waist in a grip that was almost painful, and she tried to focus on what he had said, wondering suddenly if they were still speaking of Stefan and Greta. One thing was certain. She didn't agree a man must shoulder the future alone. Not in America. Not in the land of equality where a man and woman could stand together. Surely Jamie didn't believe her sole duty was to stand aside and wait.

She would have asked, but he kissed her again and again, and the tiny alarm of warning fell silent. Their conversation, interspersed with passionate kisses, turned to the conversation of lovers everywhere. When did you know? How long...? Have you loved before? And they whispered the words again and again.

ALL TRACE OF THE SNOW had vanished by Saturday. When Jamie locked the shed the night sky was clear and cold, hidden behind the soft glow of Broadway's new electric street lamps.

"Finally man has conquered the night," he observed to Stefan as they examined the electric lamps before they turned away from the brightness and walked toward the Bag and Boodle.

"There's a future in electricity," Stefan commented as he carried their pail of ale to the table Jamie had located.

"Aye, the time will come when night will be banished all over the world." Jamie accepted the glass of ale Stefan poured. "Have you been watching the electric men at the site?"

"They claim they don't know how electricity works. Maybe they're feigning ignorance to keep their jobs secure."

The ale was cool and strong and Jamie sighed with pleasure. "I don't think anyone knows. I've been reading on the subject. If you're interested, I'll give you a list of library titles."

Leaning backwards in his chair, Stefan rubbed his eyes. After a moment he looked at Jamie and shook his head in frustration. "No, I don't want to spend my life stringing wire. I don't know what I want to do." He turned a moody face to the window.

"You're good at what you're doing now."

"I don't share your love for construction. I've watched you, Jamie Kelly. No perfume on earth is as seductive to you as the tang of wood shavings. To you that building we're building is a living thing with a life and a character. I've seen you so wrapped in the prints that you forgot your lunch, watched you stand on the first floor and stare up at floors that don't yet exist. I don't feel those things. To me it's a job, that's all."

"You haven't found the right thing yet. It will come."

Stefan looked into his glass and a humorless smile curved his mouth. "How will opportunity find me when I'm nowhere near it?" Both men smiled. They had discussed this topic before and would again. Stefan cleared his throat. "There's something I want to say to you." He met Jamie's eyes and drew a deep breath. "Most of the men at the site objected to your promotion."

"I know." Comments had been made that he was intended to overhear.

"The men didn't believe an Irishman would be fair. I agreed with them, but I was wrong. You're doing a hell of a job as foreman, Jamie. The supplies are there when we need them, the crews are coordinated, we're back on schedule and you've treated the men squarely." A flush of color infused his cheeks. "I just wanted to tell you that."

"Thank you," Jamie said after a minute. "You and Wilbur deserve most of the credit for making those things happen."

They drank in silence, each uncomfortable with the turn the conversation had taken. When the pail was empty, Stefan abruptly pushed back his chair and stood. "I have to be getting along. Lucie and Greta are waiting supper."

Jamie frowned at the sausage and pickled eggs. The pub food was filling and free as long as he kept buying drinks. But he thought of Stefan's home-cooked meal and nudged the tray aside.

When Stefan reached the pub door he paused and looked back with an expectant expression. Jamie lifted his glass in farewell, then raised his eyebrows as Stefan answered the salute with a scowl. He looked over his shoulder to discover if the scowl was directed at someone behind him. But

Stefan's stare intensified on Jamie. He waited beside the spittoon, clearly expecting something and seeming annoyed that it wasn't forthcoming.

Jamie rose to his feet as Stefan wound back through the Saturday night pub crowd. "What is it? Is anything wrong?"

"Didn't you forget something?"

For a moment he didn't understand. He gazed at Stefan with a blank expression. Then he slapped his forehead and swore. "Good Lord." Pulling to his full height, he straightened his waistcoat, smoothed down his hair and cleared his throat. "Mr. Kolska, I respectfully request your permission to call upon your sister."

"All things considered, Mr. Kelly, I wouldn't say no to it."

What he heard was the usual "no." He returned to his chair and was reaching for his pint before he realized what Stefan had said. By the time he grasped that a miracle had transpired, Stefan was pushing through the door.

Jumping to his feet Jamie threw some money on the table, grabbed his hat and dashed through the crowd, catching up to Stefan on the street outside.

"Good God, man," he shouted, gripping Stefan's broad shoulders. "Do you mean it? You're finally saying yes?"

"I'm saying yes." Grinning, Stefan clasped his hand. Then he leaned forward and stared hard into Jamie's exuberant expression. "But there's something I want to know. Have you been seeing my sister behind my back?"

The excitement faded abruptly from Jamie's eyes. "Aye," he admitted when the silence between them lengthened. "I love her." They stared at each other. "I accept full blame. I instigated the deception and I didn't allow Lucie any choice in the matter. Both of us deeply regret the necessity for deceiving you."

Stefan's dark eyes narrowed and his fists tightened against his sides. "You bastard mick! I should clean your clock, Kelly. I should pound you into sawdust."

A twinkle softened Jamie's answering stare. "Aye, that you should," he agreed firmly. "If I were you, that is exactly what I would do." He fell into step beside Stefan, matching Stefan's furious stride. "But I wouldn't do it immediately, like tonight. I'd take my time and plan my strategy."

"Where do you think you're going?" Stefan demanded as they crossed the street and passed beneath a sputtering gas lamp.

"Why, I'm going home with you so we can discuss when and where you'll clean my clock." Jamie grinned at him. "We can negotiate the details over supper."

Stefan stopped and blinked. "You're inviting yourself home for supper?" An exasperated smile spread beneath his mustache. "Jamie Kelly, the Irish were thinking about you when they invented the word blarney. If—and I say if—I don't come to my senses and change my mind, Lucie will still be there tomorrow."

"Aye, but she's there right now, tonight. And consider this, Kolska. Before I commence serious calling doesn't it strike you as imperative that I learn if the lass can cook?" His grin widened. "I can uncover this vital information in an unobtrusive manner while we're discussing clock cleaning. Surely you agree common prudence demands that a man learn if his lass can stir up an oat cake."

Stefan threw out his hands. "Blarney. Utter blarney. I really should clean your clock."

Jamie's expression sobered. "I truly regret deceiving you, Stefan. I sincerely wish it could have been otherwise."

For a long moment Stefan said nothing. Then his shoulders rose and dropped in a gesture of resignation. "In your place I'd have done the same."

GRETA ADJUSTED THE RAG stuffing the hole in the window pane, then pressed her lips together and studied the geranium on the sill with an unhappy expression. "If I move it away from the cold, it won't receive any sunlight at all," she said uncertainly. "But if we leave it on the sill, it may freeze. I can't decide what to do."

Glancing up from the stove, Lucie smiled at her with affection. "Would it help if I move the pot to the table when I come home at night?"

Removing her glasses Greta absently polished them against her apron hem. "We could try that," she agreed. "I've cut two starter slips and placed them in water..." After replacing her glasses on her nose, she leaned again to peer out the window.

"Greta Laskowski, you can't sit still tonight. If you're looking for something to do, bring in the butter."

"I'm watching for Stefan," Greta explained. After cautiously removing the stuffing rag, she reached through the broken pane and lifted the butter bowl inside. "I have news and I'm having a terrible time waiting for Stefan to tell it!" After placing the butter on the table, she stuffed the rag back to block the rush of frosty night air.

"What's your news?"

"I'm dying to tell you, but you'll have to wait. I want to tell you and Stefan together."

"I tell you all my secrets, you have to tell me yours." Laughing, Lucie chased her around the table, pelting her with a towel. "I won't stop until you tell me."

"Lucie Kolska, don't make me laugh, I'll start coughing again."

"You're already laughing. So tell me your news."

Greta paused behind a chair, coughed into her hand, then, when she had caught her breath, she looked at Lucie with shining eyes. "Well...Mr. Church gave me a raise. Oh, Lucie, I'll earn ninety-five cents a day starting Monday! Isn't that wonderful?"

"Ninety-five...?" Lucie rushed to embrace her. "Greta, that's wonderful, congratulations!"

"If I don't increase my expenses, I can save fifteen cents a week. Think of it!"

"Or you can buy new winter boots. Or a felt toreador hat." They both looked toward the door as footsteps sounded in the corridor.

"Oh, my, look at us," Greta said, her hands flying to her head. "Our hair is falling down, and we look a mess."

Lucie laughed and touched her cheek. "Stefan won't care how you look as long as you're here and supper is almost ready." Stepping to the stove she reached for the supper plates on the shelf as the door opened.

"Oh, my!" Greta gasped, jumping to her feet.

"Lucie? I've brought someone home for supper."

She heard the astonishment in Greta's gasp, heard the smile in Stefan's voice. And her heart sank. The last time Stefan had brought someone for supper it had been Mr. Pachecko. The evening had proved an endless ordeal. Drawing a deep breath she squared her shoulders and slowly turned, dreading what she would see.

Jamie Kelly stood in the doorway behind Stefan, grinning at her expression. The gasp that sent her hands flying to her mouth, sent the supper plates crashing to the floor.

"Jamie!" Heat flooded her face with radiant color before she made herself look at Stefan. "Does this mean...?"

Jamie crossed the room in three strides and caught her hands in his. "Stefan has learned of our Tuesday trysts and he's rightfully enraged. He and I are agreed he definitely should beat me bloody." Another gasp broke from Lucie's lips and her eyes widened like dark pansies. "We're negotiating the whens and wherefores now." Lucie heard Stefan laugh near the door, saw him grin and shake his head.

For an instant she didn't understand, then she comprehended that somehow, in some miraculous way, they had resolved their differences. Disbelief widened her eyes, then, as the realization of what this meant filled her mind, elation illuminated her expression. She could not look away from Jamie's warm twinkling smile. It was so hard to grasp that he was actually standing where she had imagined him so many times before.

"In the meantime," Jamie continued, his eager brown eyes caressing her face, the chestnut strands floating about her cheeks, "I am permitted to call on you."

Closing her eyes, Lucie swayed on her feet, unable to believe what she was hearing. Surely she was dreaming. When she opened her eyes, Jamie still stood before her, gripping her hands and grinning his delight. She leaned to one side to look at Stefan who waited near the door, his arm around Greta's waist. They both smiled at her.

"Oh, Stefan," she whispered, blinking to see him through tears of happiness. "Thank you. Thank you from my heart!"

"This man, Kelly, is a blarney artist, not worth the powder to blow him to kingdom come," Stefan insisted, transferring his grin to Jamie. "I'll never understand why you want him."

Jamie laughed into Lucie's shining eyes. "With such a shiftless no-good brother, lass, I can't think how you turned out so fine."

Laughing and crying she walked into his arms and rested her forehead against his chest. Suddenly the room didn't smell of coal smoke and lamp oil and decaying plaster. With Jamie's arms around her, the stained brown walls seemed warm and intimate. In the emotion of the moment, she imagined she heard Miss Delfi's Gramophone playing a waltz in her ear.

Jamie must have heard it too because he bowed before her, then danced her around the table, gathering speed as Greta and Stefan clapped and cheered and her hem and apron strings flew out behind her. And in his warm smiling eyes, the eyes she could not look away from, she saw the future she had crossed an ocean to find.

Chapter Eight

Winter's early darkness had descended and the damp air promised snow, Lucie thought as she emerged from the Ropers' kitchen door. She pulled her thin collar close around her throat and hurried toward the side of the house and the hazy glow of the gas lights lining Madison Avenue.

The thought of seeing Jamie tonight warmed her despite the chill of the evening air. Nearly a month had elapsed since Stefan had granted them permission to see each other, but she still marveled at their changed circumstances and her own happiness.

"Miss Kolska?" A disembodied whisper floated out of the night darkness, anxious and urgent.

Lucie's gloves flew upward and pressed hard to her pounding heart. Spinning, she peered into the shadowed garden. "Miss Augusta?" A pale blur moved forward. "You gave me such a start!"

Augusta Roper stepped into the golden light that fell from the kitchen window and Lucie noticed her cheeks and nose were red with cold as if she had been standing outside for some time. This surprised her as, aside from being clad in a silk dinner gown too thin and bare shouldered for outside wear, everyone knew Mrs. Roper had confined Augusta to the house. The contest of wills between Mrs. Roper and her headstrong daughter continued unabated.

Lucie cast a hasty glance toward the light falling through the window, then stepped off the walkway into the frosty garden shadows, wondering what catastrophe would result if Mrs. Roper spied Miss Augusta standing outside.

"You really must return inside. It's too cold to be out without a wrap." She spoke gently, knowing she over-stepped her bounds. But Augusta's frothy sapphire silk offered no protection against the damp bitter cold. Silver vapor concealed Lucie's lips as she spoke, and the night breeze penetrated her coat as easily as a needle passing through paper.

"Please, Miss Kolska. I require a word with you." Augusta passed a hand over her eyes, then wrapped her arms around her bare powdered shoulders. A violent shiver rustled her skirts and caused her diamond earrings to flash in the dim light.

"With *me*?"

Biting her lip to prevent her teeth from chattering, Augusta gave Lucie a searching look, then turned her head away. Indecision tightened her profile. "Oh, dear, perhaps this is a mistake." Her hand shook as she raised it to her lips. Leaning back against a dark tree trunk, she closed her eyes and let her head fall forward. "Heaven help me," she whispered. "I'm so confused, I just . . . I don't know where to turn or what to do."

After a quick glance to reassure herself the garden was deserted, Lucie stepped closer. Now that she was permitted to see Jamie, she felt increased sympathy for Augusta Roper's unhappiness. Everyone in the laundry followed the saga of Miss Augusta's thwarted romance with great regret and much clucking of tongues. Miss Clement had glimpsed Baron Grieple and described him in terms that made everyone shudder.

"Are you ill?" Lucie asked.

Augusta worried a lace handkerchief between her fingers. "I wish I was! I'd rather die than marry the baron!" Tears glittered on her cheeks in the frosty moonlight. "Miss

Kolska, forgive me for burdening you with my troubles, but that day in the laundry you seemed sympathetic to my plight. I don't know where else to turn.'' The words poured forth in a rush. ''Mama has forbidden me any contact with friends. You must know—you've seen which gowns I wear—that I'm not permitted to go out or to accept invitations. My friends are informed I'm indisposed, and my correspondence is monitored. I'm a prisoner in my own home!''

It was true. The entire household responded to the tension straining the family and knew of the dreadful scenes that daily transpired between Mrs. Roper and her daughter.

''I'm sorry,'' Lucie murmured, feeling genuine regret.

But she didn't understand why Miss Augusta had waylaid her in the garden. While they were about the same age, and it was true Miss Augusta had been denied a confidante, it was also true the social gap between them was too vast to be bridged. Any overture of friendship would have shocked them both.

''Do you pity me enough to help me?'' Augusta whispered. Pleading dark eyes fastened on Lucie's startled expression.

The need for assistance explained the puzzling encounter. But Lucie couldn't comprehend how she might be of service. ''Help you?'' she repeated.

Leaning forward from the tree trunk, Augusta grasped Lucie's hands, the gesture an indication of her agitation. ''Please, Miss Kolska, I beg you. I don't know where else to turn.''

''But what could I possibly do?'' An uneasy frown disturbed Lucie's brow.

Augusta reached into her bodice and withdrew a sealed envelope, which she pressed into Lucie's glove. ''Charles— Mr. Whitcomb—is waiting at the el station. If you would just give him this message.'' A look of despair filled the young woman's pleading gaze. "Please! Please, Miss Kolska. If you refuse me, I truly do not know what I shall do!"

Lucie blinked at the cream-colored envelope. If Mrs. Roper discovered she had acted as an intermediary between her daughter and the hated Mr. Whitcomb, Lucie would lose her position in the laundry. It wasn't a consequence she expected Miss Augusta to consider; she doubted Augusta Roper had given a moment's thought to the terrible position in which she was placing Lucie. Her own misfortune was all absorbing.

"I don't think—"

"Oh, please don't refuse!" A tear spilled down Augusta's pale cheek. "I appeal to you, Miss Kolska. If ever you have loved, if ever you have known the anguish of being separated from one you care for like life itself, I implore you to take pity on me!"

The suffering in Augusta Roper's eyes tugged at Lucie's generous heart. In the end it didn't matter that Augusta didn't recognize the enormity of the risk involved. What mattered was the young woman's pain. Turning aside from Augusta's despair, Lucie scanned the white frost coating the garden branches and considered the anguish she would feel if she could not see Jamie again. The pain would be unbearable.

Slowly she turned the envelope between her fingers. There truly was no one else to help. Perhaps she exaggerated the risk. A sigh formed a puff of silver before her lips as she tucked the envelope into her reticule. She need never again wonder if she possessed a romantic streak, she thought with a wry smile. "How shall I recognize Mr. Whitcomb?"

"Oh, thank you! Thank you!" Tears of gratitude sprang to Augusta's eyes. Her grip on Lucie's hands tightened painfully. "I'll pay you."

"That won't be necessary." Pride stiffened Lucie's small shoulders. To profit from Miss Augusta's misery impressed her as dishonorable.

The winter moonlight was bright enough to reveal Augusta Roper's distress. "Forgive me if I've offended you. I assure you that was not my intent." She drew a breath. "As you won't accept payment, I can only assume you must have endured a similar circumstance. May I inquire—how did your situation end?"

Thinking of Jamie raised a buffer against the cold breeze and brought an unconscious smile to her lips. "It ended well."

"I'm happy for you. I only wish..." Augusta raised a hand to her temple, then released a sigh before she informed Lucie how to recognize Mr. Charles Whitcomb. "No one has a smile as wonderful as his," she finished, her voice soft. Then she looked at Lucie and bit her lip. "I do wish you would allow me to repay you in some manner." Her eyes brightened. "I know. I found some cream Mama said you made. It was wonderful, truly it was. Perhaps you would allow me to purchase some?"

It had not occurred to Lucie that anyone might pay for her cream. But the longer she considered the suggestion, the more it appealed. Moreover, to her great delight Mrs. Roper had requested another sample thus she already planned to mix another batch. Purchasing the cream would fulfill Miss Augusta's desire to repay her and Miss Augusta would receive value for value given. Lucie wouldn't feel she took advantage.

"I'm pleased you enjoyed the cream," she said carefully. Her mind raced trying to decide a fair price. "Does twenty cents seem too high a price?" she asked shyly.

"Twenty cents is perfectly agreeable." Augusta glanced anxiously toward the kitchen windows. "Mama will be searching for me. Thank you, Miss Kolska. From my heart, I thank you!"

Standing beside the skeletal-looking elm, Lucie watched Augusta bolt toward the kitchen door and vanish inside into the light and warmth. Then she pressed her reticule to her side and hurried around the corner of the house, walking rapidly toward Madison Avenue. The envelope lay in her reticule like stolen goods. Guiltily, Lucie looked over her shoulder half expecting Mrs. Roper to jump from the shadows and apprehend her.

She didn't relax until she completed her mission by delivering Miss Augusta's envelope to a haggard-looking young man whom she located smoking and pacing near the ticket chop-box. He gazed at the envelope with such rapture that Lucie's reluctance at being involved evaporated like morning mist.

"Thank you, Miss . . . ?"

"Kolska," she said, enjoying his elation. Charles Whitcomb wasn't as handsome as Jamie but she could see how his blond boyishness had stolen Miss Augusta's heart.

During the train ride to the Bowery Street station, Lucie smiled, anticipating Greta's reaction to the romantic tale and her own small role.

Three days later she discovered her role was not to be as small as she had imagined. When she emerged from the el, hurrying not to be late to work, Mr. Whitcomb was waiting, eagerly scanning the crowds. His expression lit when he spied her and he rushed to intercept her before she descended the station stairs. After thrusting a dark blue envelope into her hands, he instructed her to place it under the stone beneath the kitchen elm, and he did so in a manner that suggested he believed she had agreed with Miss Augusta to be the lover's regular go-between. He was gone before Lucie could correct his impression.

Biting her lip Lucie regarded the envelope with a troubled expression. Then she sighed and pushed it into her reticule. Plant a seed and reap the harvest, she reminded herself. If trouble ensued, she would have no one to blame but herself.

"THIS IS SO EXCITING!" Lucie whispered, inhaling the intoxicating scent of bay rum as she leaned near Jamie's ear.

Eyes wide she gazed about the Cavendish Music Hall, uncertain what to expect.

Rows of wooden chairs were arranged to face a small curtained stage and Lucie noticed a piano positioned below and to the left. The moving picture show, an astonishing idea, was scheduled to begin any minute.

"The reels will be shown on the Edison Vitascope, a marvelous improvement over Edison's Kinetoscope," Jamie explained. "Only one or two people at a time could watch the Kinetoscope."

Abruptly the lights dimmed. A man in white tie and tails stepped into a spotlight and requested all ladies remove their hats, which Lucie and Greta did, placing their winter toreadors in their laps. Next came fanfare as the curtain slowly rose to reveal a blank white wall. Suddenly images flickered on the wall and Lucie forgot it was a wall at all. Her mouth dropped open and she convulsively gripped Jamie's hand as two men wearing boxing gloves and shorts stepped into a ring and circled each other, glowering. The piano player filled the hall with music that also seemed to glower and threaten.

For fifteen breathtaking minutes the boxers slugged it out, and the action was so real that Lucie and Greta gasped at each punch and hid their faces against each other's shoulders while Jamie and Stefan cheered and waved their fists in the air.

When the lights came up, Jamie and Stefan grinned and shook hands across Lucie and Greta, recalling their own violent first meeting. "I don't know what to say," Greta breathed, fanning her face. "It was so *real*. Didn't you think so, Lucie?"

Lucie continued to stare at the descending curtain in speechless wonder. She could not believe what she had seen with her own eyes. A juggler ran on stage to amuse them while the projectionist changed reels—Stefan explained it to them—then a trained dog act followed and after that the lights went down again.

This film portrayed a perspiring fat man who tried to carry an armful of eggs down a chaotically busy street. The audience roared with laughter as the fat man was jostled, almost lost an egg, caught his balance, lost an egg and slipped on it, tottered, stumbled, caught an egg in his hat, and finally, accompanied by a merry crescendo on the piano, arrived at his destination with one egg left, which he placed on the table, then smashed when he fell forward. The audience was weak with laughter.

Afterward, Stefan and Greta left to meet some friends, promising to catch up with Lucie and Jamie later, and Lucie and Jamie linked arms and walked toward Elizabeth Street.

When Stefan first gave them permission to see each other, they had reveled in their new found freedom, spending every evening together until Stefan, yawning and protesting, sent Jamie home so he, as their chaperon, could go to bed. Eventually, and reluctantly, they conceded the late nights interfered with rising early for work and agreed to see each other on Wednesdays, Saturday evenings and Sundays. The certainty of knowing they would be together made the schedule acceptable.

"Didn't you enjoy the picture show?" Jamie asked as they turned into the wintry courtyard and approached the tenement door. "The more I've talked, the quieter you've become."

"Oh, yes," she assured him hastily, squeezing his arm before she preceded him up the dark staircase, then lighting the lamp while he hung their coats on the pegs beside the door. "It's just . . . isn't it strange that we laughed at that poor man with the eggs?" Frowning, she set a loaf of poppy-seed bread on the table and a bowl of pickles. "And it was funny, I'm not saying it wasn't. Except I also felt sorry for him. He was trying so hard to save his eggs and get them home. I wanted him to succeed."

Jamie studied her in the glow of the table lamp. "Maybe you're reading more into the piece than was intended, lass," he said finally.

"Perhaps," she agreed, running her fingertips along the edge of the table. "I feel so frustrated about how little I've progressed in achieving my own goal, that I want other people to achieve theirs."

"We're back to that, are we?" Jamie leaned back in his chair.

Lucie stiffened. Repaying her passage money had gradually evolved into a sustaining factor. When life seemed hard, she reminded herself that she worked toward achieving an important goal. When the wind sliced through her thin coat or stung like needles against her cheeks, she remembered that her endurance moved her nearer to a satisfying accomplishment. When the hot irons weighed like concrete, when she returned to the tenement thinking herself too exhausted to clean and cook, it was good to have a goal to put starch in her resolve.

But Jamie did not seem to comprehend how important and necessary her goal had become.

"On this subject you sound like Stefan at his stubborn worst," she said with a sound of exasperation. "Why do you object to my having a goal?"

"It's the nature of your goal, lass." His voice rang with a note of sharpness. "Women bring linens and cookery utensils to a marriage; they don't provide the house and furnishings or buy the wedding clothes. This is not yours to do, Lucie."

Lucie threw out her hands and paced toward the range. "Stefan can use the money however he likes. To save toward a stormy day or pay for his wedding. But he spent his marriage money on me and it's important to me to repay his sacrifice."

"There's something unseemly about a woman focusing so intently on repaying an imagined debt. I can't think Stefan agrees to this."

"But that isn't the point." Though they had discussed this before, he couldn't seem to grasp her position. Frustration furrowed her brow. "My goal has little to do with Stefan. It has to do with me! *I* feel I owe this debt. Repaying it is something *I* need to do." She faced him across the kitchen table, drew a breath, and lowered her voice. "Dear Jamie, please try to understand. I've passed from father to brother and one day I'll pass to a husband." Twin dots of color blossomed on her cheeks. "Before that happens, I want to accomplish something on my own." This was a bold new idea, a distinctly American idea. And it was one she embraced wholeheartedly. "If I can repay Stefan, I'll feel I've achieved something valuable that's mine alone."

He tried to understand, she could read the effort in his troubled expression. "But, lass, why distress yourself by setting your heart on a goal you can't achieve?" Raising a hand, he cut off her protest. "Think of it, Lucie. Twenty-seven dollars. It took Stefan two years to save twenty-seven dollars. Is it your plan to place your own future in abeyance? How much of this money have you saved? How do you intend to accomplish this goal?"

His questions embarrassed her and made her feel foolish. "I'll find a way," she insisted stubbornly, knowing the words sounded lame. Jamie's expression suggested she attempted to defend an indefensible position.

"Lucie, let's not argue."

Immediately the anger vanished from her eyes and she gasped. Her fingers flew to her lips and she stared at him. "My heavens! We're *arguing*!" Her eyes widened. "Oh, Jamie, I'm so sorry."

He stood and opened his arms and she ran to him, hiding her face against his lapel and murmuring apologies. "I'm as much at fault as you, lass." He stroked her hair. "I've wasted a rare hour alone with you." Tilting her face up to him, he gazed deeply into her eyes, then he kissed her.

This kiss was unlike any that had gone before. Perhaps it was an inevitable result of the high emotion charging the previous moments, or perhaps it sprang from the realization they were finally and truly alone, away from prying eyes and "tsking" tongues, or perhaps it was the sudden release of pent-up passion.

When his lips claimed hers, firm and insistent, something hot and turbulent erupted within, igniting Lucie's body like a flash fire. It was as if she had slumbered through life until this moment, then awakened swiftly, passionately, inhabiting a woman's body with a woman's needs.

Her breath quickened and her lips parted, inviting exploration and possession. When Jamie's mouth hardened on hers, when she felt her breasts crush against his chest, felt his hands tighten on her slender waist, her arms wound around his neck and she did not step away, but pressed closer, tighter against him. Her tongue met his and an explosion of sensation weakened her limbs, leaving her hardly able to stand.

Giving herself to the moment, she tangled her fingers in his silky hair as his kisses grew more demanding, more possessive, and it didn't occur to her to object. No thought entered her mind except the electric thrill of his kiss, the almost unendurable excitement of his hands moving up her shirtwaist until she could feel the heat of his palms through the material, almost touching her breasts.

And she wanted him to touch her. Her breasts felt swollen and ached with desire. Her body trembled in anticipation. Her head fell back, offering her throat to his lips. And she waited, panting slightly, until his palm covered her breast and she gasped and felt the nipple thrusting hard through her chemise and shirtwaist.

The sensation was like nothing she had ever experienced. Her whole being centered on Jamie's hand cupping her swollen breast, thrilling to the yearning heat that sped outward from his caress. A light sheen of perspiration appeared on her brow, and his, and their kisses deepened and assumed an urgency that blotted all else from her mind.

She didn't know what might have happened if Jamie had not placed trembling hands on her shoulders and gently stepped away.

That was not true. She did know. She was innocent of experience, but not innocent of knowledge. No village girl could be. But she had not known it would be like this. How could she have guessed? How could she have suspected a moment would be reached when practicality and propriety flew out the window? When mind and body united in urgent heated need, disregarding all else?

"Forgive me, lass." Removing a handkerchief Jamie touched it to his forehead. He appeared as shaken as she. "I've acted the cad. I've taken advantage of your innocence and the tender feelings you hold for me. I apologize, dearest Lucie."

Her knees felt as if they could collapse at any moment, and she steadied herself by placing a hand on the top rung of the nearest chair. When she caught her breath and her breast quieted, she smiled at him.

"Dearest Jamie," she said softly, loving him. "Why do you insist on taking full blame for the faults of two?" Stepping forward she framed his dear face between her hands, wondering if he felt the tremor in her fingertips. "I could have said no," she reminded him gently. "Nothing happened that I haven't dreamed a hundred times."

A hoarse sound issued from his throat and his arms tightened around her. She understood he intended his kiss to be tender, and it began that way, but they had opened a door that could not be easily closed again. Their passion reignited. Only the sound of Stefan and Greta returning with a growler of ale prevented a repetition of what had exploded before.

ON NEW YEAR'S DAY, a holiday for everyone, Lucie, Jamie, Stefan and Greta rode the Sixth Avenue elevated to Central Park and carried rented ice skates to Ladies Pond. Flashing Starlings wheeled against a clear cobalt sky. A bright red balloon floated above the center of the pond signaling the ice was thick enough for skaters, but they knew that because the city horse cars and omnibuses all flew the park's ice flags.

For the price of a penny the boy in the pond house laced on their skates and stored their boots in the numbered racks along the wall. When it was Greta's turn, she tucked her boots under her hem and shook her head.

"I believe I'll just watch."

Lucie, who held onto Jamie's arm to balance herself, looked up in concern. "Are you still tired from last night?"

To celebrate the passing of the century they had bundled in several layers of clothing and took a horse car to Battery Park to enjoy the fireworks display and cheer as the ships in the harbor fired their cannon. Bells pealed over the city; exploding stars spread across the night sky. It seemed everyone in New York took to the streets to celebrate a new year and a new century. Bonfires blazed in the streets, and music and dancing. Men with carts selling chestnuts occupied every corner, and every saloon door dispensed hot rum and good wishes.

"A little," Greta admitted. Lowering her head she frowned at the tips of her boots. "Mostly it's my feet. Several of the women at the factory suffer swollen ankles and sore legs. I was so glad it hadn't happened to me." She looked up at them and bit her lower lip. "Now it has."

Stefan sat on the bench beside her and peered at the purplish circles smudging her eyes. "Greta, I think we should see a doctor."

Removing a hand from the muff in her lap, she coughed into her mitten. When the spell eased and she caught her breath, she rested her head on Stefan's shoulder. "I have," she said quietly. "The doctor said to continue taking the catarrh medicine and to eat even if it comes up later."

"Did you tell him about losing your hair and how brittle your fingernails have become? How your spectacles don't stop your eyes from aching?" Lucie asked, frowning with concern. "Did you show him your rash?"

Greta's laugh was as light and tinkly as the harness bells jingling on the spans parading through the park. "Oh, Lucie, what does thinning hair have to do with swollen ankles? Or a rash with an upset stomach?" A golden curl dropped beside her cold-pinked cheek as she made a shooing motion with her mittens. "Go on, all of you. The ice is waiting."

Stefan cut figures in front of Greta's bench, showing off for her and Jamie invited Lucie to couple skate, slipping his arm around her waist and taking her mitten in his hand.

"Beware of my hem," she warned him, looking up with a smile. "It's sent me toppling once already."

"I didn't notice," he said gallantly, admiring the roses blooming on her cheeks. The cold air raised a sparkle to her eyes and a becoming flush to her cheeks.

"Liar," she said, grinning. "I saw you laughing."

The curve of her waist beneath his palm, the cherry pink of her lips and the teasing smile dancing in her eyes conspired to make him ache with wanting her. She was not a flirt, and he doubted that she realized the effect she produced when her long dark lashes swept her cheeks, or when she smiled into his eyes as she was doing now.

Resisting the urge to pull her close and kiss her until they were both breathless, he tightened his arm about her small waist and skated around the edges of the pond, slowing when they approached the bench on which Greta sat smiling at Stefan's antics on the ice.

Lucie's saucy smile faded abruptly and anxiety darkened her eyes. "Greta is very ill," she said softly.

They looked toward the bench, examining the weariness and pain drawing Greta's pale face. "Is there nothing we can do?"

The bright new century held such promise for Lucie and Jamie, but for Stefan and Greta the future had become uncertain. Tears welled in Lucie's eyes and she shook her head.

SOMETIME AFTER MIDNIGHT she awoke to discover Stefan was not in his blankets. Slipping from bed, Lucie tied on her wrapper and hurried into the kitchen room. In the dim wintry light she saw him sitting at the table, his head held in his hands.

Tears flooded her throat and she sagged against the door, knowing she witnessed a pain no one was intended to see. When she could bear to open her eyes, she cleared her throat and went to him. Blindly, like a child reaching for comfort, Stefan turned and wrapped his arms around her waist. For several minutes he held her in a tight embrace, his shoulders shaking.

"Oh, Lucie." His strangled voice tore at her heart. "I don't know what to do." Holding him, swallowing repeatedly at the knot in her throat, she stroked his hair, felt the tremble in his arms. When finally he released her and groped for his handkerchief, she crossed to the stove and poked the embers, then poured them both a mug of warmed coffee.

"Stefan?" she said quietly, pushing the mug across the table. She could see her breath in the icy darkness. "I'm so sorry. I wish there was something..."

"I'm worried out of my mind, and I don't know what to do." Cupping his large hands around the hot mug, he dropped his head and closed his eyes. Anxiety hoarsened his voice. "Some days she's so sick she can hardly get out of bed. She's started limping."

"I know." Leaning forward, Lucie clasped his shaking hand.

"I'm going crazy with this." He stared at her in the dim glow from the stove and his fingers tightened around hers in a crushing grip. "I want to help her so badly I hurt inside with it. I want her here where I can watch over her and take care of her." His fist slammed down on the table and sent the mugs jumping. Once again his head dropped and he dug his fingers through his hair. "If we just had some money! Or a larger place. If there was just something I could *do*!"

"Stefan—"

"But there isn't! All I can do is pretend I don't notice she's failing, assure her that she'll get better, when I can see she's not getting better. Oh, God, Lucie, I love her so much. There's never been anyone else. No one else made me feel like I mattered. When Greta smiles, I feel ten feet tall, as if with her beside me, I can do anything, endure any hardship as long as she's there. Just knowing she's there!"

"I know," Lucie whispered. She would have moved heaven and earth to help him, but there were no words that could comfort either of them.

"There's nothing to say. Nothing to do. All we can do is wait, hope and pray." His head fell back and he looked at the ceiling, blinking rapidly. "I wish to God I could take her out of that damned factory. All this started after she began at the factory. I know it sounds stupid and I can't support it, but I can't help believing the factory has something to do with this."

Lucie didn't see how that could be, but she said nothing. In the silence her thoughts drifted to the future, Stefan and Greta's and her own and Jamie's. Tonight the future seemed depressingly distant.

They sat together in the cold darkness trying to comfort each other, aching because comfort was not possible, until dawn glowed above the rooftops.

At some point a startling idea occurred to Lucie, an idea born of desperation and one that impressed her as bold and audacious. But the more she turned the thought in her mind, the more she gradually became convinced it was an idea she had to pursue.

CHEWING HER LIP in agitation, Lucie entered the kitchen door and turned toward Mr. Grist's office instead of entering the laundry. If she didn't proceed immediately, she suspected she might lose her nerve.

"I'll relay your request," Mr. Grist said, after learning she desired to speak to Mrs. Roper. He peered at her curiously. Although Lucie liked Mr. Grist and ordinarily would have experienced no discomfort confessing her errand, today she kept her business to herself. She felt too unsure of herself to discuss her idea with anyone. She only hoped she would not lose her courage when she stood in front of Mrs. Roper.

Each time the laundry door opened she thought it was Mr. Grist come to fetch her, and her heart banged painfully against her rib cage. The midday meal came and went; the clock hands crept toward quit time and still Mr. Grist did not come.

Finally, when the dial showed twenty minutes to six and Lucie had all but given up, Mr. Grist appeared in the laundry doorway and crooked a finger at her.

Swiftly she straightened her cap and donned the fresh apron she had prepared hours ago and followed him through the house and up the staircase to Mrs. Roper's private parlor. Heavy velvet draperies were drawn against the snow blowing outside; a cheery fire crackled in the grate.

Mrs. Roper wore a new Paris wrapper, studded with the finest Whitby jet. The beads captured the firelight like tiny jewels. At another time Lucie would have examined the beads with interest, wondering if they would be injured by cleaning. But now she swallowed nervously as Mr. Grist ushered her inside the room and Mrs. Roper uttered an exasperated sound and banged her embroidery frame against her knee.

The entire household had cause to know Mrs. Roper's temper boiled near the surface. Her cherished baron had become impatient with numerous delays and demanded a commitment. Other mothers with eligible daughters circled with predatory interest. The prize threatened to slip from Mrs. Roper's grasping fingers.

"Really, you could have given the cream to Mr. Grist," Mrs. Roper snapped with a grimace of irritation. "It isn't necessary to traipse through the house."

"I . . ." A burst of heat exploded on Lucie's cheeks as she extended the twist of newspaper. A large greasy stain circled the paper, evidence of the richness of her recipe and the extra amount she had packed into the twist. "I thought..." Her voice died in her throat and her hands trembled nervously.

"Yes, what is it?" Scowling, Mrs. Roper jabbed the needle through the embroidery frame. "I don't have all day, you know."

"Well, I thought . . . you see, the ingredients cost . . . well, not a lot, but they do cost something . . . so I was thinking . . ."

A sigh of exasperation raised Mrs. Roper's jet beaded shoulders. "For pity's sake. Put the cream on the silver tray and just go." She flicked her fingertips at Mr. Grist.

"The thing is—" Perspiration appeared on her brow and Lucie wet her lips before she plunged ahead. "My cream is good enough to sell and I've decided to sell it instead of giving it away!" There. Thank God, it was done. She had said it.

"I beg your pardon?" Mrs. Roper's penciled eyebrows rose toward her hairline. She stared at Lucie, then waved her needle in a gesture of impatience. "Oh, very well. What price are you asking?"

Elation sent Lucie's heart soaring. The first fence had been jumped. Mrs. Roper didn't object to paying! She exhaled slowly and pressed her hands together. Settling on a fair price had been an agonizing process. Too small an amount might suggest inferior quality. But if the price was too high, Mrs. Roper would stop using Lucie's cream and return to purchasing her emollient at one of the ladies' emporiums or from a chemist.

"Forty cents," she blurted. The words ran together and emerged as one.

"Forty cents?" Mrs. Roper smiled at the greasy twist of newspaper and one eyebrow lifted in a arch. "I think not," she said coldly. "For forty cents one would expect a crystal jar at the very least. Perhaps a Paris label." A flat chill turned her gaze as hard and unyielding as the jet beads. "You flatter yourself, Miss Kolska."

As if Lucie had abruptly ceased to exist, Mrs. Roper returned her attention to the embroidery frame. Crimson flamed on Lucie's cheeks. When Mr. Grist, whom she had forgotten, gently touched her sleeve, she wanted to fall through the floor with embarrassment knowing he had overheard and the conversation would be repeated below stairs. Whirling, she started from the room, telling herself she must not run.

Mrs. Roper's voice called her back. "Take that—that thing with you." Another flick of her fingertips indicated the twist of newspaper. "Forty cents! How amusing."

Amusing. Lucie grasped the twist of newspaper to her breast and wondered if human beings could die of humiliation.

When Miss Augusta whispered her name from the dark garden shadows as she left the Roper mansion, she was so upset she almost didn't hear. Without a word she accepted the envelope Augusta handed her, thrust it into her reticule, then lifted her skirts and ran around the side of the house fleeing the scene of her defeat.

Chapter Nine

"She could have declined graciously," Jamie said angrily after Lucie confessed the disastrous audience with Mrs. Roper. "It wasn't necessary to embarrass you."

It was Sunday afternoon and they stood outside the Mercantile Library doors, bending against a cold wind. Jamie tucked the books they had chosen under his arm and assisted Lucie down the icy steps to Astor Place before they turned onto Broadway and walked toward Canal Street.

"Thank you for not saying I told you so," Lucie murmured, taking the arm he offered and pressing it close. She had not confided her plan to approach Mrs. Roper until after the fact, but they had frequently discussed the occasionally belligerent attitude displayed by the rich toward the not-so-rich, speculating whether all or only a few of the wealthy felt it their obligation to keep the lower orders in their place.

"Don't offer me too much credit, lass. That's exactly what I might have said if I'd known of this plan beforehand. Regardless, Mrs. Roper had no call to treat you as she did." They paused, waiting for a break in the Broadway traffic, then dashed across the frozen street dodging the four-in-handers who used Broadway as a racecourse on Sundays.

Cold wind stung Lucie's cheeks as she stopped to smooth her skirts and watch the elegant equipages racing down Broadway, the whips shouting cheerful insults back and forth. Then Jamie took her arm and they gravitated toward a crowd circled around an astonishing three horsepower Fiat. Both Lucie and Jamie gaped at the machine as the crowd shouted jeers and advice to the coachman who labored to repair one of the Fiat's tires.

"Do you suppose it's true that one day there will be as many machines on the road as there are horses?" Lucie asked, trying—and failing—to imagine herself or Jamie riding in such a conveyance. The experience would frighten her half to death.

"Absolutely," he said, and laughed at her horrified expression. When he suggested they duck into a coffee house to catch their breath and warm their hands and feet, Lucie gave him a grateful nod. The damp air was bitter cold.

After they were served steaming cups of coffee and small plates of Liberty cake, Jamie returned to the subject of the Ropers. "Forty cents is nothing to Axa Roper, a few grains on a wide beach!" Fuming, he pushed the cake aside. "It isn't enough the old harridan works you like a man for coolie wages, or the daughter uses you to further her deception, she expects you to provide the cream at no cost!"

His anger on her behalf did more to warm Lucie than the hot coffee and milk. Her lovely dark eyes shone when she lifted her head.

"I wish to God you didn't have to work in that place!" The intensity of Jamie's emotion raised a dark flush above his wool scarf. "I live for the day when I've saved enough money to take you out of there! By God, after we're married you will never again wash other people's soiled laundry! I promise you that."

Hot coffee splashed over Lucie's fingertips as she looked up at him. Her mouth dropped open.

"The idea!" His furious stirring created a tiny whirlpool within his cup. "Doesn't that foolish woman realize you have to buy ingredients to make the cream? Doesn't she think your labor is worth compensating?" He spread his hands. "The least you deserved was a bit of common courtesy!"

"Jamie—" Lucie stared at him, her heart thudding painfully in her chest.

"Hasn't she heard? Slavery ended thirty years ago!" Lifting his head, he frowned at her. "The whole selfish passel of Ropers isn't worth your little finger!" Her expression penetrated his anger and he blinked, then his features shifted to a look of concern. "Lucie? Is something amiss, lass?"

"You said..." Surely she had not heard incorrectly. "You said, 'after we're married...'"

He stared at her, then a sheepish smile stole across his expression. "Did I say that?" The Irish twinkle she loved animated his gaze.

"Indeed you did," Lucie said softly, her eyes shining. "I believe you just proposed, Mr. Kelly." She tilted her head and smiled. "In a rather backhanded manner, if I may say so."

"Dearest Lucie."

They gazed into each other's eyes across the tabletop, thrilling to what they saw. When Lucie finally dropped her gaze, she discovered they were both leaning forward, gripping each other's hands. There was so much to say, but her heart was too full to permit speech.

Jamie cleared his throat and cast a dazed glance around the coffee house. An awkward laugh broke from his lips. "I've imagined this moment a thousand times, and never once did I picture it occurring in a public coffee house. I envisioned going on my knees before you, flowers in hand and—" He blinked at her. "Good heavens. I haven't done this at all properly. Lucie, I haven't spoken to Stefan. I don't have—"

Sensing he spoke from nervousness, she squeezed his hand and smiled tenderly into his eyes. "Yes."

"Yes?" Joy illuminated his features. "Lucie, lass. You're saying yes to me?"

Lucie laughed. "Did you ever doubt?"

Jumping up, he rushed around the table and pulled her to her feet in a crushing embrace. It was so unlike him to mount a public display of affection that Lucie laughed again and buried her flaming cheeks in his tweed coat collar.

Jamie didn't notice the waiter's frown of disapproval. He grinned broadly and announced with pride, "She said yes!"

"To a marriage proposal," Lucie added shyly, ever practical. Heaven knew what the waiter supposed she had agreed to. But today she didn't care what anyone thought. Happiness glowed on her cheeks and in her radiant eyes.

The waiter's scowl dissolved into a grin. "More coffee, sir? Or would you prefer something stronger?"

"Neither," Jamie said, gazing down at Lucie with proprietary pride. "Let's get out of here."

On the street he swung her in a high circle, bringing her boots to the pavement to the accompaniment of a fierce embrace. When he could bear to release her, he tilted her face up to his. "I love you, Lucie Kolska. You've made me the happiest man on this earth."

"Oh, Jamie, Jamie dearest." Tears of happiness sparkled like tiny prisms on her lashes. "I love you, I love you, I love you!"

Throwing back his head, he tossed his hat into the air and laughed with joy. But his expression sobered when he looked down at her again. "I didn't plan to propose today..."

"I know," she said, smiling. "But you did, and I intend to hold you to it."

He dropped a kiss on her nose, then hastily looked at the traffic slipping and skidding down the icy street. "I'm disgracing us both, aren't I?"

Smiling, Lucie pressed her forehead to his chest, then tucked his arm firmly against her side. "Today is special. I think we can be forgiven any shameless display." She gazed up at him, her heart in her eyes. "Tell me again that you love me, Jamie Kelly. I'll never grow tired of hearing you say it."

"I love you, lass. I do love you!" She saw the truth of it in the glowing dark eyes that caressed her lips, her throat, her hair. "But I've spoken precipitously." A frown clouded his happiness. "I have nothing to offer you but ambition and potential. By rights, Stefan should withhold his permission."

"If he does," Lucie said, unperturbed. "I shall never speak to him again."

Stopping on the snowy pavement, he turned her to face him. "Lucie, it could be years before we're financially able to wed. We'll need furnishings, a decent place to set up housekeeping, a cushion against emergencies..."

"However long it takes, Jamie Kelly, I'll wait."

"Oh, my dearest." Again he embraced her, oblivious of the stares and smiles directed at them from Sunday afternoon drivers. It was the happiest day of Lucie's life and she reached trembling fingertips to stroke his jaw, brush his lips. A tiny thrill electrified her. If they lived together for a hundred years, she would never tire of touching him and being touched by him.

A hoarse groan sounded against her temple, then he stepped back to look at her and straightened her hat with shaking fingers. "Waiting is so hard, dearest. So hard."

"For both of us," she whispered, feeling the heat in her secret parts, longing to know him as a wife knows a husband. She thought about the possibility of years passing before they could wake in each other's arms, and a bit of the brightness faded from her happiness. The promise to wait came easily, but she suspected the reality of denial would be a torment.

"I'D LIKE TO HEAR your opinion about something I've been considering," Lucie said two days later. After stacking the supper dishes on the shelf above the stove, she untied her apron and sat at the kitchen table with the others.

Without being aware, she reached beneath the table and clasped Jamie's warm hand as a rush of thankfulness and gratitude momentarily overwhelmed her. She was so fortunate. Sometimes she experienced a twinge of guilt that she could be so happy in the face of Stefan and Greta's mounting desperation.

"An opinion costs nothing," Jamie commented with a wink and a squeeze of her hand. "We await the opportunity to give it."

Aware of the enormity of what she was about to suggest and not sure how they would respond, Lucie drew a long breath to steady her nerves. For a moment her resolve wavered. Was this a door she truly wished to open? Yes, yes it was. She had thought of little else for several days.

"I've been thinking..."

"Oh, no," Stefan groaned, summoning a wan smile. He raised an eyebrow toward Jamie. "Trouble's ahead."

Lucie laughed with the others, then returned to her subject. "Even if Mrs. Roper wouldn't buy my cream, Miss Augusta does."

"I think she buys the cream to repay you for delivering her letters to Mr. Whitcomb," Jamie interjected in a gentle voice.

"Perhaps. But she does use it. I've smelled the scent on her clothing when it comes into the laundry. So she must like it."

"It's a wonderful cream," Greta insisted loyally. "I wouldn't use any other."

"Mrs. Roper was willing to pay for the cream, too, except she wanted it in a pot or a jar." She looked at each of them, feeling the excitement build in her chest. "So, I've been thinking...what if I bought some rouge pots and filled them with cream?"

"Pots?" Stefan asked. "How much cream do you think Mrs. Roper would buy?"

"Well..." She didn't look at Jamie because she sensed his surprise and, more importantly, his resistance. "I thought I'd try to sell the cream elsewhere, as well." When she dared glance at him, she saw Jamie's reaction was worse than she had feared and her breath caught in her throat. He looked utterly appalled.

"You intend to peddle your cream door to door like a drummer?" he asked incredulously, staring at her.

"I can't agree to that." Stefan frowned and shook his head.

"I wasn't thinking about going door to door," she said, discarding that idea on the instant. "I thought I might approach the druggists in Mercer Street and ask if they would accept the cream on consignment."

"Consignment?" Jamie's stare deepened.

"I learned about it at the Settlement House. It means I would leave several pots with—"

"I know what consignment means. I didn't realize you did."

Turning away from his opposition, she appealed to Stefan and Greta, speaking in a rush before her nerve failed her. "I think I could be successful. The cream is good, I know it is. Stefan, please, just hear me out." She swallowed and cleared her throat in the abrupt silence. Snow hissed against the window panes. The tin coffeepot bubbled and spit on the stove.

"Go on," Stefan said, his reluctance visible. She guessed from his expression that he had already rejected her idea.

From her pocket she slowly withdrew the sums she had figured earlier and pressed the paper flat against the table-top. Having progressed this far, she felt obliged to see it through. "As nearly as I can determine, each pot of cream would cost four cents to produce. Two cents for the ingredients, one and a half cents for each pot, and half a cent for a label."

"You've priced pots and labels?" Jamie leaned forward. "You've gone that far with this?"

"I believe the pots would sell at thirty-five cents," she persisted, not looking at him. "That's a profit of thirty-one cents a pot."

The words hung in a pocket of silence as each considered the implications of thirty-one cents profit per pot of cream.

"Lucie!" Greta breathed. "You would only have to sell three pots to make more money than you could make in a whole day at Mrs. Roper's laundry!"

"Yes." She made herself look at Jamie now. "Does anyone see any reason why we shouldn't try this?" Silently, she pleaded for his support, wanting him on her side in this as in all things. But he was looking at her as if seeing her for the first time.

It was Stefan who answered. "In the name of heaven, Lucie. Even if what you propose could be done, and I'm not convinced anyone would pay thirty-five cents for a little pot of cream, women don't peddle goods!"

"Then you do the peddling," she suggested evenly, shifting on her chair to face him. Why didn't Jamie speak? His silence grated across her nerves. "Remember the year you managed Mr. Holstoffer's stall at the harvest fair? When you set your mind to it, Stefan, you can sell anything."

"Not women's face and hand cream," he said, raising his hands and shaking his head.

"We could all be partners. If Greta feels well enough, she could design a label for the cream. Stefan could sell it. Jamie could arrange for the ingredients and pots. And I'll make it." She made herself turn again to Jamie and released a slow breath.

"You told me you had no interest in business."

Noting that he had crossed his arms over his chest, Lucie wet her lips and spoke carefully. "I'm not a businesswoman nor do I want to be, Jamie. I didn't deceive you. If the cream is successful, and I think it could be, I would expect you and Stefan to take it over and Greta and I would withdraw."

"Stefan and I are already employed," Jamie replied stiffly, watching her.

Stung by his lack of enthusiasm, Lucie directed her appeal to Stefan and Greta. "Whenever we're together we talk about opportunity. We look for it, long for it. Isn't it possible the cream could be our opportunity?'' She spread her hands and leaned forward, struggling to persuade them. ''Are we limiting our future by assuming opportunity can come only to Stefan and Jamie? Maybe that isn't how it will happen. Maybe our opportunity is here, now, right in front of us.'' She placed trembling fingertips on the page of figures. ''Please. Couldn't we just try?''

''I object to your proposition for several reasons,'' Stefan said finally, leaning his elbows on the table and looking at her. ''First, I loathe the idea of having a sister in business. It isn't decent.''

''But, Stefan, I'm proposing a partnership—''

''Second, I don't have time to sell your cream. Frankly, I don't think you do, either. Everyone here works six days a week. Sunday is our time to see each other, to catch up household chores. You do most of the week's cooking and baking on Sunday, Lucie. And the laundry and marketing and so on. We all have Sunday chores enough without taking on additional obligations.''

''I'm willing to—''

He raised a hand. ''But as you spoke I kept remembering something you said several months ago. You said: 'Have we brought our limitation with us?' I've thought about that, Lucie, and the answer is yes, we have. When we came to America, we shed laws and customs we found restrictive or unjust. And we rejoiced in the freedom to do so. But we kept much also, attitudes and beliefs we seldom realize we hold until they're challenged.''

He spoke slowly, thoughtfully, but as Lucie gradually recognized the direction of his thoughts, excitement mounted within her and she could hardly make herself sit still. Stefan was going to agree. He did so with deep reluctance and against his better judgment, but he was going to permit her to proceed.

''My beliefs are wrong for what you propose. I don't approve of women involving themselves in business. I oppose your working seven days a week. I feel a man's shame that someone in my house must work two jobs. I can also guess why you want to do this, but you know I don't agree that you must repay your passage money."

"But?" she encouraged in a soft voice.

"But if you wish to pursue this—" He paused and met her eyes with a troubled gaze. The effort to rise above conflicting cultures and attitudes tightened his jaw. "If you wish to test the limitations you oppose, then I won't stand in your way." He studied the excitement lighting her expression. "But I won't be a partner, Lucie. It would be dishonest to participate in something I don't believe in."

"Thank you, Stefan." She knew how difficult the decision was for him. Squaring her shoulders, she turned to face Jamie. One glance at his expression and her excitement plummeted. "Please, Jamie. Will you be my partner? You know I want you to be."

"No." His reply was curt.

An uncomfortable silence ensued. The pain and surprise of rejection colored Lucie's cheeks and she dropped her head. Though she had not expected Jamie's wholehearted approval, neither had she anticipated he would so flatly oppose her. The awkward silence seemed to endure forever.

"I'll be your partner."

Greta spoke quietly in a voice hoarsened from coughing. Leaning toward Stefan, she placed her hand over his. "Our Lucie has a wonderful idea. Surely she has a duty to follow her dream, doesn't she? The death of a dream is a terrible thing. We must not allow that to happen." The gentle admonishment shamed the frown from Stefan's expression. Turning to Lucie, she smiled. "I'm honored to be given the pleasure of designing a label. As I've been listening, I've thought of a name. That is, if you—"

"I hadn't thought of that! Of course we need a name."

"I thought perhaps we could call it Countess Kolska's Superlative Face and Hand Cream."

Lucie clapped her hands and laughed. "So, I've become a countess after all," she said to Jamie. His thin smile erased her pleasure and sent her heart dropping toward her toes.

"There's something else," Greta continued when she had recovered from another attack of coughing. "We'll need money to buy increased amounts of ingredients and the pots and labels."

"Yes." A frown appeared above Lucie's eyes. She couldn't very well request a contribution from Stefan and Jamie as they had washed their hands of the affair.

Lifting a hand to her throat, Greta withdrew a waxed string from her bodice and untied it. A gold ring slid into her hand. "This was my mother's wedding ring. When she gave it to me, she told me to use it well. What finer use can there be than to finance a dream?" Leaning across the table, she pressed the ring into Lucie's palm and closed her fingers around it. "I believe in dreams, Lucie dearest, and I believe in you."

Tears sprang to Lucie's eyes as she stared at the gold ring. "Thank you," she whispered. She would have given anything if this gesture of support had come from Jamie.

Jamie's continued silence cast a pall across the evening, and very soon Stefan rose to see Greta home. The moment the door closed Jamie leaned back in his chair and his dark eyes narrowed.

"Do you have so little faith in me, lass?"

"What?" She had risen to brew more coffee, but she dropped back onto her chair and stared at him.

"Don't you believe I can provide for our future?"

"Of course I do!"

"Then why do you insist on going into business?"

"My dearest Jamie." Leaning forward she reached for his hands, but he pretended not to see and remained aloof, his arms folded firmly out of reach. A flush of heat stained her cheeks. "More than anything in this world, I want to help Stefan and Greta marry. Afterward, if the cream should prove successful.... Does it really matter if our future come more quickly from my efforts or yours? Or a combination of the two?''

''No self-respecting man takes money from a woman. Or allows her to support him.''

This line of reasoning impressed her as frustratingly limiting and solely based on pride. Long ago Lucie had concluded pride was a rich man's conceit and a poor man's prison. ''Then join partners with me,'' she entreated, presenting what seemed an obvious solution. ''The business can be ours together.''

Dark curls of smoke wafted from the lamp chimney and his moody gaze followed the drift toward the ceiling. ''No, Lucie. My business is construction, not face cream.''

Both spoke in carefully modulated voices, suppressing the anger they each felt. But Lucie sensed the importance of the conversation and the rift opening between them. How could it be otherwise? She couldn't help feeling resentful that he refused to support an idea that even Stefan agreed to, an idea that could, if successful, significantly speed their future.

''Can you really believe my idea to sell the cream indicates a lack of belief in you?'' she asked, her gaze begging him to see how absurd such a thing was. With all her heart she believed in Jamie's abilities; given time, he would provide everything they dreamed of, she didn't harbor a single doubt.

''It would seem so,'' he replied in a tight voice.

''Oh, Jamie.'' She stared at him. ''You must know that isn't true! How could you think such a thing?'' But he did. She saw it in the stiff set of his shoulders, heard it in his clipped words. Swallowing further comment, she bit her lip and tried to sort through the confusion muddling her thoughts.

''If you tell me not to proceed, I won't,'' she said eventually. Her disappointment was intense and tinted by anger. However, nothing was worth jeopardizing their love for each other.

For several uneasy moments he did not respond. "I'll never forbid you anything, Lucie. That isn't the direction I want our lives to take." A troubled smile acknowledged her murmur of gratitude. "It is my hope we can discuss our differences and in the event of a deadlock, arrive at a compromise to suit us both."

"You've rejected the compromise I suggested," she quietly pointed out. "You refuse to share in the venture."

A flush of discomfort rose from his collar. "Then you intend to proceed?"

"Perhaps you don't believe in my cream, but I do." That wasn't what she had intended to say but having said it, her chin lifted. At some level she understood her stubbornness was a defense against the confusion and upset swirling in her mind.

"So there we are." Frowning, he looked toward the snowy window and Greta's geranium drooping on the sill. "I'll say this. I admire your spirit and determination." Rising to his feet, Jamie reached for his coat and cap. "If you believe you can provide for our future better than I, Lucie, then I wish you well."

"Oh, Jamie," she whispered, shocked. "That isn't it at all. Please don't believe that."

For a moment they gazed at each other. "I have saved sixteen dollars. Would you accept it toward your goal?"

"No." Moisture gathered in her eyes. "You don't understand at all, do you? Please, Jamie—"

"Good night, lass." The door closed behind him with a sharp sound, like that of a breaking heart. Lucie lowered her face to her hands.

MIDWAY TO HIS LODGINGS, Jamie halted beneath a street lamp and rubbed his eyes with an irritated gesture. For a moment he stood motionless, listening to the hiss inside the gas globes above. Instinct urged him to return to Lucie's tenement and apologize for behaving like an ass. But why should he apologize for speaking his mind? He had spoken the truth as he knew it to be. His jaw hardened and pride directed his steps forward, away from Elizabeth Street.

Blowing snow swirled around his shoulders and he tugged his cap over his ears and sank his chin into his scarf. Things had come to a pretty pass when a man's future bride felt she had to provide for their future. His teeth ground together. Maybe she was right. He was a hell of long way from being able to offer her a home.

The issue was not simple. He had not deceived her when he praised her spirit and determination. Both were qualities he admired in Lucie Kolska. But he had not anticipated how such qualities might manifest themselves. He hadn't imagined her spirit would ever shame him or make him feel inadequate.

Hands thrust into his pockets, his head bent against the wind and snow, he turned into Canal Street. If Lucie failed in her endeavor with the cream, he would feel relieved. That was mean spirited, a quality he loathed and did not associate with himself. But, shamed by the admission, he knew that was how he would feel. And if she succeeded, he would feel like half a man, a failure in her eyes and in his own, unworthy of her.

"Damn it!"

He kicked at a frozen horse dropping. He loved her and he honestly wanted to support her endeavor. But he couldn't. Damn it, he couldn't.

THE PLAN CAME TOGETHER more swiftly than Lucie had imagined it would. By Saturday evening Greta had painstakingly drawn twenty labels, which she affixed to the rouge pots Lucie had purchased the previous night. Before Saturday supper the pots were filled with cream and sealed.

Greta studied the row of small pots with pride, her beautiful blue eyes shining behind her spectacles. "They're quite nice, aren't they?"

"Thanks to your exquisite labels!" To please Greta, Lucie had scented this batch of cream with geranium oil, and

Greta had drawn a border of twining geranium blossoms. Greta's eyes were reddened and tearing from bending over the labels, though she insisted it had been a pleasure. Lucie slipped her arm around Greta's waist. "Now you sit down and rest."

When Stefan returned, bringing a growler of Marva ale and a gust of chill air, his gaze fastened immediately on Greta, noting her exhaustion and lack of color. Before she could see his anxiety, he hung his cap and coat on the nails. "Is Jamie coming for dinner?"

Lucie turned to measure more lumps of coal into the stove. "I don't think so," she said.

"Give him time," Greta advised softly.

There was nothing else she could do. But if he was stubborn, so was she. The plan had progressed too far to abandon now. Besides which, there was Greta. Greta believed in her, and Greta's unquestioning faith kept her going when thoughts of Jamie's disapproval planted seeds of doubt.

On Sunday morning Lucie rose before dawn to complete her household chores before the noon whistle sounded. Looking about the tenement at the freshly laundered clothing hanging on nails and chair backs drying, she tried to think if she had forgotten anything. The cooking and baking was finished, she had emptied and cleaned the slop bucket, scrubbed the table and floors, filled the lamps, fetched a bucket of fresh water from the partially frozen courtyard pump; she would iron tonight. Stefan and Greta had agreed to do the weekly marketing.

There was nothing to delay her further. But as she placed the twenty small pots inside her bulging reticule, her heart filled with trepidation. Why was she doing this? Why on earth was she doggedly continuing along a course that opened an abyss between herself and her beloved Jamie?

No clear answer jumped to mind as she pinned on her hat and tied her scarf beneath her chin. There was her goal, of course. And a genuine and intractable belief in her recipe. And there was Greta, who had drawn the labels at such cost to her poor eyes. But there was something more, something she responded to but could not adequately define.

It had something to do with America. With tales of golden streets and silver platters, of opportunity awaiting every man. And woman. Whatever drove her also owed something to the recognition that never again in her life would she have the freedom or the chance to act on her own, to pursue a dream solely of her own creation. This was her moment, and it was likely to be the only such moment she would ever have. That above all, compelled her to try. If she did not at least try, she would never forgive herself.

And surely, she would succeed. One could not want something this badly, or be this committed, and fail. Determination and the quality of her cream would see her through.

At the door she gripped the handle of her heavy reticule, squared her slim shoulders, and sailed forth to carve out her small share of the pie.

"ARE YOU THIS . . . this countess person, honey?" The man behind the tall oak counter turned a pot of cream in his hand, then peered over the countertop with an oily smile.

His familiarity shocked her. Lucie had been into Sheldon's Drug Emporium to purchase remedies for Greta and the white-coated man behind the counter had never before taken liberties with her.

"I—I suppose I am," she said stiffly. "I make the cream from my own recipe."

"You? A countess?" His gaze swept the tips of her muddied boots and hem before swerving upward to her mended coat and the felt hat she had purchased at the rag fair. She knew herself to be dressed neatly and respectably, but his sly gaze made her feel shabby and second-rate.

"My recipe won first prize at the harvest fair back home."

"Did it now?" He dropped the pot over the edge of the counter and she jerked forward to catch it before it shattered on the plank floor. "Then maybe you should peddle it back home. No thank you, honey. My ladies use soap and water like any decent woman should. No fancy dancy creams for my patrons.''

Silently she turned and walked out the door, aware of several customers observing her with lifted eyebrows. On the street outside she paused to inhale deeply, then tilted her face toward the sky. Today had been clear but cold, the weak sun turning the streets into slush that would freeze overnight. Already she felt the chill of approaching evening.

She had not placed a single pot of cream. Not one. For a long moment she considered the weight of the reticule wrenching her arm, thought about her aching feet and the cold slush seeping through the hole in her boot. She thought about the smirks and smiles, the refusals, polite and not so polite. And she knew she wasn't going to sell any of the cream. She also knew she had to see it through to the end. There were still a few minutes before the shops closed.

For most of her life she had associated courage with heroic deeds, with large acts of valor or sacrifice. But she saw now that an act of courage could be as small as drawing labels when one's eyes ached and streamed, as small as stepping through a doorway into a dry goods store.

She closed her eyes, squeezing her lashes against her cheek, then she drew a breath and pushed through the door before her, hearing the bell jangle above her head. Dreading each step she approached the proprietor of the store, an older balding gentleman who wore an old-fashioned frock coat and a heavily starched standing collar.

"May I help you find something, miss?"

She fumbled to open her reticule. "You wouldn't want to sell my face and hand cream, would you?" How many times had she asked the same fruitless question? Suddenly she felt endlessly weary. "It's very good."

Surprise widened his eyes. Then he drew back from her. "What is the world coming to when young women take to the streets as drummers?" His stare hardened. "Shame on you, miss!"

Lucie moved backward a step. "If I could just leave a pot or two with you . . . on consignment."

"You should be at home, tending to your house and family! Who is responsible for you? Who sanctioned this offense?"

"I—I live with my brother, sir."

"Your brother should be horsewhipped for permitting you to behave like a man and a drummer at that! Do neither of you have the least sense of decency?"

It was the last straw. Lucie turned on her heel and fled, her skirts billowing behind her, tears glistening in her eyes, knowing she had failed so utterly devastating her.

Darkness had fallen by the time she reached the Elizabeth Street tenement. In the blackness she stumbled over the bodies of those homeless souls who crept into the icy stairwell to sleep huddled on the steps. Their curses followed her as she pulled herself upstairs, murmuring apologies.

She had never been so happy to see the inside of the dark smoky rooms. Closing the door she fell against it and strangled on a sob of defeat. Facing Greta, who believed in her foolish dream, would be the most painful moment in recent years. She couldn't bear to think about it.

"Lucie? Are you all right, lass?"

"Jamie!" Running across the room she threw herself into his arms and buried her face against his shoulder. Relief choked her voice and brought tears to her eyes. She held tightly to his solid strength, reassuring herself that he was really here. "Oh, Jamie, you were right. It was terrible, awful! You can't imagine what people said to me, they—"

"There, there," he murmured, unpinning her hat and tossing it toward the table. He stroked her hair and kissed her temples. "Dearest, you're half frozen. Sit down and I'll pour you some hot beer. Good Lord, your reticule weighs a cartful. Stefan, take this, will you?"

She allowed them to cosset her because she needed cosseting as seldom before. And she was so glad that Jamie had swallowed his pride and reappeared that it diminished the humiliation of her defeat. But she had glimpsed the relief on his face as he hefted the weight of her reticule and understood what it meant. To her shame a wave of unwanted resentment clouded her joy at seeing him again.

Then, as his arm slipped around her waist and she rested her head on his broad shoulder, her resentment eased. She was intensely disappointed that her venture had failed but—and this was difficult to admit and accept—perhaps it was for the best. She couldn't quite bring herself to believe this entirely, but she did recognize success might well have created as many problems as it solved.

"I'm so glad to see you," she murmured against Jamie's shoulder, clasping his hand. It meant the world to her that he had returned before he knew if her efforts to sell the cream had been successful. Surely that fact was more important than his fleeting expression of relief.

"I love you, lass," he said gruffly.

"I love you, too. I don't want us ever to fight again," she whispered against his collar.

Now that her feet and hands had thawed and the lump in her throat diminished, it was time to face Greta and confess her failure, admit that all their labor had gone for naught. Lifting her head, dreading the moment, she gazed about the room.

"Stefan, where is Greta?" She had been so distraught over her defeat, so overjoyed by Jamie's return, that she had failed to notice Greta's absence until now. But it didn't make sense. Greta was her partner and her ally. Her heart stopped in her chest and her brows clamped together. Greta would have moved the earth to be here tonight to learn the results of their efforts and dreams. She would have been here to cheer a success or soften a defeat. "Stefan?"

"She's having a bad day, Lucie. It's everything. Her eyes, vomiting, the cough. Her legs pain her too much to walk." Stefan pressed his lips together as he reached for his coat and cap. "She asked me to apologize that she isn't here to congratulate you." He squeezed Lucie's shoulder in a gesture of sympathy. "I'm under strict instructions to report back at once."

"Tell her I'm sorry," Lucie whispered. She remembered their excited speculations, the half-formed plans for the extra money. "Tell her . . . tell her I tried."

"She knows that. We all do."

After Stefan left, Lucie rested in the circle of Jamie's arms and listened as he tried to take her mind off the day by telling her of the progress on the Tucker Building. She sensed the rift between them was not entirely mended, but the distance had narrowed. After a time she bit her lip, then blurted the question she had sworn not to ask. "Are you glad I failed?"

"No, not glad," he said after a moment. "I know how upset and disappointed you are."

"Relieved then?"

His eyes met hers. "I'm not proud of my feelings, lass," he admitted slowly. "But I can't help them, either. It's my task to protect and care for you. That's the natural order of things. Not the other way around. 'Tis a mark of shame when a man's woman must take to the streets to earn a few coins."

Gently disengaging herself, Lucie looked up at him. "In Wlad they say two horses can pull a heavier load and pull it farther than one."

"In Dublin they say he who travels fastest, travels alone."

As this conversation could easily have escalated into something Lucie did not want, she released the moment and concentrated on the joy and comfort of having him with her tonight. But eventually her thoughts drifted toward an inner vision that revealed a horizon that had slipped farther into the distance. Not only had she failed to earn a profit, but she had depleted her cache beneath the loose board. All that to finance what she now thought of as Countess Kolska's folly.

Chapter Ten

Before Lucie had time to remove her coat and change into her uniform, Mr. Allison, the coachman, burst into the Roper kitchen shouting for Mr. Grist. Clumps of mud showered from his boots and cuffs as he ran past the laundry room and threw open the door to Mr. Grist's office.

Sensing something important was afoot, Mrs. Greene, Lucie and Hilda lingered curiously in the laundry room doorway. Two minutes later Mr. Grist and Mr. Allison burst out of Mr. Grist's office and hurried down the corridor.

Leaning into the hallway, Mrs. Greene caught Mr. Grist's sleeve. "Whatever is going on?"

"Not now, Mollie," he said, shaking off her hand. But he couldn't resist sharing the news. Before he dashed after Mr. Allison he swiftly confided, "Mr. Allison's found a ladder against the house." He cast Mrs. Greene a knowing look. "It's beneath Miss Augusta's bedroom window."

Mrs. Greene's reddened hands flew to her mouth and her eyes widened. "Lord a'mercy! They've done gone and eloped!"

Lucie gasped. She had not foreseen this possibility.

When Mr. Grist returned inside, smoothing down his hair and straightening his cravat as he sped past them, his face was pale. "The ladder is confirmed," he called over his shoulder. "Now I must inform Mrs. Roper." A light shudder disturbed the perfection of his morning coat.

Although Lucie hastily donned her uniform, there was no question of anyone setting to work. The news of the ladder spread through the household like a case of the pox. The kitchen staff crowded the end of the corridor, the household maids and chars gathered in excited knots, Lucie, Mrs. Greene, and Hilda hovered in the laundry room door and everyone held her breath and waited.

Within minutes the charged silence was splintered by a shrill scream, then another and another until the screams ran together into a great rush of rage and betrayal, punctuated by the intermittent crash of smashing glass.

"Good God," Mrs. Greene marveled. "That woman has a set of lungs on her, don't she? We can hear her clear down here."

"Clear down here" was no longer the laundry room. Without being aware they did so, everyone had crept into the main house and gathered at the foot of the central staircase.

The screams continued unabated, accompanied by shattering glass and slamming doors and the urgent sound of running feet. Briefly Miss Clements appeared at the top of the stairs, dressed in a wool wrapper, her hair still braided. She stared at the crowd of upturned faces, lifted her palms toward heaven, then she dashed off again.

In short order Mr. Allison was summoned to tell his story before he was dispatched to fetch Mr. Roper home from his law firm. The constable was sent for, as well as a doctor to calm Mrs. Roper. Orders were issued to remove the ladder lest the neighbors see. Mr. Grist sent down for coffee and brandy. Miss Clements, still not dressed, wrote and dispatched a dozen notes canceling Mrs. Roper's afternoon tea party and her evening appointments. Miss Delfi fleetingly appeared at the top of the stairs where she clasped her hands over her head and grinned down at everyone before Mrs. Roper's strident shout summoned her.

The moment Lucie observed Miss Delfi's triumphant gesture, she understood Miss Delfi had participated in the plot. Now she could guess how Miss Augusta delivered her letters to the rock under the kitchen elm and how she had retrieved the missives from Mr. Whitcomb. The in-house conspirator had been Miss Delfi. Lucie twisted her hands and worried her lower lip between her teeth. She wondered uneasily if Miss Delfi knew who had delivered the letters to and from Mr. Whitcomb.

Mr. Roper arrived at the same time as the constable and the doctor, and everyone pressed back to open a path. The gentlemen ran upstairs and the door to Mrs. Roper's chamber slammed shut to sighs of disappointment from below.

By now it was known Miss Augusta had left a letter for her parents with Miss Delfi. It was also known the lovers had not confided their destination to Miss Delfi for fear Miss Delfi would crumple under the pressure applied by furious parents.

Within the hour the constable hastily departed to commence a search for the lovers, Miss Delfi had been confined to her room, Mr. Roper had instructed his law firm to file suit against the Whitcomb family, and Mrs. Roper had slapped Miss Delfi, Miss Clements, the doctor and her husband. Or so it was whispered.

And then . . . Mr. Grist appeared at the top of the stairs, paused, and his dark gaze settled heavily on Lucie.

"You are wanted upstairs, Miss Kolska."

Thirty feverishly curious eyes swung toward her in astonishment. Mrs. Greene sputtered. "They want Lucie!" Swinging about, she studied Lucie's bloodless face and shaking hands. She swore softly. "And I thought you had sense, Lucie Kolska. I thought you was a blowed in the glass daisy." She shook her head and clucked her tongue. "Shows how wrong a body can be."

Lifting skirts that weighed as heavy as lead, Lucie slowly climbed the stairs, feeling the stares against her back. Mr. Grist studied her a moment, but she couldn't read his expression. It was as if she had become a stranger.

"This way." He opened the door to Mr. and Mrs. Roper's private chamber, ushered her inside, then closed the door behind her. This was the first time Lucie had faced Mrs. Roper without Mr. Grist's solid assuring presence at her side.

Both the Ropers stood before the fireplace, staring at her. It flashed through Lucie's mind that Zeus probably resembled Mr. Roper, severely clad and thunderous of expression, as rigid and unyielding. It provided small comfort to notice it was brandy he held in his hand, not a lightning bolt. Mrs. Roper still wore her burgundy dressing gown, the color ghastly against her blotched face. Her iron-gray hair had not been dressed and sprang out in messy tendrils from the braid that unraveled down her back.

"We know the entire appalling story," Mr. Roper said in a tightly controlled voice. Each word was as cold as his frozen eyes. "You needn't deny your role. I have but one question to put to you: How long have you been delivering letters between my daughter and that blackguard? When did this travesty begin?"

Lucie wet pale lips and wrung her hands together. The seed she had planted had grown. Now the scythe was raised and poised for harvest.

After she answered, her voice a dry whisper, Mrs. Roper rounded on her, spittle flying from her lips. "How *could* you! How could you betray this family after we took you into our home? After we gave you work, fed you, treated you well! We've never beaten you or nicked your pay. We—"

"Axa! Take hold of yourself. Remember who you are!"

Mrs. Roper's eyes flashed bitter hatred. "Well, look at her! Standing there as brazen as you please, not a word of apology or regret! She should be horsewhipped and tarred and feathered!"

"I do regret your distress, Mrs. Roper, truly I do." Lucie bit her lips and pressed her hands together until her knuckles whitened. "But when Miss Augusta approached me, I thought—"

"I am not the least interested in what you think about anything, Miss Kolska." Mr. Roper's cold look cut through her flesh. "You are dismissed without character. You have twenty minutes to change your clothing and leave my house."

Absurdly, in view of the circumstances, she bobbed her head to them and backed out of the chamber as if they were royalty. Dazed, she blinked at Mr. Grist and meekly submitted as he led her downstairs into a pool of absolute silence. No one spoke as Mr. Grist guided her through the assembly, through the house, and left her without a word at the laundry room door.

Inside the deserted laundry she removed her cap and apron and slipped out of her uniform. Events had occurred too swiftly for her to fully comprehend her altered circumstances. Later, she would think about the scene with the Ropers and experience the chill beginning of despair.

But now, as she hastily buttoned her shirtwaist and pinned on her hat, Lucie thought about Miss Augusta and her cherished Mr. Whitcomb. She had not seen Miss Augusta smile or heard her laugh in longer than she could remember. But she could imagine it. And the vision was gratifying.

Mrs. Greene and Hilda burst through the door as Lucie donned her coat and looked for the last time at the warm steam puffing up from the tubs on the stove, at the wonderful inside water taps. She knew each iron and what quirks to watch for, knew which drying racks could withstand the weight of a damp quilt and which could not. She had enjoyed her time here, and she would miss this room and these people.

"Lordy, Lucie," Hilda said breathlessly. Her eyes were as wide and round as lumps of coal. "Is it true? Was it you who ran the letters back and forth?"

Lucie pulled on her gloves, glancing at the knot of people staring at her from the door. It seemed the entire household had shifted from the staircase to the laundry room door.

"Yes, I did it," she said firmly. Breathing deeply, Lucie lifted her bosom. "And I'm glad. My only regret is I won't be here when Mrs. Roper informs the baron."

Then, raising her small chin in a show of bravado, she left the laundry room, walked through the silent kitchen and out the back door.

It wasn't until she was sitting on the train, returning to the tenement at midday that she began to fully consider her situation. An unpleasant prickle flowed over her scalp. Her failed venture with the cream had nearly depleted the coins saved beneath the loose board. They could not survive on Stefan's earnings alone. Her romantic foolishness would cost them dearly. What hurt more was knowing Stefan would suffer for her actions.

A hard knot formed in the pit of her stomach and began to grow. "Dismissed without character." Without character. The devastating words circled in her mind, seemingly repeating in time to the click of the wheels.

"STEFAN, HAVE YOU HEARD anything I've said?" Lucie asked in a low voice. She cast a quick worried glance toward Jamie, who watched Stefan with an expression as puzzled as her own. "I've placed us in a terrible situation."

When Stefan did not respond but continued to look unblinkingly at his untouched portion of water-bread, Jamie leaned forward to take her hand.

"It's done, lass." He looked at Stefan, waiting for a word that did not come, then returned to her. "For the past hour you've flogged yourself without mercy. Even if you wished to turn backward and change the beginning, you can't do it."

"That's the worst of it," she admitted, turning moist dark eyes to him. "I'd do the same again. And look where it's put us!'' A shudder twisted down her spine. "He said without character, Jamie. Without a character I can't obtain another job.''

Jamie stroked her hands. "Not a job on Madison Avenue anyway. Not work in a private laundry. But there are other jobs, and you'll find one.'' He didn't add that he loathed the necessity of Lucie working outside the home at all, but the impractical thought was written across his expression.

"Oh, Stefan, I do wish you would say something!'' Wringing her hands, Lucie turned her pale face to her brother. "Shout at me, yell and stamp your feet. But *say* something, I beg you!''

At last he lifted his head and looked at them with dull eyes. "Greta is too ill to get out of bed. She couldn't go to work today and Mr. Church sent word that she's sacked.''

"Oh, no!'' The breath rushed from Lucie's body. She sat very still, only now noticing Stefan's face was as chalky as her own.

"There's more.'' After pushing aside his plate, he drained his mug of weak coffee. Lucie saw his hand was shaking. "The Janics, the people Greta boards with, they're leaving next week to try their luck in a place called Wisconsin.''

"She's lost her job, she's too ill to find another and she has no place to live,'' Jamie repeated, his voice strained. "Stefan, does Greta have any savings?''

"Four dollars and thirty-two cents.''

No one spoke. In the silence Lucie could hear her heart thudding against her ribs. Last week the world had been filled with promise and hope. Now it seemed as if bits of sky crashed around them. She inhaled deeply, filling her lungs with the acrid smoke drifting from the table lamp.

"Greta will come to us, of course,'' she announced firmly. There was no other solution. Standing, she dusted her hands across her apron front, and eyed the room. "We'll fix a bed for her here, near the stove so she'll stay warm. You can pull apart one of the wagons in the street, Stefan, and make a platform. We can't have her sleeping on the floor, not with the mice and vermin so bad this winter. A platform will help. I'll sew a mattress out of my curtain and Mrs. Blassing will sell me enough rags to stuff it. Let's see, how shall I pay her?'' She spoke more to herself than to the men. "With bread loaves, I think. Yes, Mrs. Blassing praised my loaves.''

"Thank you, Lucie." Relief flooded Stefan's features and for a moment he could not speak. Then he spread his hands and frustration clouded his expression. "With you out of work, God knows how we'll eat or buy coal or pay for Greta's medicine. Damn it!'' He ground his teeth. "A man ought to be able to care for his own! He ought to be able to provide more than two closet rooms and he should be able to put food on the table. Damn it to hell!''

"We'll manage." Lucie noticed Jamie's expression and knew he understood she was not nearly as confident as she sounded. He had observed the flash of fear behind her eyes. "I'll find work soon, you'll see." Leaning over Stefan's shoulder, she pressed her cheek to his and kissed him. "Now go to Greta and tell her what we've decided. She must be feeling so frightened and alone.''

The instant the sound of his footsteps receded, Lucie buried her face in her hands. "Oh, Jamie, what have I done? This is the worst time to be out of work!''

He came to her and gently guided her into his arms. "There's never a good time, lass." Smoothing back her hair, he tilted her face up to his. "I still have our sixteen dollars.''

"Stefan would never agree to accept it.''

"That's why I'm offering it to you instead of to him.''

She shook her head. "Stefan is as stubborn and prideful as you are. He would rather starve than borrow a penny.''

Jamie held her close and rested his chin on top of her hair. "The time may come when Stefan must swallow his pride and accept a wee bit of assistance from a friend. Just remember the money's there.''

"Thank you," Lucie whispered. Knowing a small cushion existed was a comfort. But not a solution. Tonight she saw no solution. Tonight she saw the rag stuffed in the broken window pane, the stained brown walls, the sagging stove. She inhaled the reek of coal and kerosene and the musty odors behind the walls. Even in winter, she could smell the school sinks in the courtyard.

What she could not see or smell or touch tonight was the future. She, who could usually see sunshine where others saw darkness, saw only shadows. This, as much as the actual situation, frightened her.

"Everything will work out," she murmured against Jamie's chest. Blotting the shadows, she pressed her face against the shoulder of his waistcoat and inhaled the reassuring scents of wool, starch, bay rum and the soapy scent of his hair. Good smells that overwhelmed the others. "It will work out, won't it?"

"Aye, lass."

They stood before the stove, holding each other in a loose embrace that tightened as their thoughts turned to their own immediate future. What small measure of privacy they enjoyed was about to end. They had tonight and possibly tomorrow, then there would be no place where they could be alone.

"It was good of you to insist Greta come here," Jamie murmured against her shining chestnut hair, holding her close against him.

"Of course she must come to us."

They held each other tightly, combating the selfishness of need and feeling the charged urgency of impending loss. This kiss might be the last for weeks, certainly the last that could be uninhibited and private. This touch, so intimate and deeply personal, would not be repeated before Stefan and Greta. Mouths could not cling, nor hands linger. There was only tonight.

Their kisses deepened, made sweeter by a hint of despair, by the knowledge tonight must sustain them through the coming weeks. The restraint they so carefully maintained weakened beneath the stress in hands that flew to stroke and to remember, in lips that clung and murmured fevered endearments. In bodies that strained and ached and ignited in need and passion.

Pleasantly shocked by her boldness, driven by a need she did not dare analyze, Lucie shyly opened Jamie's shirt and slipped her small hand inside, pressing it flat against the hard muscles on his chest. A soft moan parted her lips. Beneath her palm she felt his heartbeat accelerate, felt the soft mossy growth of auburn hair. The touch of his skin was as she had imagined so many times, but firmer and smoother, possessing a warmth that shot through her body and left her trembling.

Covering her hand and holding it in place inside his shirt, Jamie kissed her, and his tongue explored the sweet innocence of her mouth, then gently traced the tender contour of her lips. A gasp issued from Lucie's throat and she withdrew her fingers from his shirt to circle his neck with both hands, pressing closer, closer to his body and feeling the frustration of layers of clothing, of empty spaces crying to be filled.

Holding each other so tightly it was impossible to identify which heartbeat belonged to whom, they sank to their knees on the floor. When Jamie's lips released hers, he whispered her name and ran his hands down her sides to her waist, then over her hips, smoothing down the dark skirts that puddled around them. The fluid movement of his hands, the heat that tingled behind, left her weak and lightheaded.

"I can span your waist with my hands," he murmured in a thick voice.

Lucie's head fell back and her eyes closed as the warmth of his hands slid from her waist to her breasts. He hesitated and her breath caught in her throat, her back arched slightly. Then the heat of his palms covered her breasts, and she gasped, suddenly aflame with heat and light and an explosive need that quivered through her body.

He kissed her, deeply, urgently, his hands still cupping her small aching breasts. When his mouth released hers, he looked into her eyes, and she felt his trembling fingers on the buttons of her shirtwaist.

"Lucie?" he said hoarsely.

"I love you," she whispered, trusting him, needing him. She wanted him to hurry, to hurry, wanted his fingertips where her own had been, yearned to know the thrill of his caress on her naked skin. But the strength had bled from her body. She knelt before him, trembling in anticipation, her arms at her sides, as he fumbled with the seemingly endless row of small buttons marching from her throat to her waist.

When the shirtwaist fell open, he leaned to kiss her mouth, his fingertips resting lightly against the pulse beat throbbing in her throat. Only after he kissed her again did he allow himself to look down at the creamy flesh swelling above the tiny lace edge of her chemise. Now it was he who seemed paralyzed.

Emboldened by his sharp intake of breath, Lucie touched a shaking fingertip to the perspiration on his brow, then smiling a woman's smile, loving him so much it hurt inside, she opened the top buttons of her chemise and raised her eyes in shy hope that she would please him.

"Oh, God," he murmured hoarsely. "You are so lovely. So incredibly lovely!"

Relief and joy softened her expression, raised a moist shine to her eyes. "I was so afraid I'd disappoint you," she whispered.

"Disappoint me?" Shock darkened his eyes almost to black before he caught her and held her so close against him that she could not breathe. "Never! Never, Lucie lass!"

Kisses rained over her hair, her face, her throat, then his lips were on her offered breast, moving in tender exploration, circling, circling until his tongue found her thrusting nipple and a tiny cry of pleasure caught in her throat. Heat raced through her body. Perspiration rose like dew on her naked skin. Every instinct urged her toward the floor that she might feel his possessive weight on her and the bliss of completion.

"Lucie." Passion roughened his voice. But he deliberately forced himself to ease away from her. Shaking hands lifted to frame her face. "My beautiful, Lucie." He kissed her, gently, struggling to restrain the passion that sucked at his breath, roared in his blood.

"I love you."

"I love you, Lucie Kolska. The earth shakes with it." Tenderly he stroked a damp strand of chestnut hair back from her cheek, fighting to establish control. Trust and disappointment mingled in her gaze as desire and duty mingled in his. "'Tis a cruel wait, lass." His whisper emerged as a groan.

On one level she admired his control and his respect for her, understood he withdrew while it was still possible, which it might not have been a moment later. That he did so against his will was evident in his intense gaze, his trembling lips and fingertips. On another level his withdrawal, as gentle as it was, devastated her and left her feeling bereft, shivering on the brink of a fulfillment she longed for.

Taking her hand, Jamie helped her to her feet, then tactfully, he turned aside as she buttoned her chemise and shirtwaist and lifted her hands to straighten her hair and touch the rosy heat still pulsing in her cheeks.

He removed the rag from the broken window pane and reached outside for a handful of snow, which he rubbed over his face and forehead and throat, watching her as he did so.

"Someday, lass," he said quietly, his voice deep and husky, "I will wake with you beside me. And know you will be waiting when I return at night. I live for the joy of that day, my dearest, for the moment I can truly call you mine. I want nothing more than to spend the rest of my life making you happy."

"You want nothing more?" she asked, smiling. Her arms slid around his waist and she lifted her head with a teasing look, the taste of his kisses still on her swollen mouth. "You don't want a snug little house, perhaps? Or a horse and trap? Or perhaps a building to build?"

Laughing, he dropped a kiss on her forehead. "If those things would make you happy, I could force myself to endure them." He held her close, then tilted her face up. "What do you want, Lucie? What will make you happy?"

"You," she said simply, meaning it. When he protested, telling her that wasn't what he meant, she smiled. "My wants are simple, dearest Jamie. I hope for a home of my own someday, and a kitchen garden and perhaps a tree to shade the afternoon." Pink bloomed in her cheeks. "And healthy laughing children with their father's auburn hair."

She touched his shoulder as she placed a mug of coffee and a loaf of potato bread on the table before him. "Sometimes I grow impatient, too," she said softly, cradling his head against her breast. "Sometimes I want to go to sleep and wake when my goal has been accomplished and your goal has been accomplished and we can be together always."

"I know, lass. I know." A frown drew his brow. "I'm doing all I can to hasten that day."

THE ELUSIVENESS of the future consumed Jamie with frustration. When he thought about Lucie and his love for her he was overcome by impatience, by a deep-seated desire to leap into tomorrow. He couldn't endure the possibility of waiting for years before they could marry; he wanted and needed her now.

Although he had not received the raise in pay he requested, it was promised for spring, and he could look forward to small but regular increases. On several occasions Jonas Tucker had declared himself well pleased by Jamie's performance and indicated Jamie had a secure future with

Tucker Enterprises. But his progress occurred in small increments; it would not be swift.

Leaning back from his worktable, he rubbed his eyes and pinched the bridge of his nose. The sound of hammering rang through the floors above him. He inhaled the scent of wood shavings and wet mortar.

Recently, without telling Lucie, he had priced household furnishings and had checked the cost of family housing. What he discovered appalled him. It wasn't only the cost of necessary items, like a bed and a stove, that shocked him, but the lack of adequate space.

Consequently, choices narrowed to a small hideously overpriced home far outside the city or adding oneself to the lengthy list of those waiting for the few mid-priced homes available within the city or settling for a tenement. Assuming one could afford any of the choices, which presently he could not. An impatient sigh collapsed his chest.

Moreover, there was a second truth he had deliberately delayed facing until recently. He could save to marry Lucie . . . or he could save to finance his dream, a business of his own. Kelly's Design and Construction Company. But he could not do both. Not even with a generous raise in pay.

By continuing a regimen of austere frugality, he believed he could save enough to launch a business within six to eight years. Or he could save enough to marry within the next three years. He didn't have to think twice. Lucie was more important to him than any business. But he wanted Lucie *and* his own business. He wanted all of the pie, not just a slice. Was that so wrong? Not wrong. Merely impossible.

Bending forward, he dropped his head into his hands and dug his fingers into his scalp. For a moment he visualized the sign he saw so often in his thoughts: Kelly's Design and Construction Company. He pictured the sign made of polished oak, the letters cut in Roman script, a circled JK in the upper right-hand corner. The vision shimmered briefly, then slowly began to fade.

He did not regret his choice. But what had Greta said? The death of a dream is a terrible thing. That was also true.

LUCIE CONCEALED HER SHOCK as best she could when Stefan carried Greta inside the tenement and gently laid her on the platform mattress. During the flurry of activity that accompanied Greta's arrival, Lucie tried not to stare, tried to swallow a scalding lump that threatened to strangle her.

Swiftly, shockingly, Greta had lost the weight she had gained. Gone were the rosy rounded cheeks, the hourglass curves of bosom and hips. The woman Stefan covered with the blankets from home was drawn and wasted, perilously thin and pale. The fashionable Gibson fullness had also gone. Now Greta wore her thinning hair pulled straight back and coiled on her neck. But the color was more white than golden and the rich luster had vanished. She could not walk without agonizing pain. Her stomach cramps were so severe she could not sit upright or sleep without doubling over. She couldn't eat without vomiting afterward.

Greta was desperately ill. "Oh, Lucie," she whispered after an attack of coughing that left her gasping and too weak to sit up. "I'm so sorry to intrude." A shine of tears moistened her eyes. "The last thing I wanted was to be a burden."

Lucie sat on the platform bed and unpinned Greta's hat and smoothed back the brittle strands of hair. "You're not intruding and you're not a burden. My dearest sister, I've wanted you here for months. Now that you are, we'll have you well in no time."

For a moment Greta's glistening blue eyes met Lucie's and held. In her gaze lay a truth neither of them could bear to admit. Then, panting slightly from the exertion, she opened her reticule and withdrew a worn cloth bag, which she pressed into Lucie's hand. "My savings. I wish it were more."

It was useless to pretend Greta's savings would not be needed. Nodding, Lucie kissed Greta's gaunt cheek and tucked the small bag into her apron pocket.

Then, because she didn't want Greta to see her tears, she rose and turned blindly toward the stove. But not before she saw Stefan's despair as he removed the geranium from the windowsill and placed it on the table where Greta could see it.

For a full minute Lucie stood staring at the pot of vegetable soup, not seeing it, listening to the soft murmur of voices behind her: Stefan's anxious questions, Greta's gentle assurances.

The soup pot blurred and a tear dropped on her hand. One by one their dreams were crumbling. The realization frightened her.

Chapter Eleven

For the first time in memory, spring arrived without Lucie taking notice. From her chair beside the window she could see only the side of the opposite tenement and a small slice of sky. When she emptied the slop bucket or fetched water from the courtyard pump, her thoughts were too distracted to notice the weeds pressing up along the base of the tenements, or to register the children playing outside, or the laundry tubs several of the women had moved into the courtyard.

Every third day Mr. Klaxon delivered three roped bundles of men's coats and a tin bucket of buttons. He counted the coats Lucie had completed, paid her, then took the finished coats away. By working from dawn until nine at night, Lucie could finish sewing buttons on one bundle of coats a day and earn seventy cents, less the cost of the thread and wax to coat it.

Spring, when Greta called it to her attention, meant little more than better light for longer periods. But it startled Lucie that she had not noticed. Her life had narrowed to an endless parade of cuffs and lapels, to needle pricks and stains on her hands and skirts from the dye used on the coats.

But life was not all drudgery and long hours wielding her needle. To everyone's joy, Greta steadily improved. As the weeks passed, a golden sheen gradually returned to Greta's hair and a suggestion of color reappeared on her lips and cheeks. Her stomach cramps eased and more and more frequently she was able to hold down her food. She remained unable to walk as her legs continued to pain her but she could sit up for longer periods, and the redness began to fade from her eyes.

Smiling, Lucie glanced up from the heavy coat spread across her lap. "It's so good to hear you laugh again." Now that Greta's hoarseness had all but vanished, her clear laugh again reminded Lucie of tiny pealing bells.

"It's the children," Greta said from the platform bed. Supported by pillows, she sat where she could see the window and a scrap of sky. "Do you hear them playing?" she asked, smiling.

The children's occasional visits brightened the day and so did Jamie and Stefan's arrival at twilight. After supper, while Lucie sewed buttons and Greta rested, Stefan and Jamie read from the newspaper or a library book. Sometimes they talked until late, enjoying each other's company, discussing the day's small events, or remembering their childhoods and friends and family now far away. They seldom spoke of the future.

"It's Sunday," Greta said, interrupting Lucie's train of thought. "Dearest Lucie, you finished the laundry before dawn, supper is simmering on the stove . . . can't you set the coats aside and rest? When is the last time you and Jamie spent any time alone together?"

She couldn't remember. First, Greta had been so desperately ill that Lucie did not dare leave her even for a moment. Then, she had succumbed to panic as the money steadily dwindled until only a few pennies remained in the small bag beneath the loose board. Finally she had persuaded Mr. Klaxon to allot her the piecework and from that moment it seemed she had scarcely had an instant to breathe. Each idle moment represented a coat that was not being finished, coins that were not being earned.

"Lucie? Jamie will arrive in a few minutes. And he will ask you to walk out with him. Please, this time say yes. The two of you need some time alone."

Lucie's gaze darted to the bundle of coats beside the door, her mind calculating the sum it represented.

"You don't know how terrible I feel," Greta said in a low voice, "watching you work so hard and being unable to help."

"Without your encouragement, I would go utterly mad sitting here day after day pushing this needle in and out, in and out."

"If it weren't for me, you would have different work, maybe something you could enjoy."

Setting aside the coat, Lucie went to the platform bed and took Greta's hand. "Listen to me, Greta Laskowski. You must stop thinking you're an imposition. Stefan and I are your family now. If your illness has been a burden, it has been a burden of love." She leaned to kiss Greta's cheek. "We're managing, aren't we?"

"Oh, Lucie. Stefan sold his pocket watch to buy my medicine. Did you know?" Distress filled Greta's lovely eyes.

So that was how Stefan had paid for the bottles standing in a row on the shelf. Lucie drew a breath. "Excellent," she said, smiling. "Now we know what to buy him for his next birthday gift. In the past I've never known what to get him."

Greta stared at her, then laughed her chiming laugh. "I love you so much," she said, embracing Lucie. "Soon I'll be well enough to find work, too."

"Indeed you will be. Even Stefan, who worries enough for all of us, admits you're much, much improved."

A sudden shyness entered Greta's eyes. "Dearest Lucie. Will you step out with Jamie today? If not for your sake, then for mine?"

"Oh! I see." Surprise lifted Lucie's eyebrows, then a look of delight. "You *are* feeling better!" Then a thought occurred and she peered into Greta's face. Greta's health was greatly improved but she was a long way from full recovery. "Or are you putting your suggestion in a way you know I can't refuse?"

"Perhaps a bit of both," Greta admitted. "But Jamie needs you, too," she said softly. "And I am feeling better."

Lucie bit her lip and her gaze again strayed to the bundle of coats beside the door. Such a thin line separated safety from disaster.

"You haven't worn the shirtwaist with the leg-o-mutton sleeves since last summer...and you look so pretty in it," Greta gently prompted. "It would please Jamie so much to have you all to himself for a day."

Indecision flickered behind Lucie's eyes. The coats beckoned. But it was spring. And it had been so long since she had shared any privacy with Jamie. Suddenly she felt the weariness slip from her shoulders, replaced by a youthful eagerness she had not experienced in weeks. "Yes," she breathed, turning to look at the window. "Yes, if you're certain..."

When she told Jamie of her decision, the joy in his eyes told her she had made the right choice.

AFTER CONSIDERING and rejecting several alternatives, Jamie took her to Central Park to show her the spring flowers. Starlings and sparrows wheeled overhead, as numerous as the Sunday strollers who passed one another on the promenades exchanging murmurs of appreciation for the fine warm day. The elms were in full leaf and the spring air smelled of cut grass and emerging blossoms.

"Oh, Jamie!" Lucie pressed her gloves together and gazed around the park with wide eyes. "I'd forgotten how green it can be! Isn't it lovely?"

"Lovely," he said, smiling at her happiness and tucking her arm inside his. He suspected today's outing had been Greta's idea, and he silently thanked her for it. They had all begun to worry about Lucie, about the long relentless hours and the purplish circles beneath her eyes. She never complained, but the strain of caring for Greta while trying to work manifested itself in broken thread, burned loaves and in another dozen small ways all of which she apologized for and turned in on herself.

The helplessness of standing by, watching the struggle without being able to assist had proved a strain for Jamie, as well. He could guess what it must be for Greta and Stefan to know the heaviest weight fell on Lucie and there was nothing anyone could do.

That was the worst part, the helplessness. Again and again as he moved through the Tucker Building, watching it grow and come to life around him, his thoughts drifted to the Elizabeth Street tenement, knowing Lucie sat in the gloom, her fingers numb and stained with dye, her back aching from bending over the coats, her eyes straining to see.

At such times his teeth clenched and his muscles tightened in frustration. Sometimes he remained at the site after the others had gone, hammering nails in a fury until the tension began to ebb from his body. He wanted to rescue her; he wanted to bump time ahead to a period of safety and peace. He wanted to change the world and fashion it into a place where lovely young women didn't waste away from mysterious maladies, where hearts didn't silently weep over buckets of buttons. He wanted a quiet world, a safe world, where a man and woman could face the future with confidence and a small degree of comfort. Where the price of a doctor's house call didn't equal several days of a man's labor.

"Jamie?"

He blinked. "What? I'm sorry, dearest, I was thinking of the world to come. And it will come, surely it will. People like us will make it happen."

She smiled at him from beneath the brim of her little straw boater. "My, such lofty thoughts!"

"And what are you thinking, lass?" he asked, covering her glove on his arm with his hand. "That a lemonade would sit well about now?"

"Actually, I was wondering if we're allowed to pick the flowers. See the geraniums there? And the forget-me-nots? And tulips! It's late for tulips, isn't it? I'd like to pick them all and take them home." She gave him a wistful smile. "But I'll settle for lemonade."

"We'll have both." After darting a glance over his shoulder to see that no one watched, he grinned, then stepped into the flower bed.

"Jamie!" Her hands flew to her mouth, but her eyes sparkled. And when she laughed, the first time he had heard her laugh in weeks, he knew he would have plucked every flower in the park and suffered the consequences gladly.

"For you, madam," he said grandly, bowing before her and presenting the stolen bouquet.

Closing her eyes, she pressed her face into the blossoms and inhaled deeply. "Thank you. Oh, thank you."

For one stunning moment, he felt like weeping. It took so little to make her happy. A bright sky, a bit of greenery. His smile. He wanted to spread the world at her feet.

Instead, he took her to the dairy for a lemonade and light refreshments. It twisted his heart that she chose the least expensive items. "No," he said to the waiter, "bring the lady the butter cake instead. With ice cream."

When the waiter left, she leaned forward with a worried expression. "Jamie, can we—"

"I received my raise in pay. It wasn't as much as I'd hoped, but welcome no less."

She stared at him. "You said nothing!"

Immediately he understood he had hurt her by not sharing his news on the instant. "It didn't seem appropriate to mention my good fortune when you and Stefan are having such a struggle."

She lifted her head and forced a smile. "Congratulations on your raise. I'm proud of you and happy for you."

"For us, lass. Be happy for us."

"For us," she said, pressing his arm possessively as they left the dairy.

They went to the romanesque American Museum of Natural History where Lucie exclaimed over the war canoe suspended from the ceiling, and they toured the Peruvian collections and the Alaska and Northwest coast series. They saw the skeleton of Jumbo, Mr. Barnum's giant African elephant, and inspected the collections of stuffed monkeys and insects. Afterward, he suggested supper in a nearby chophouse, but Lucie declined.

"It's been a wonderful day, but this is the first time I've left Greta . . ."

"I understand." They spoke little during the return ride on the elevated. Lucie sat beside him holding his hand beneath the concealing folds of her dark skirts, her face turned to the window. Her silence worried him, but she would not be tempted into conversation. As the Bowery Street station came into view, she finally spoke.

"I wanted today to be perfect, but I almost spoiled it. I'm sorry."

"It was the raise, wasn't it?" he asked, leaning to look beneath her hat brim. "I was wrong not to tell you."

She didn't answer immediately, then she raised her head from the flowers she still carried. "I love you, Jamie. I believe you love me. We love each other enough to share our dreams and our disappointments." She spoke quietly, gazing into his eyes. "Don't we love each other enough to share our successes, as well?"

Her statement startled him. "Even if news of that success may make the road seem rougher for the other?" he
asked after a moment. She nodded. "Even if a heartfelt
'congratulations' might strain the goodness of a saint?"

She smiled and squeezed his hand. "Even then. No matter my situation, dearest Jamie, I will always be glad for
your successes. I hope you would feel the same about my
successes."

"Of course!"

They returned home to discover Greta dressed and sitting at the table. She laughed and clapped her hands when
she saw their astonishment, then exclaimed in delight over
the flowers.

"Lucie, about today..." Jamie said later. They stood in
the black hallway, stealing a moment for a passionate kiss
before he departed. "And my raise—"

"Shhh," she said, placing her fingertip across his lips.
"It's been a marvelous day and I love you. That's all that
matters. Love me, Jamie. Just love me."

GRETA'S PROGRESS seemed rapid and remarkable, though in
truth it occurred in small daily increments. The day came
when she could brush and dress her own hair. When she
could sit up all day. Then she could read the newspaper
without her sore eyes streaming tears. Her legs still bothered her, but when Stefan carried her up to the rooftop she
told the children stories for hours without becoming exhausted. And one Sunday afternoon in early summer, when
Lucie returned from a band concert with Jamie, Greta had
peeled the supper potatoes.

"Soon," she said, gazing at Stefan with shining eyes, "I'll
be able to run up and down to the courtyard pump! And go
to the market again." Teasing him, she pointed to the geranium he had brought her to replace the one that had died.
"The dear man bought white, Lucie. Imagine it, white when
he could have had red!" When the men departed to carry

their chairs up to the cooler rooftop, Greta touched Lucie's sleeve. "I hate to ask this, but would you and Jamie give Stefan and I a moment of privacy after supper?"

"Of course." She looked at Greta with raised eyebrows, waiting to learn if Greta would explain her anxiety.

"I've made a decision I doubt Stefan will accept easily," Greta said, biting her lip. "I sent Mr. Church a letter last week inquiring if I could do piece work here." When Lucie protested, she raised a hand. "Please don't tell me I haven't been a burden, Lucie. Of course I have. I'll feel much better if I can bring in some money. Even if it's just a little at the start."

Lucie didn't immediately see where they would put Greta's supplies. Unless Stefan cut a door in the platform bed and Greta could keep her supplies beneath the platform. "Are you absolutely certain you feel well enough to attempt this?"

"I'll be paid by the piece, so I can rest whenever I wish. Whatever I earn would help."

That was true. The extra coins were desperately needed. There had been weeks when Lucie, her cheeks pale with fear and embarrassment, had been forced to beg the landlord's agent to return later because she didn't have the rent money in hand.

When Stefan and Greta did not return to the tenement rooms until after midnight, Lucie guessed a row had ensued over Greta's decision. Lying on her mattress in the sleeping room, she heard the shortness in their voices as they said good night to each other. Stefan appeared in the sleeping room so swiftly Lucie understood they had not kissed, an omission that shocked her and indicated the seriousness of the argument.

But in the end Stefan acquiesced. Greta's doctor waved aside Stefan's questions about arsenic in the dyes, saying he thought it nonsensical to suppose the Hudson Factory would poison its employees. He took umbrage that Stefan dared question his expertise.

"Haslip could be wrong," Stefan insisted, brooding in a last attempt to have his way. He cast an unhappy glance at the papers and beads and wires covering the kitchen table.

"Bunkum," Greta responded firmly. "Dr. Haslip's remedies have almost cured me of whatever made me ill."

Greta did look lovely today, Lucie thought, happier than she had been in weeks knowing she had work again and could contribute to her upkeep. Before Lucie returned to the coats and buttons, she smiled at Greta's eager expression.

"Stefan will come around," she assured Greta the next day as Greta arranged her supplies across the table and seated herself before them. The next time Lucie looked up from her bucket of buttons, Greta had completed three exquisite paper roses. "They're beautiful!" The color was a deep glowing red that seemed to chase the shadows from the room.

At the end of the week, Lucie paid the rent on time. She added a nickel to her cache. A hank of mutton waited in the salt box for Sunday supper. At Greta's insistence, she agreed to the extravagance of a net of oranges. Her heart soared. The worst was over.

"EVERYTHING IS GOING to be all right!" she informed Jamie, taking his arm. Her cheeks still ached from laughing at the vaudeville comedian. She suspected she had laughed even when the jokes were mild and she remembered wearing a silly happy smile during the musical numbers. But she felt so good, so happy. It had been weeks since she felt this wonderful.

Jamie smiled at her and covered her hand with his own. "Do you know your eyes sparkle when you're happy? It's like looking into diamonds. I'm blinded."

She laughed. "Diamonds aren't brown."

"The only diamonds I care about are. It's still early, would you like a glass of wine?"

"Wine? Good heavens! Did you receive another raise?"

"Not yet," he said, grinning. "But when we start excavating the new building next month, Mr. Tucker has promised a ten-cent-a-day increase."

"That's wonderful! Oh, Jamie, I'm so proud of you," she said, giving his arm a squeeze.

They turned into the coffee house on Bowery Street, the one they had once thought of as their own, where they had spent so many wonderful, if guilt-ridden, moments. They had not returned here until tonight.

"Do you suppose we were sitting at this very table a year ago?" Lucie asked when their wine had been served. If so, she might have been wearing the very same straw hat and striped shirtwaist. Aside from the new, fashionable belt he wore, Jamie would have been dressed the same, too, wearing his summer bowler and lightweight vest. And she would have wanted him then as much as she wanted him now.

"August? Aye, we might well have been here a year ago." Leaning forward, the gaslight behind him forming a halo around his head, he touched his wineglass to hers. "To a year of happiness past, and to years of happiness ahead," he toasted solemnly. Then he mouthed the words "I love you" and she smiled with happiness.

The year had passed so swiftly. Now when she said "home" she meant the tenement on Elizabeth Street, something she wouldn't have believed a year ago. She no longer thought of herself as Polish, she was an American. She followed the current presidential campaign with great interest because she believed it was something all Americans should be interested in whether or not they could vote. It pleased her that the incumbent, President McKinley, "her" candidate because of his full-dinner-pail slogan, seemed to be gaining ground over William Jennings Bryan and Eugene Debs. A year ago she hadn't been entirely sure who was President and had never heard of a newspaper poll.

Stefan had returned to her life bringing her a dearly beloved sister. And, most importantly, she had found Jamie.

Looking at him now, she tried to decide if he had changed in the last year. He was suntanned and the lines on his forehead were a bit stronger, she noticed. He was more handsome but that did not surprise her. Jamie Kelly was the type of man the years would touch lightly, who would grow more handsome, more distinguished with each coming year. She read a new frustration in his gaze and impatience, but also increased confidence. He knew his direction now and had settled into himself.

Suddenly it crossed her mind that she had not heard Jamie mention Kelly's Design and Construction Company in a very long time. A frown creased her brow. Then it occurred to her that she had not mentioned her goal in a long time either, and her expression relaxed. Daily events intruded; they had not had much time alone. Now that Greta was feeling well enough to work a little Lucie had ceased sewing buttons on Sundays and there would be time to dream aloud again.

When Jamie cleared his throat to capture her attention, she looked at him across the table and saw his eyes twinkled with anticipation.

"Jamie Kelly! There is a special reason for the wine!"

"I've been waiting all evening to tell you." Leaning, he caught her hand in both of his and smiled.

One thing that had not changed throughout the last turbulent year was her response to Jamie's touch. When he touched her something hot and shameless ignited inside, and she longed for him as much or more than ever she had. Many a sleepless night had she lain awake on her thin mattress remembering the night he kissed her breast, feeling herself blush in the darkness and wishing it would happen again.

"Tell me!" His news was good, maybe wonderful. She could see the excitement fairly dancing in his gaze. "I'm about to faint with suspense!"

"As it seems the Kolskas' fortunes have rebounded and you won't be needing my nest egg, I thought it safe to invest in the Kellys' future..."

"Jamie Kelly, you're teasing me! If you don't tell me your news this instant, I don't know what I'll do, but something!"

He laughed, then pressed her fingers and gazed at her mouth. "I bought our bed!"

"Jamie!" She stared at him, then her face lit. "We have a bed? Of our very own?" Falling back in her chair, she blinked at him in amazement, stunned by the news. "Oh, Jamie." Tears of happiness strangled her voice. "We've begun our household."

It was unthinkable that she would visit his lodgings even to inspect the bed she would sleep in for the rest of her life, the bed where her children would be born. Such impropriety could not be countenanced.

Leaning forward, her expression ablaze with excitement, she gripped his hands and asked a dozen questions. "Have you slept in it? Is the mattress filled with goose down? Not chicken feathers, oh, I hope not. Good. What does it look like? Oh, tell me, Jamie! Here—" she rummaged in her reticule until she found a pencil "—draw me a picture!"

When he did so, she stared at the drawing in breathless awe. "It's beautiful! Such a large headboard, and the footboard curves around like a cradle. Oh, Jamie, I love it!" A wave of heat burned her cheeks as she imagined them lying in this bed together. It was what she wanted more than anything else. "And cherry wood! It must have cost a prince's ransom."

"That it did, lass," he said, giving her a rueful smile. "Thirteen dollars."

"No!"

"But we'll have it all our lives. It seemed better to purchase well now than sleep poorly the rest of our days for the want of three dollars."

This, her practical mind understood. She agreed, praising his wisdom. She could hardly take her eyes from the drawing long enough to give him a dazed smile. "We have a bed!"

Tonight of all nights she longed for a place of their own, where they could kiss and touch in private bliss, sharing dreams of their future together. But there was only the deserted doorway, a partial refuge from the pedestrians enjoying the warm summer night.

When they stepped into the shadows, she lifted her hand to his cheek, her eyes shining. "Oh, Jamie."

His kiss was almost chaste, filled with tenderness as if she were a dream from which he might awaken if he held her too tightly. The passion that simmered between them was there as always, but tonight was a night for tenderness, a night to cherish each other and the future they longed for.

"Atta boy, bingo," a rude voice called. "Put the boots to 'er."

Jamie broke from their kiss to scowl as the man laughed and walked away. "I hate this," he said in a low voice. "Sometimes I think we'll never have a place of our own!"

Lucie gently placed her hand on his jaw and smiled at him with shining eyes. "But, dearest, we're so much nearer than we were last week!"

"Someday," he said, his dark eyes making love to her.

Tonight, someday seemed just around the corner. Hugging him close, Lucie covered his dear face with kisses, not caring who might see. The future was theirs again.

GRETA'S FLOWER PAPER shed a filmy gray dust that settled on her clothing as she worked and spread a fine, almost invisible coating across the platform bed.

"I wish you could see the factory," Greta said as she scrubbed the dust from the table before she put down the cloth for supper. "The dust is everywhere, it's unavoidable. It piles in the corners, under the worktables..."

Lucie looked up from the pot of peas she was shelling. "Did you get some in your eyes? I noticed you've been squinting again and rubbing your eyes." For a time Greta had not worn her spectacles, insisting she no longer needed them. But two weeks ago she had begun wearing them again.

"Perhaps I did. Does the dust bother you?"

"Not that I've noticed. You wear yourself out sweeping it up." In truth Lucie hadn't been feeling one hundred percent of late, though she hardly thought the paper dust had anything to do with it.

But Greta's ankles had swollen again. And the rash had reappeared on her hands. Last night Lucie had opened one of the little pots of cream stored on her shelf in the sleeping room and rubbed it into Greta's hands until the tenement rooms smelled pleasantly of geranium oil.

"I think the cake is almost done," Lucie said, turning away from worrisome thoughts. "Can you smell it?" Actually it was a recipe of her mother's that combined the sweetness of cake and the sturdy consistency of bread. Lucie had purchased raisins and candied cherries and the cake would be iced, as well.

"You shouldn't have gone to all this trouble," Greta protested. But her eyes glowed behind her spectacles.

"Bunkum! You don't have a nineteenth birthday every day. You must have a cake. Besides, we haven't properly celebrated your restored health." Immediately, she knew it was the wrong thing to say. The light dimmed in Greta's eyes and they looked at each other for a long moment before they turned aside and hurriedly busied themselves with preparations for the evening ahead.

STEFAN GAVE GRETA a new winter hat trimmed with velvet ribbon in a shade of blue that matched her eyes. "A *new* hat," he emphasized proudly and grinned as they teased him about walking into a milliner's shop on Ladies Mile. "They recognize a man of consequence when they see one," he explained grandly, sending them into gales of laughter. "It's all in the attitude."

From Jamie Greta received two flourishing geraniums and a packet of seeds. "To grow your own when these die," he explained, grinning. "And I thought Stefan and I were stubborn!"

Lucie's gift was a pair of everyday black stockings and a pair of white for best. "I wish it could have been more," she said, enclosing Greta in a tight embrace.

They opened the wine Jamie had brought and sang the Polish birthday song, then again in English. And laughed when Greta blushed and fluttered up on her tiptoes to give everyone grateful kisses.

Finally, with much ado and a shout of fanfare from Stefan and Jamie, Lucie produced the iced cake with a flush of pride. The crust was golden and bursting with swollen raisins. The drizzled icing was smooth and sweet.

"To the angel among us," Stefan said softly, raising his wine glass to Greta.

"To my dearest sister!"

"May your nineteenth year be the best year ever," Jamie said, smiling.

Tears of happiness glistened in Greta's eyes. Unable to speak, she opened her arms as if to embrace them. Then she mopped her eyes and gave them a radiant smile. "I love you all," she whispered.

"Lucie, darlin' lass, are you ever going to cut that cake? The fragrance has had my mouth watering from the moment I arrived."

Laughing, chattering happily, they devoured Greta's birthday cake, leaving not a single crumb.

Afterward, Greta vomited; she was sick all night. The illness had returned.

Chapter Twelve

Greta's decline was swift and absolute.

Lucie, Jamie and Stefan watched in helpless horror as Greta's previous symptoms returned with stunning virulence. For a time she sat against her pillows and continued to make the paper flowers, ignoring bouts of fevers and chills, but the day arrived when work was no longer possible. Her hands shook too badly; her eyes could not withstand the strain. Mr. Church rejected more of the paper flowers than he accepted. Silent tears rolled down Greta's cheeks as she pushed her supplies under the platform bed for the last time.

She could not eat, experienced difficulty sleeping. Her legs were numb. Each movement required an enormous expenditure of energy and left her gasping. Dr. Haslip proclaimed himself baffled by Greta's steadfast deterioration.

Lucie and Jamie stood on the tenement rooftop watching a dying sun glowing against the clouds. Someone nearby was burning rubbish and the sour smoke drifted on the evening air. Lucie tightened her shawl around her shoulders and leaned back in Jamie's enclosing arms.

"The smell of an early winter is in the air," she murmured, trying to read omens in the cloud patterns and trying to quell the hopelessness thinning her whisper. "Maybe the cooler weather will help. She felt better last year when the weather cooled, I'm sure she did. It's been so hot this summer, don't you think?" She was babbling. Cracking her teeth as Mrs. Greene would have said. Pressing her lips together, she stared at the clouds. One of them was shaped like a rose. Surely that was a good sign. It had to be. She fastened her gaze to the rose cloud, clenched her jaw, and willed it to mean Greta's health would improve.

"Dr. Haslip is with her now," Jamie said quietly, resting his chin on top of her head.

"I'm so frightened. I love her so much."

"I know, lass. We all do."

"And Stefan—"

"Shhh. Let's wait and see what Dr. Haslip has to say."

They remained on the rooftop another five minutes, then silently descended to the tenement, arriving as Dr. Haslip emerged. In the room behind him, Lucie glimpsed Stefan kneeling beside Greta's bed. She sucked in a hard sharp breath and her heart went cold. For the rest of her life, she would remember Stefan's ruined face, the agony in his eyes.

"No," she whispered, shaking her head violently. Her throat closed as she spun toward Dr. Haslip and examined his expression, searching for hope. "Oh, God, no. No!" Jamie's strong arm caught her before her knees collapsed.

"There's nothing more I can do," Dr. Haslip explained in a low voice. He settled an expensive bowler upon his white hair. "Mr...?"

"Kelly. I'm a friend of the family."

"Mr. Kelly, I'd suggest you advise Mr. Kolska that further doctor visits are a waste of three dollars. I've left some opiates. All we can do now is make her as comfortable as possible until—" He glanced at Lucie who turned sobbing into Jamie's arms. "Until the end," he finished quietly.

"Will she suffer much?"

"The opiates will help. In any case, it won't be long."

"No!" Lucie sobbed. "Not Greta. Not Greta!"

Dr. Haslip gave her shoulder an awkward pat. "I'm sorry."

Jamie looked inside the room as the doctor lifted his bag and walked toward the stairwell. His heart wrenched. Lamplight fell across the bed, across Stefan's heaving shoulders. Then, as Greta reached to comfort him, her thin arms closing around him, Jamie quietly closed the door. Their faces tore at his soul.

"Jamie..." Lucie raised drowning eyes. "I must go to her!"

"Not now, lass," he said, gently guiding her to the stairs. "Not just now."

THE IDEA CAME TO LUCIE that night on the rooftop. Shaking with rage, she cursed what was happening, cursed her powerlessness to stop it. But there was something she could do. She could give Greta her dream.

But the wedding had to happen swiftly. Greta and Stefan's wedding would be a paler version of what they had imagined, but Lucie was determined it should happen.

The first consequence of her decision was the loss of her work. Her voice edged with desperation, she explained to Mr. Klaxon that she urgently needed a week off for personal matters, but personal tragedies meant nothing to Mr. Klaxon. He collected his coats and buttons and slammed the door behind him. The coats and buttons—and the money they represented—were gone.

Greta struggled up from her pillows and coughed into her handkerchief. "Oh, Lucie,..." She waited, gathered her strength. "The cost is too high."

"No," she said firmly, staring at the door. "I'll not give up on this. The only thing you ever dreamed of was marrying Stefan." She bent to stroke a strand of hair away from Greta's burning forehead. "It's the only thing I ever heard you say you wanted. And by heaven you shall have it, my dearest sister."

If she let herself think about money now, she would shatter into pieces. As it was, the effort to hold herself together grew more difficult every day as she helplessly watched Greta grow weaker, slipping further away from them. She could not give Greta the children she longed for, but she could give her Stefan. If only for a short while.

Burying her pride she borrowed three dollars from Jamie and added it to the three dollars taken from under the loose board. Through meticulous searching and relentless bargaining at the rag fair, she purchased a vest and coat and tie for Stefan and an ivory gown for Greta.

A stubborn grass stain stained the back of the gown, as if the original owner had slid across a lawn, and it defied Lucie's skilled efforts to remove. But this was not an insurmountable problem. The gown had to be altered to fit Greta's wasted figure, so Lucie trimmed out the panel containing the grass stain and rebuilt the skirt.

When she spread the altered gown across the platform bed, Greta touched the material with trembling fingers. "I've never worn silk before. It's so soft!" Awe glowed on her translucent skin. "Describe it to me, Lucie, I can't see well enough...tell me if it shimmers. Is the color as lovely as it appears?"

Lucie swallowed and shut her eyes against scalding tears. "It shimmers, dearest, like a waterfall. The color is almost the same as your hair. Lace trims the bodice and cuffs. You'll be as beautiful—" a lump closed her throat, strangling her "—as beautiful as the day Stefan met you."

Greta fell back into the pillows, gasping for breath, the fever burning on her cheeks. "Father Norlic agreed to waive the reading of the banns? And he doesn't mind coming here?" When Lucie confirmed it, Greta struggled against the effect of the opiates to open her eyes. "I don't know how you've managed everything. How can we thank you for all you've done?"

"Get well! Oh, Greta, get well!"

Gently Greta stroked her hand. "Don't cry, dearest Lucie," she whispered. When she could speak again, her weak grip tightened around Lucie's fingers. "I know this isn't fair, but you must be strong for all of us. We depend on your strength. And dearest sister..."

"Don't try to sit up. Please, just rest."

"Help our Stefan." Her lovely eyes begged. "He seems so strong, but he's not. He will need you, Lucie."

"I know." Lucie wept.

"When some time has passed..." A fit of coughing left her pale and trembling. "Help him find someone to love." When she had rested a moment, she opened her eyes and a single tear slipped down her cheek. "Help him understand it's what I wanted. He's such a good man. He needs someone to love him. And someone to love."

"Oh, Greta! I can't bear this!"

"Remember, dearest. Promise me and remember."

That night Stefan sat beside Greta on the platform bed, holding her hot hand, his face as pale as hers. His dark eyes burned with grief and bewilderment. To depart for work was torment; to sit beside her and feel her slowly leaving him was agony.

"Everything is arranged, my love," he murmured, stroking her fingers. When she managed a smile, his face constricted in an effort to return the joy in her gaze. "Do you mind terribly that you won't have a ring?"

"But she will!" Lucie slapped her forehead, then rushed to her shelf in the sleeping room. When she returned she sat on the platform bed and opened her palm to show them the gold wedding ring Greta had given her for the cream. "Your mother's ring, I saved it. I didn't sell it to buy the ingredients for the cream. I sold my hat pins instead. You gave me the ring for my dream, dearest Greta, now I give it to you for yours."

Tears of happiness flowed down Greta's cheeks as Stefan helped her sit up so she could embrace Lucie.

As Greta had to rest frequently, it required most of the afternoon to dress her and arrange her hair. Lucie did so with silent tears streaming down her cheeks. The once lush body was thin and wasted, each gesture an exhausting effort. But eventually Greta was ready minutes before Father Norlic arrived. And she was lovely.

The artful magic of a hot curling iron and three or four false curls created an illusion of golden fullness framing her face. Fever and excitement tinted her cheeks with rose. The ivory silk captured the light from the table lamp and shimmered like champagne across the platform bed. Adoration filled Stefan's wet eyes as he gazed down at her.

"You look beautiful!" he said gruffly, his throat full.

"Oh, Stefan, look at you!"

Lucie had trimmed his hair and mustache. He wore the new coat, vest and tie. Lucie stared at him, her handsome brother, and knew the years would distinguish him and he would wear them with dignity.

"Are you all right?" Jamie murmured. He and Lucie sipped the wine he had brought, not tasting it, standing at a discreet distance from the platform bed while Father Norlic spoke to Stefan and Greta.

Tears flooded Lucie's throat, choking her. "She's so terribly ill, but even now she thinks of others. She worries about Stefan. She asked me to—" But she couldn't speak.

Jamie touched her cheek. "You accomplished your goal after all, lass," he said gently.

Father Norlic nodded to them then, but before they stepped forward Lucie plucked the single blossom from Greta's fading window geranium and gave it to her to hold.

"Please," Greta whispered, looking up at them. "I can't be married in bed. Stefan? Will you help me to stand?"

But her legs would not support her. In the end Stefan held her in his arms, cradling her tenderly to his chest as Father Norlic spoke the words that made them man and wife.

Afterwards, Stefan placed her gently on the platform bed, propped up by pillows, then stretched out beside her, holding her in the circle of his arms while Jamie toasted them with a new bottle of wine.

"Thank you," Greta whispered. "This is the happiest day of my life!" Eyes bright and dilated by opiates, she rested against Stefan's shoulder and smiled joyfully at the gold ring on her finger. "Oh, my dearest, I've waited so long for this happy day!"

Father Norlic finished his wine and tasted the wedding loaf, then he wished the newlyweds well. Before he departed, his sad eyes lingered on Stefan and Greta. Quietly, he shut the door behind him.

Shortly afterward Jamie and Lucie tactfully departed to take supper at a small German restaurant in Bowery Street. The moment they left the tenement their festive expressions dissolved into anguish. In the alleyway between the courtyard and Elizabeth Street, Lucie turned into Jamie's arms and wept until no more tears would flow, until she felt limp and drained.

"All she wanted was Stefan. And a home and children of her own. She never hurt anyone, never spoke a harsh word. I don't understand! Why is this happening?"

Jamie held her shaking body tightly, stroking her back. "I don't know, lass," he said quietly. "It isn't fair."

"She's only nineteen! She had a whole life in front of her, she—" But the words suffocated her.

Neither had much appetite. Their thoughts strayed to the Elizabeth Street tenement and Stefan and Greta. What would Greta and Stefan say to each other, they who had no future? How would they spend this, which should have been the happiest night of their lives?

And they stared across the table at each other, desperate in their need to celebrate life, and in their guilt at having such thoughts and in having each other. Each thought longingly of Jamie's nearby lodgings and the new bed, though neither stated these thoughts aloud, or spoke of the hungering need to love and touch and know the thrill of rushing blood and pulsing nerves and life. Life.

But the urgency was there in their stolen moments within the deserted doorway, in fevered kisses and clinging caresses. In endearments that carried an edge of desperation and immediacy. In their reluctance to part, as if tomorrow were an uncertain mirage. It was nearly midnight before they wrenched apart and Lucie reluctantly entered the tenement to stay with Mrs. Blassing and her family.

Sometime during the night, Greta slipped away.

MRS. BLASSING WOKE LUCIE to inform her Stefan was acting strangely. He had departed the tenement before light but not before battering holes in the stairwell wall with his fists. Staggering as if drunk, weeping, he kicked in the side of one of the reeking school sinks and very nearly wrenched the handle off the pump. Shortly after dawn he returned, his arms overflowing with flowers, his eyes savage and wild.

Lucie's shoulders collapsed and she buried her face in her hands, sobbing.

"It's Greta, isn't it," Mrs. Blassing said with a heavy sigh of understanding. Wrapping her large arms around Lucie, she tried to offer comfort though none could be given. While Lucie dressed, Mrs. Blassing quietly collected several women in the building to do what must be done. They accompanied Lucie to the door.

When her key did not work, Lucie wiped her streaming eyes and stared at the door. "Stefan?" There was no answer, but she could hear him moving about inside. "Stefan? I've come with Mrs. Blassing and the others. Please, dearest, let us in."

"Go away!"

She closed her eyes against the hoarse agony searing Stefan's grief. Tears ran down her cheeks. "Stefan, please. There are things to be done."

"I'll do what's necessary. Go away."

She tried the handle of the door. But he must have thrust a chair beneath the handle. Behind her, she heard scandalized murmurs from the gathered women. She knocked and called again, but Stefan refused to respond. Grief blinded her and she could not think. Finally, because she didn't know what else to do, she sent one of the children to the new construction site on lower Broadway to fetch Jamie.

When Jamie arrived he took one look at her face, then his broad arms enclosed her and crushed her against his body. "I'm sorry," he murmured, his voice thick. "God." When he learned Stefan refused to allow the women inside, he squared his shoulders, then knocked on the door. "Stefan? It's Jamie. The women are here. Please open the door."

The silence lengthened inside. "The wagon will come at noon. They can have her then." His voice cracked. "But not before."

The women studied Jamie's expression, then silently moved away down the dark corridor, clucking their tongues. Jamie's arm slid around Lucie's waist and he led her to the rooftop where he held her shaking body and they waited, standing silently as the pale sun climbed the sky.

Shortly after the noon whistle blew they heard the body wagon rattle to a stop in the street below. Jamie looked over the rooftop, saw the pine coffins destined for Potter's Field, and nodded to Lucie who bolted for the stairs.

"Oh, Jamie! Don't let them take her until I've said goodbye!"

This time Lucie's key opened the door and she ran inside, then stopped abruptly. What seemed like a hundred candles burned on the table and surrounded the platform bed.

Stefan had dressed Greta in her ivory silk wedding gown and had arranged her golden hair over the pillows like a halo. Her slender fingers held a single red geranium. Thousands of geranium petals covered her silk skirt, her breast, her hair, and the bed, each petal placed with exquisite patience and loving devotion. She lay as if asleep in a bower of flickering candles, surrounded by the fragrant petals she had loved so much.

Stefan had gone.

THE FOLLOWING DAYS passed in a blur of grief and anxiety. Because she sensed Stefan would want them, Lucie kept many of the geranium petals, placing them in her treasure box on the shelf in the sleeping room. Jamie dismantled the platform bed and sent Greta's flower supplies to Miss Elfin on the ground floor whom they had learned was now working at the Hudson Factory. Lucie packed Greta's few belongings into a pillowcase and placed it in the sleeping room for Stefan.

Whenever she thought of Stefan her heart tangled in painful knots. Greta had been the center of his life. Without her, he would be like a ship without anchor. Lucie knew him well enough to know his grief would be a savage storm, brutal in its intensity. But she discovered she didn't know him well enough to guess where he might have gone.

"It's been four days," she murmured to Jamie, her white face lowered over a cup of coffee so pale it looked like tinted water. But the heat felt good beneath her palms. The nights were sharp and chill now and yesterday she had awakened to frost coating the courtyard floor. "Please, Jamie," she said, lifting her face. "I've never asked for anything... please don't give Stefan the sack. I beg you, grant him a little more time."

She saw the pain her request caused him. Knots rose like stones along his jawline, his hands curled into fists.

"I would give the world if I could do as you ask," he said in a low voice. "But I can't. I had to notify Mr. Tucker's office that Stefan is off the site. I'm sorry, lass. But it's done."

"Oh, God," she whispered. A long breath collapsed her chest and her fingers whitened around the mug. Now neither she nor Stefan had work.

"God, lass. Don't look at me like that." He tried to take her hands, but she sat as if she were granite, unable to move. Jamie swore softly. "Don't you think I would have kept Stefan on the roll if there was any way I could? If he were anyone but Stefan, I would have given him the sack the first day! Lucie, please. For God's sake, try to understand. Stefan would. He knows I can't show favoritism. Wherever he is, he knows his job is gone."

"The agent came for the rent," she said in an expressionless tone. "I persuaded him to come back the day after tomorrow." Her head dropped. "But I won't have the money then, either."

Throwing back his chair Jamie paced across the space where the platform bed had been. "I have a dollar, that's all." He kicked at the stove, then stood staring down at the top.

Lucie thought of the money he had lent her for the wedding. For an instant the memory of that day blinded her. She shook her vision away with difficulty. Even if she ended in the street, she did not regret the wedding. Given the same circumstances, she would spend the money the same way again.

"I'll sell our bed," Jamie said, turning to look at her.

"And then what?" Lucie asked in a dull voice. She shook her head. "No, Jamie, keep your bed."

"*Our* bed, lass."

"You wouldn't get full price for it now. And the money would only prolong whatever is going to happen. Without work, and with jobs so hard to find…" Her shoulders lifted then fell, and she covered her face in her hands.

"Lucie, Lucie lass." Jamie dropped to his knees beside her, trying to look into her face. "Damn it, I feel so helpless! So damned helpless!"

"Please. Just hold me." She felt so cold.

AND SHE FELT BETRAYED. Worse, she understood Jamie knew she blamed him for giving Stefan the sack.

Her practical mind understood Jamie had no real choice. To make an exception of Stefan would damage his credibility with the other workmen on the site, and ignoring procedure would anger Mr. Tucker and possibly jeopardize Jamie's own employment.

But in her heart, she blamed him regardless. This was Stefan, alone and lost and floundering in a world turned dark and bitter. He needed their help, not another loss.

Where was he? What was he doing? Lucie closed her eyes and bowed her head in the silent rooms. She knew she should be out looking for work. But she wanted to be here when Stefan returned. Besides which, she could not earn all the rent money before the agent reappeared tomorrow.

Tomorrow evening she would be standing in the street, her few belongings tied in bundles at her feet. The scene rose before her with chilling clarity. She could almost feel the cold night air, could almost smell the scent of her own fear.

This then was what happened between Ellis Island and Elizabeth Street. The hope, the shining promise, slowly eroded one speck at a time until one day the dreams dissolved and gave way to the demands of simply surviving. Did the dreams return? She didn't know.

If they did she suspected they returned in a different form. What was once personal would surely expand to a larger scope. The dreams would include change beyond the individual. The dream would include building a better, safer world.

For the moment her own world had slowed to a halt. She wanted to turn back or jump forward, but she did not want to be here now, numbed by grief and despairing over Stefan, confused by her feelings toward Jamie, missing Greta so much she hurt inside.

It stunned her to gaze about the tenement rooms and see so little to recall Greta's presence. It was as if Greta had never occupied these rooms, had never existed to brighten her small portion of the world. Only the pot of geraniums on the window sill, turning brown from the cold, suggested that once a lovely young woman had passed this way.

"Stefan!"

Jumping to her feet, she flew to the door as it opened, then halted and her hands flew to her mouth.

He leaned in the doorway, a wreck of a man, swaying on his feet as if drunk. And she saw that he was. He reeked of cheap barrel gin. Five days of beard roughened his chin. His hair and clothing was dirty and wild as if he had slept where he had fallen. If Lucie had seen only his eyes, she would not have recognized him. His eyes were sunken and the light had died behind them.

For one long despairing moment they stared at each other, silently sharing the agony of loss, remembering Greta and the love she had brought to each of them. Words could not convey the grief that filled their eyes and wounded their hearts.

When Lucie, blinded by tears, opened her arms, Stefan fell forward and caught her in a bone-crushing embrace.

"She's gone," he whispered.

WHEN JAMIE ARRIVED they sat together waiting for Stefan to waken, not speaking until Jamie made her look at him.

"I've listed our bed for sale." When Lucie did not respond, but turned her face away, he tightened his hands around the mug of ale he had brought. "Lucie, we have to talk about this."

"I know I'm being unfair," she murmured finally. "But I trusted you! I didn't believe you would give Stefan the sack."

"No, lass," he said gently. "You knew I had to. You're angry right now, and frightened. And you have much to be angry about. But it's circumstance, Lucie, not me who has betrayed you.''

"I know…" There was no way to tell him what she was feeling, because she knew she was being unfair.

"I won't let you sleep in a doorway or starve. You must know that."

Her immediate urge was to scream and shout and throw things. This was so unlike her that she was shocked into silence, using the excuse of Stefan's stirring to leave Jamie and swallow the words scalding the tip of her tongue.

First she fed both men, finding comfort in the performance of simple tasks, then she asked Jamie to take Stefan to the public baths near the East River.

When they returned Stefan was sober and restored to some semblance of his former self. Subdued, he sat at the table while Lucie shaved him and Jamie silently watched.

"You must not blame Jamie for my actions," Stefan said when Lucie had patted his face dry and replaced the razor and basin on the shelf over the stove.

She turned accusing eyes to Jamie. "Did you—"

"Jamie told me nothing. I can guess."

Lucie turned flaming cheeks toward her lap and clasped her hands tightly. "He didn't have to sack you."

"Yes, Lucie, he did." Stefan spoke in a hollow voice devoid of expression. It was as if he had forgotten how to speak and formed the words with difficulty. "If you can set your fear to one side—and I know that isn't easy—you'll understand that Jamie acted properly."

"Thank you, Stefan," Jamie said, looking at Lucie.

"You don't understand how desperate our situation is!" She explained there was no food in the house, and the rent agent would return tomorrow evening for money they did not have.

"If the bed sells—"

"Thank you, Jamie Kelly, but I am still responsible for myself and my sister." Stefan stared at the space where th platform bed had been. "Hell, what am I saying? I couldn't save Greta. Maybe I can't save you, either," he said to Lucie, dropping his head.

"I don't know what we're going to do." She wrung her hands until she noticed what she was doing, then she flattened her palms against her knees. "There's nothing left to sell."

In the ensuing silence Jamie rose and moved to the window, staring out at the cold night. Stefan looked at the geranium on the sill and his eyes filled. Lucie scanned the room seeking a solution she had sought a dozen times before.

"There is something we can sell," Lucie said suddenly. Stefan and Jamie looked at her. "The cream. I used one of the pots, but there are nineteen left." Pushing to her feet she found a pencil and a scrap of paper and laboriously worked the ciphers, not looking at either man. "Yes. This will work. If I can sell nine pots, that will give us the rent money. I only have to sell nine. And I have all day tomorrow to do it."

Jamie was the first to speak. "Dearest, please don't misunderstand, but you didn't sell a single pot when you tried before. Why should it be different now?"

Hope surged into her chest. "Because...let me think. Yes. The primary reason I couldn't place the cream is because I couldn't get past being a woman. No one would take me seriously." She focused pleading eyes on Stefan. "They would listen to you, Stefan. You could sell the pots, I know you could."

"Me?" His laugh was harsh. "Right now I couldn't give the pots away." She continued to look at him. "For the love of God, Lucie. I can't think, I can't function. My mind is dead. When I can think, all I can think about is Greta. I keep asking why? Why, God? What did she do that was so terrible she had to die? What did I do that was so terrible that she was taken from me? I'm hollow inside. Can't you see that? Don't ask me to take this shell into the world and pretend it's whole!''

She dropped her head. "Then I'll do it." Jamie sat in the chair beside her and took her hand in his. But the warmth of his presence was not enough to chase the chill of memory. Her fingers gripped his as she remembered the last time she had tried to sell the cream. "I can't let them throw us into the street without at least trying."

Stefan's fist crashed down on the tabletop. "All right. I'll sell the damned cream!"

"Thank you," Lucie whispered. The cream was their only hope.

In the morning Lucie gave Stefan water-bread for breakfast, then supervised his attire. Though he protested, she finally persuaded him to don his wedding suit. For several moments she studied him, critically debating whether she should trim his hair and only now noticing the thick sprinkling of white that had appeared in the last week. In the end she decided to leave his hair as it was, similar in style to Count Bartok's.

The similarity did not end there. Stefan's resemblance to Count Emil Bartok was more startling than before. In the last week something had died inside leaving Stefan stiff and straight, quieter somehow than Lucie remembered. She saw the shell he had mentioned; but others would see a somber dignity. Suffering had sharpened his features into aristocratic aloofness.

She embraced him at the door. "If there was any other way . . ." But there was not.

"Greta believed in your cream," he said against her chestnut hair. "She believed it would sell. So it will."

"He should be back by now," Lucie said to Jamie. They stood beside the tenement window, staring down at the street. As they watched a lamplighter ambled into sight and placed his ladder against the pole.

"I'll speak to the rental agent when he arrives," Jamie said. His reflection in the window wore a worried expression. "I have a dollar and a half. If he's half human, that should buy you another day."

Lucie drew a long breath and turned to face him. During the last few days a lump of fear had lodged in her throat and she had difficulty speaking around it. "Jamie, I've treated you badly and I'm sorry." She lowered her head and bit her lip. Now that she could hope again, her mind had cleared and she felt ashamed of herself to the point she could not meet his eyes. Jamie was the one solid thing in her life right now. He didn't deserve to be blamed for simply doing his job. It hurt to know she had been so unfair. "Can...can you forgive me?"

Cupping her chin he tilted her face up to his and gently kissed her lips. "Of course I forgive you, dearest. These have been trying times for us all."

"I used to see hope where no one else could," she whispered, resting her head on his shoulder. Recently she had felt so tired, exhausted in mind as well as body. She wished she could rest in Jamie's arms and sleep. "But lately...all I seem to see is the present moment. And it frightens me."

"It's the helplessness," he murmured, stroking her hair. "Seeing the path so clearly but being unable to reach it."

"Oh, Jamie, I've missed you." Wrapping her arms around his neck, she held him tightly. "I hated the distance between us. I was thinking such spiteful things and—"

"Shhh, lass. It's all right now," he said, smoothing a strand of hair from her cheek.

Instantly the fear returned, because it wasn't all right. Being in Jamie's arms helped, but the terrible problems still existed. Her fingers dug into his shoulders.

"What if Stefan wasn't able to sell any of the pots?" she asked, staring up at him. A shudder traced down her spine.

"What if the rental agent won't give us another day?" Panic rose in her throat and she pushed her face into the warm hollow at Jamie's neck, drawing strength from his solid body.

"We'll know momentarily, lass," Jamie said, his voice grim. "There's Stefan."

Lucie whirled to the window, trying to read Stefan's expression as he strode past them on the street below and turned into the alleyway. Her heart sank. He wore the look of a man who has lost all he values and cares for nothing.

Gripping Jamie's hand, she turned to face the door and waited, holding her breath.

"Stefan?" Her voice was choked.

For a moment he looked at them, his expression unreadable, then he walked to the table, pushed aside the kerosene lamp and upended his worn tapestry bag. Coins and papers spilled over the table.

Lucie gasped and covered her mouth, her eyes widening. "Oh, my God!" Swaying, she threw out a hand and steadied herself against Jamie's arm. "You sold them all! But—" She moved to the table, her mind racing. "But there should be less than six dollars." She raised her eyes. "And there's almost ten!"

"I raised the price," Stefan explained wearily, sinking to a chair. "I sold them for fifty cents a pot."

"Fifty cents!"

"Congratulations," Jamie said softly. Relief flooded his features as Lucie hastened to answer the rap at the door. No one spoke as she counted six dollars into the rental agent's palm, paying the week past and the week ahead.

When she returned her hands were shaking, but her face was more relaxed than it had been in days. "I don't know what to say, Stefan. Thank you." Still trembling, she poured hot water into three cups, using the same tea bag for each, then returned to the table. "Where did you sell them? How did you do it?"

As he explained he had sold the pots primarily to Bloomingdale's and Wanamaker's, Lucie studied his expression. Something hard and determined flickered in Stefan's eyes as he spoke. It was the first spark of life she had observed since his return. Selling the cream had given him a foe to fight, a challenge to take his mind off his beloved Greta. For so long he had been forced to sit in helpless frustration; selling the cream was something he could *do*.

"This is wonderful news," Jamie said, smiling with relief. "The rent is paid ahead and there's a bit left over to carry you until you find work."

Whenever Lucie let herself remember that neither she nor Stefan were employed her heart stopped, then lurched into a gallop around her chest. "What are these slips of paper?" she asked eventually, pushing at one of the papers with her fingertip.

Stefan shrugged. "Occasionally a proprietor asked me to call again when he was not as occupied. Or the proprietor was not in. If I hadn't made a show of noting the names, it wouldn't have looked right."

Lucie considered his explanation. "Are you saying you could have sold more of the pots than you did?" she asked slowly.

"Possibly. Who can say?"

"My heavens." Cautious excitement flared in her eyes as she studied the array of paper slips. "Stefan, hear me out. Suppose, just suppose we use the extra money to buy more ingredients... wait, don't say no just yet." Leaning forward she spread her hands and looked at him and at Jamie. "Do you realize you brought home nine dollars and fifty cents? In one day? Even if we deduct the cost of the ingredients, the remaining sum is more than you could earn in a *week* of working at the construction site!"

They stared at her. "What are you saying, Lucie?" Jamie asked after a quick glance at Stefan.

"I think I'm saying we have work right here." She leaned forward. "Stefan, if you sold only ten pots a day, that would come to…" Her mind raced. "Thirty dollars a week! Think of it. We'd never again have to worry about rent or food or coal or winter boots or—"

"Wait a minute. You're suggesting I shouldn't look for work? That I should sell women's face cream for a living?" Stefan scowled and slowly shook his head.

"Listen, please. Last night you told me you wanted a marker for Greta's grave. You said if it took years, you would save the money for a marble marker. Stefan, it will take years. Or… you could buy the marker immediately, in less than a week if you sell only ten pots of cream a day!"

He stared at her. Then his gaze dropped to the papers scattered across the table. "In less than a week…"

"And, Jamie," she said, turning to him, her mind whirling with the excitement of possibilities. Dreams did return. "You could have Kelly's Design and Construction Company sooner than we dared imagine." His stony expression tempered her enthusiasm. "Dearest, please don't be stubborn. Think about this." Drawing a breath, she took his hand between her own. "You haven't mentioned Kelly's Design and Construction Company in so long. Have you abandoned your dream, dearest? That wonderful dream of building housing for people like us?"

"Some dreams are not realistic, Lucie. Or maybe the time is wrong. Other dreams take precedence."

"But it doesn't have to be like that! Please, Jamie, don't look at me that way. Stefan has proven we can succeed with the cream. We didn't go about it right before, but now we know how to do it! We needed Stefan as our drummer."

"Bloomingdale's and Wanamaker's said they would order more if the cream proved a success with their ladies," Stefan said thoughtfully, continuing to regard the slips of paper.

"It will! Mrs. Roper said my cream is as fine as any on the market." Her grip tightened on Jamie's hands. "I know we can be a success! Please join us, Jamie. The future can be ours again."

"Isn't it possible you're grasping at straws, lass? An hour ago you didn't know if you would have a roof over your head. Now, you're buying stone markers and construction companies." He shook his head. "You're setting yourself up in business."

"No, Jamie. This isn't grasping at straws. Look at these papers. Didn't you hear what Stefan said?"

"I heard. I'm not stupid, Lucie."

She gasped. "I didn't mean to imply you were. I only meant to point out an unmistakable opportunity. We've been given a second chance to see what's under our nose! My cream can give all of us everything we ever wanted! I'm sure of it. I feel it."

"So, you've set your mind to this. You're determined to go into business."

She looked at Stefan, knew he was thinking about the marker for Greta's grave. "Yes," she said simply, softly. "Countess Kolska's Superlative Face and Hand Cream can give us everything we've dreamed of. Safety, and a future for us and for our children. Dearest Jamie, say you will join us."

"How would I contribute, Lucie? You make the cream and Stefan sells it. Do you think I could accept a portion of your profits for doing nothing?" Pride stiffened his jaw and hardened his eyes. "No, lass," he said, standing. "The cream is your dream, perhaps your opportunity. I wish you well with it."

But he looked at her as if she had betrayed him. As if a near horizon had slipped suddenly into the far distance.

"Jamie—" She felt the blood drain from her face. His expression was one she had not seen before.

"You're right," he said quietly, glancing at the paper slips Stefan was sorting into piles. "I think you and Stefan have found your opportunity. I have a feeling you'll be a tremendous success. Someday I will read about you in the newspapers."

"Oh, God," she whispered, falling back into her chair. "Jamie, I beg you . . . don't do this. Don't let foolish pride destroy us. Please."

"Now I'm foolish?" Jamie stood beside the door, his coat and cap in his hand. They stared at each other across the room. "Do you see the changes that will come, lass? If I'm foolish now, what would you think of me if I took money from you?"

"You know I spoke in anger . . ." She spread her hands, her eyes imploring him. "Jamie, don't put this between us. Please. Share our good fortune, be part of it!"

"One day," he said in a thick strange voice, staring at her as if memorizing her features, "if Kelly's Design and Construction Company becomes a reality and if it becomes a success . . ." He drew a breath then opened his eyes, "and if you haven't found a better man than I, I'll find you again. When I can come to you as an equal, as a man."

"You're saying goodbye!" She rose on trembling legs, staring at him. "No. Please, Jamie . . ."

"In the meanwhile, wish me the same success I predict for you." But she couldn't speak, so he quietly let himself out and shut the door behind her.

Lucie's knees collapsed and she fell back on her chair. Tears blinded her, tears as gray and cold as her world had suddenly become.

Chapter Thirteen

Stefan wholly immersed himself in selling Countess Kolska's Superlative Face and Hand Cream. In Stefan's mind the cream was inexorably intertwined with memories of Greta. Greta had believed in Lucie's cream; she had believed in the dream. Making the cream a stunning success was something he did for Greta, her victory as much as his. But as weeks blended into months he discovered he enjoyed selling. Selling was a game that offered interesting new challenges every day. At the back of his mind something clicked into place, and Stefan understood he had found his life's work, his opportunity. Without Greta, it was a hollow triumph.

For Lucie the cream's enormous success proved a mixed blessing. On the one hand, she could scarcely believe the money that poured in, a virtual waterfall of funds the sum of which surpassed comprehension. As it quickly became unthinkable to keep such large sums beneath the loose board in the sleeping room, she and Stefan proudly opened a bank account, the first bank account in the Kolska family. Each week when she updated the books, she stared at the growing bank balance with incredulous disbelief.

In a remarkably short period the business had earned what seemed to Lucie like a fortune. Now she and Stefan could move to a small furnished house. They could purchase a horse and trap if they wished. She gazed into the future and could see that the cream's potential was unlimited. The thought made her head spin.

The mixed side of the blessing was the lack of time. Ironically, there was no time to spend the profits that poured into their bank account. Stefan had moved Greta to a private cemetery and erected a marble stone, and Lucie insisted he purchase clothing at a haberdashery suitable for the representative of Countess Kolska's Superlative Face and Hand Cream. Lucie purchased three new work aprons, and they had meat in the supper pot every night. Otherwise, little changed in their lives except they worked longer hours than ever before.

There wasn't time to locate and move to better housing. No time to stroll along Ladies Mile and know she had funds to purchase a new hat if one should catch her eye. There was hardly time to sit a moment and catch a breath.

Repeat orders flooded Stefan's sample bag, along with requests for varied scents. Bloomingdale's requested a rose fragrance; Wanamaker's preferred violet; Lord and Taylor wanted lily of the valley. Stefan refused all orders for geranium scent.

Lucie rose before dawn and made cream until well after darkness had fallen. Following a late supper, she drew labels and pasted them on the pots. Day after day she rushed to keep up with the orders, and slowly fell behind as the orders outpaced her.

And every day as she stirred the tubs occupying every inch of space in the tenement, she thought about Jamie.

Throughout the first weeks her pain over Jamie's loss blended into her pain of losing Greta until she could no distinguish the two. She measured and mixed the ingredients with a blunted expression, her heart aching. There wa no pleasure in work, just the constant blind grief of be reavement.

But as autumn faded to winter and snow blew inside the broken pane Stefan had no time to fix, her grief and confusion over Jamie coalesced into anger.

Scowling, she leaned over the stove, stirring the ointment, oil and soda, waiting for a soaplike consistency to form. "Too proud to take money from a woman, is he?" She wrestled the tub to a heat-resistant platform on the floor, then lifted another pot to the stove top to warm the glycerine and boric acid. "Too proud to lend a hand! He loved me well enough when I was poor as a mouse, but he can't love me now that I can afford a new gown if there was someone to wear it for! I ask you," she said to the empty room, waving her stirring paddle, "Does that make sense?"

Jamie Kelly was as crazy as a rabid dog if he believed she didn't need him, she thought. She did. The business had become too much for two people to handle. Moreover, neither she nor Stefan had any training to handle the books. The rows of figures intimidated them both. Tired and apprehensive, Lucie consistently made frustrating errors. It would have been a tremendous relief to be spared the dreaded ledger.

Already they needed a small warehouse to store the supply of ingredients and pots if they were to keep up with the orders and hope to continue expanding. The boxes of supplies jamming the tenement rooms made it almost impossible to live here and trying to work was crowded and inconvenient. They certainly had the wherewithal to lease larger working space but not time to do it. Moreover, they needed someone to assume the burden of drawing and pasting the labels, someone to assist Lucie with making the cream, someone to fill the seemingly endless crates of pots, someone to deliver the finished pots to the emporiums.

Tears of frustration and exhaustion wet her eyes as she poured the glycerine mixture into the ointment blend and stirred as it cooled. Next she would add the remaining water and the volatile oils, then she would fill dozens of pots before she began another batch. Trying to accomplish everything alone became more daunting every day.

She missed Jamie with an ache that blinded her. She missed him the way she would have missed an amputated arm or breath in her lungs. Not an hour passed that she didn't wonder what he was doing, and if he ever thought of her, if he regretted the foolish damnable pride that kept them apart.

When she fell onto her mattress at night, too exhausted to fall asleep immediately, she remembered his tender kisses, his passion, his fingertips stroking her cheek. She remembered the dark intensity of his gaze, how he seemed to throw off sparks when excitement fired his imagination, how his lips curved when he smiled.

She recalled when she first met him, when love's elbow struck. She remembered summer sunlight striking fire from his auburn hair, and snow settling on his eyelashes and shoulders. How could he have claimed to love her then walk away?

STEFAN FOUND A MOMENT to mend the broken windowpane and to buy them both winter boots and new gloves. In the evenings he helped Lucie fill pots and draw labels, struggling to keep pace with the orders stacking on the spindle file.

"We simply must hire people to help," Lucie said, rubbing her eyes before she opened a fresh pot of paste. "Stefan, we can't continue like this. We're both exhausted."

Stefan lifted his head and studied her as if he hadn't seen her in a long while. "You do look tired."

She returned Stefan's searching look and discovered he did not appear as wearied by the frenzied pace as she. He looked almost as fresh as when he had left this morning. In fact, Stefan looked better than he had in years. The weight he lost after Greta's death had not returned and the lean hard look became him. At Lucie's suggestion he had grown a beard and trimmed it into the Van Dyke style, which made him resemble Count Emil Bartok more than ever. With the beard, his new clothing and his quiet bearing, he could be mistaken for a count himself.

"Are you feeling well?" he asked, suddenly anxious.

"I'm just tired." She pushed a hand through her hair and frowned at the kerosene lamp. "We should discuss moving into larger quarters and hiring help. We can't handle this alone."

"Can we afford all that?"

Lucie stared at him and laughed, the first time she had done so in weeks. Leaning forward, she pushed the ledger across the table so he could see.

"Good God!" Stefan blinked at the page. "Surely this must be a mistake! It isn't? Lucie, are you certain?" When she nodded, a thoughtful look chased the astonishment from his gaze. "With more people, the business can expand. In a few years we can think about opening markets in other cities." He gazed into the future.

"Dearest Stefan," she said softly. "You love the cream business, don't you?"

A flush rose from his collar and he smiled at her. "It amazes me, too. But I do. I dream of making Countess Kolska's Superlative Face and Hand Cream a household name all across this great land. Not immediately," he added hastily, laughing at her expression. "But someday."

"I know you will," she said slowly, watching him. "I think, Stefan, that you have only begun. That you have found whatever it was you were seeking."

For a long moment they said nothing, smiling affectionately at each other across the table, remembering how it began, remembering Greta.

Then Stefan took her hand in his. "What about you, Lucie?" he asked softly. "What do you dream of?"

"I have no dreams."

"I think you do." He waved a hand toward the tubs and the shelves of ingredients. "This isn't what you want, is it? You want what you always have. A home and children. Jamie Kelly."

"Once . . . but that's finished," she whispered, lowering her head.

"Odd," Stefan said, looking at her and raising an eyebrow. "I don't recall agreeing to release either of you from your betrothal. Perhaps you should think about that." Yawning, he rose from the table. "And perhaps you should think about America."

"America?" She looked up and frowned.

"Do you want your slice of the pie, Lucie? Are you hungry enough to go after it?" He stroked her cheek. "I thought you were. I thought nothing would stop you from having your Jamie."

"Good heavens! Is this Stefan Kolska talking?" She blinked.

"I've done a lot of thinking during the last weeks. And I've concluded I was wrong about many things. You were right, Lucie. I brought a closed mind to America. Because of it, I couldn't see opportunity when it kicked at the door. If it wasn't for you—and other things—we might have missed a future so splendid we can't imagine it yet. America offers everyone an opportunity, but you have to have eyes to see it and a willingness to seize the moment even if it means turning your beliefs upside down. To do this, a man—and a woman—must be alert to hidden attitudes, to limitations. We must reevaluate every thought." He lifted her face. "Beginning with pride."

"But, Jamie—"

"There are two people involved here, my dear sister. And both are acting as stubborn as mules." He kissed her cheek then moved toward the sleeping room. "Have you talked to him?"

"Chase after a man who doesn't want me?" A horrified look pinched her expression.

Stefan smiled back at her over his shoulder. "Pride, Lucie. Is that Wlad speaking, or the new American woman? How do you know what Jamie's thinking if you haven't spoken to him? Maybe he thinks you don't want him now that you're as rich as the Ropers."

She managed a smile. "We aren't *that* rich."

"Does Jamie know that?"

Long after the night turned deep and silent, Lucie sat at the kitchen table. Thinking. Getting angrier by the minute. Jamie Kelly, whom she had set her heart on, was as pigheaded as they came. And his pigheadedness was costing her the one thing she wanted. Well, that was not going to happen, not if she had a say in the matter. And she did. This was, after all, America.

THE GLASS MEN should have arrived an hour ago, Jamie thought irritably. He frowned at the fat flakes of snow flying through the empty ground floor windows. Once the glass was in the ground floor would be closed and he could relax. The thought almost coaxed a smile. He couldn't recall the last time he had genuinely felt at peace. He doubted a few windows would alter his mental state to any meaningful degree. The glass men would come and go and he would still be unsettled, pacing and feeling miserable whenever he thought about Lucie Kolska.

What was she doing today? Had she forgotten him? Did she ever pass a thought for Jamie Kelly?

Unaware he was frowning, he crossed the marble floor lobby to stand before a large fireplace. Removing a pair of heavy gloves, he warmed his hands in front of the flames and watched two workmen carry a bundle of two by fours through the lobby and up the central staircase.

He knew Lucie's cream was a stupendous success. He had met Stefan for a growler of ale several weeks ago and had learned the news. But he had known it before Stefan spoke simply by observing Stefan's appearance. It wasn't the elegant new clothing Stefan wore, it was more his demeanor. This was a man who had found his calling, who finally recognized his path and felt the excitement and challenge of success. They had not spoken of Lucie; pride stopped the questions he wanted to ask.

But he thought of her constantly. She haunted his mind with ghostlike memory. Once, he gave in to his loneliness and his need to see her, and he walked to Elizabeth Street with every intention of rapping on her door. But he halted in the courtyard and could go no farther. He didn't know what to say to her. She was a success; he was not. She and Stefan didn't need him.

In addition he had not altered his conviction that no man worth the name accepted money from a woman. Not even a woman whom he adored, whose loss had carved a hole in his heart. How could he respect himself if he accepted a penny from her? How could he hope she would respect him? How could he ask her to wait years for him to save their marriage money when she herself already banked a hundred times that amount? In the end, angry and wounded, he turned on his heel and forced himself to walk away.

"Damn it!" He stared into the fireplace flames. It would be years before he could launch Kelly's Design and Construction Company, years before he could hope to compete with Lucie's success. She would find someone else, a brownstoner as wealthy as he imagined she now was. And that bastard would hold her in his arms and kiss the smile on her lips. The image was unbearable. Thrusting his hands into his pockets, he kicked at a piece of construction debris and swore out loud.

"Jamie Kelly, I wish to speak to you!"

For a moment he believed he imagined her voice. But he had never heard that tone before. Turning, he lifted his head in astonishment, still not certain if she was real or if he had conjured her from his own longing. But it was Lucie. Against all that was proper, she had come to him.

There was nothing dainty in her movement. She strode toward him like a diminutive hurricane, her hem flaring behind her, a thunderous scowl on her lovely face. To his surprise she wasn't wearing fashionable new clothing as he had supposed she would be, but wore her old coat and mended muffler and the little felt hat she had purchased last winter at the rag fair.

"Lucie!" Hungry for the sight of her his eyes darted over her pink cheeks, the strands of chestnut hair falling from a hastily constructed knot on her neck, her ripe angry mouth. Though he had sworn he remembered her exactly, he had forgotten how truly beautiful she was. Even as upset as she seemed to be, the sight of her was enough to take his breath away.

"I have some things to say to you, Jamie Kelly," she said, stopping in front of him and placing her gloved hands on her hips.

Jamie was too astounded to speak.

"First, I want you to know what a cad I think you are! What kind of man pledges himself then vanishes into the night? You didn't ask Stefan to release you from your pledge. You didn't ask me, either! Whether you like it or not, we are still betrothed."

"You think I'm a cad?" He blinked at her, stunned by the abrupt realization that she was right. He had not handled his situation at all properly. A flush of discomfort and embarrassment heated his cheeks.

"Second, you are the most selfish man in America!"

"Selfish?" He felt like a fool repeating her words, but he was too surprised to do anything else.

"Yes, selfish! Look at me, Jamie Kelly." She pointed a gloved finger to her eyes, then at her dripping hair. "I'm exhausted. I work from dawn until midnight every day. And so does Stefan. We need help. We need a partner. But can

you be bothered to help people who believed you were
friend they could rely on? No. You're too wrapped up i
your own concerns. We need someone to manage the bus
ness, the books, the hiring of extra people, leasing a ware
house and a thousand other vital details we're too busy, to
inexperienced and too exhausted to see to!''

''But you look beautiful!''

''Bunkum! I look as tired as I am. As tired as you woul
look if you were trying to manage Kelly's Design and Con
struction Company with only two people. But that isn't
problem is it, Jamie? Because you're too proud to seize you
dream if it means accepting a hand up from someone else.
She stamped her boot on the marble floor. ''You woul
rather delay or abandon your dream than hasten it by pa
ticipating in my dream or Stefan's. It has to be *your* way c
no way at all. Even if that means you can't have your drean
for years and years. God forbid a crack should appear i
your precious pride!''

''Lucie...''

For a moment she looked like the Lucie he knew. The
she lifted her hand. ''No, don't interrupt me, or I'll lose m
nerve and I won't say what needs to be said.'' She drew
deep breath and the bosom he remembered so well ros
against her coat. ''Once you said 'the time may come whe
Stefan must swallow his pride and accept assistance from
friend.' You said that, Jamie. If you really believed you
own words, then why can't *you* accept a bit of assistanc
from a friend. Why can't you join us and help us and in th
process achieve your own dreams much sooner?''

''I said that?''

''You also promised that you and I would be happy fc
each other's success. But you've taken yourself away t
sulk.''

''Grown men don't sulk!'' he said, stung.

''Grown men don't let pride stand in the way of the
happiness! At least any man I'd want doesn't!'' Her chi

lifted and her dark eyes flashed. "You just think about that, Jamie Kelly. You ask yourself why my success should diminish you! What does one thing have to do with the other?" All at once the fire died in her eyes and her shoulders drooped. "Oh, Jamie." Then she looked at him with such despair that he reached for her.

But she moved out of his grasp. "Don't you see? Don't you think Stefan would trade all the pride in the world for one more day with Greta? Do you think he would care a fig if Greta had more money than he if he could just have her back again? Is your pride so important that you would throw aside all we've been through together, all we meant to each other? Would you rather find someone else and begin again?"

Shock darkened his eyes. "There could never be anyone else!"

"But there isn't me, either," she said simply, looking at him. "You and I are as lost to each other as Stefan and Greta. Is that what you want, Jamie?" When he didn't speak she spread her gloves, let them fall. "You loved me when I was poor. Can't you love me when I'm not?"

"Stated like that, you make me sound like a fool!"

"Well, you're behaving like one." She stared up at him, then, like an actress offering an aside to the audience, she cast a look over her shoulder and leaned forward to whisper, "I don't think I can keep this up much longer. The settlement house said Americans assert themselves, but it is difficult, you know."

"I imagine so," he said stupidly, blinking at her.

She squared her shoulders and recalled her scowl. "I've swallowed my pride by coming here. I hope you will rethink your pride. Stefan and I need you." She started walking backward toward the door and the snow blowing outside. "I love you, Jamie Kelly. I always will. If the only way to appease you is to give the business to Stefan and live in poverty until you are ready to wed, then I'm willing to do so.'' She was almost at the door.

"To walk away from your success and a splendid future would be idiotic!"

"Yes, it would be. But that appears to be the only way you'll have me, as idiotic as it is. For poorer, not for richer." Glaring at him she placed her boot through the door. "I want you to think about our situation, Jamie, and make a decision. Join us, tell me to leave the business, or ask Stefan to release you from your pledge." She turned and ran out the door.

He stared at the empty space, still seeing her though she had gone. And he knew everything she had said was correct. But still...his beliefs were deeply rooted, not easily altered. A pounding headache formed behind his forehead.

LUCIE HALF HOPED, half expected Jamie would follow her back to Elizabeth Street. But he didn't.

During the next few days she kept an eye on the window interrupting the stirring and filling to peek down at the street.

By the end of the week she finally, painfully, accepted that Jamie would not come to her. In the end his pride was greater than his love for her. That was the tragedy, the knowledge that broke her heart. Because he did love her. She had seen the joy leap in his eyes when she first appeared in the construction lobby. She had seen his love for her a thousand times and she could not doubt it. But his pride was more important.

Only now did she admit she had never completely given up, or wholly believed they would never be together again. She had grieved for him, yes. She had missed him and ached for him. But somewhere at the back of her mind, she had cherished a stubborn belief that her loss was temporary. One day he would return.

Now she began to understand that Jamie would not return. Bending over the tub on the stove, stirring it with the large wooden paddle, she tried to comprehend how she could have misjudged him so badly. She had believed that, given enough time, reason would triumph. She had believed Jamie Kelly was a man whose personal integrity would not allow a false premise for long. A man who could sort out his thinking and arrive at a reasonable, if uncomfortable, conclusion. She had believed in him and in their love for each other.

When a knock sounded at the door she wiped the perspiration from her brow and called, "Come in." It was the delivery boy Stefan had hired yesterday. Without turning from the stove she said, "Put the boxes anywhere. I'll sort them out later."

"As you say, lass. But it seems to me, you're needing more space. There's scarcely room to turn about in here."

"Jamie!" Dropping the paddle, she whirled from the stove.

"Stefan didn't tell you?"

"He said he'd hired a new delivery boy, but—"

Jamie rolled his eyes and grinned. "A delivery boy, is it! Last night I signed papers buying into the Kolska partnership." He touched his tie. "As I'm temporarily short of funds, the agreement states my share of profits will go toward the purchase price until we're square. That is, if you agree. Stefan must intend to review the documents with you tonight. I thought he would last night. I guess he decided I should tell you myself—"

"If I agree?" Joy lit her eyes. "Oh, Jamie! Of course I agree. It's a dream come true!"

They moved toward the table and looked at each other across the pots stacked over the surface. "Everything you said was right, Lucie. I've been a shortsighted fool. A selfish cad."

Crimson flared on her cheeks. "You're not a cad! I only said that—"

"No, you were right." His dark eyes caressed her face, her mouth, made love to her. "I don't claim I'm easy with the partnership yet, but I can say I'm willing to try." A smile softened his expression. "After examining your books, lass, I can spy where I might be useful. The question is: can you forgive me for being a damned idiot?"

Her eyes turned as soft as velvet. "Of course I forgive you. I love you, Jamie Kelly."

"And I love you, Lucie Kolska. You don't know what it's been without you. You're my very life, lass." He smiled and his eyes centered on her trembling mouth. "You gave me a speech, now I have one for you."

She smiled, loving him, aching for him. But there were things that needed saying. She gripped the tabletop with impatience, longing to hold him and be held, and nodded.

"I'll earn my way, and I'll make myself worthy of your trust and Stefan's. I won't accept a penny I haven't earned."

"I know that, dearest. I've always known that."

"You were right about everything, lass. Countess Kolska's cream is the opportunity we sought for so long. It makes everything possible. Stefan and I intend to eventually expand the partnership to include design and construction." He drew a breath. "My first task as managing partner of this firm will be to lease a warehouse where the cream will be manufactured. My second objective is to hire a dozen people to actually make the cream. Do you object to anything so far?"

She gazed at him with shining eyes. "Did you truly think I would?" She loved his laughing mouth, his thick auburn hair, the rich sound of his Irish *r*s.

"Next I plan to retire you." He observed her closely. "Or do you wish to continue making cream?"

She tilted her head. "I think you will make an excellent managing partner," she said softly. "The thought of retirment thrills me. But what shall I do with myself, Mr. Kelly?''

"Your brother has stated that under no circumstances will he release you or me from our pledge. Therefore, it seems you must marry me forthwith."

"I see... well, if I must," she said, laughing. Though it was impossible, she imagined a burst of sunshine lit the tenement rooms, as blazing as her happiness. Her heart pounded against her ribs as he moved around the table and caught her in his arms. He crushed her to his chest and murmured her name against her hair.

"God, Lucie. I've missed you so much!"

The distance closed and it was as if they had never been apart. She stroked his dear beloved face and felt a familiar excitement kindle within her body, leaving her breathless as his mouth possessed hers. Both were trembling when he released her.

"Lord above, lass." His shaking fingertips stroked her hair, her cheek, her lips. "When I think how close I came to losing the only thing I ever loved..."

Tears of joy glistened in her eyes. Her hands slipped inside his vest and she heard his intake of breath. "We have each other and our future. A wonderful future! Oh, Jamie, such lovely things lie ahead. If only Greta..."

He kissed her again, deeply, passionately, telling her as best he could that he would never leave her again. That he would be there always, loving her, cherishing her.

"Lucie, dearest darling," he murmured hoarsely against her parted lips. "Would it be a terribly caddish thing to... yes, yes it would."

She pressed close to him, feeling the urgency of his need and her own trembling response. "Dearest Jamie," she whispered. "I want to, I... you must know I do, but..."

He examined her violent blush, then he laughed and swept her into a tight embrace. "Precious Lucie, there's never been another like you. I love you, I love you," he said against her mouth. "Say you'll marry me. Soon. Immediately. Before I expire from wanting you."

"I agree," she whispered, blushing to the roots of her hair, "The wedding should be soon. Very soon."

"I'll speak to Father Norlic first thing tomorrow." Then he gazed adoringly into her eyes and kissed her again, slowly, deliberately, a kiss that promised delights to come, a kiss that sent her heart pounding and took her breath away.

In the street outside a wagon passed and Lucie heard the jingle of harness bells. The sound was as clear and pure as Greta's musical laughter. For a moment she felt Greta's presence beside her and sensed she would conceive a daughter on her wedding night. A small Greta to love and protect and keep from harm's way. Before the bells faded into the distance, she imagined the fragrance of geraniums scenting the room, a brief impression then gone.

Then there was Jamie, and the excitement of dreams coming true. And the joy of discovering her slice of the pie was as sweet as she had always imagined it would be.

Coming in July
From America's favorite author

JANET DAILEY

Fiesta San Antonio
Out of print since 1978!

The heavy gold band on her finger proved it was actually true. Natalie was now Mrs. Colter Langton! She had married him because her finances and physical resources for looking after her six-year-old nephew, Ricky, were rapidly running out, and she was on the point of exhaustion. He had married her because he needed a housekeeper and somebody to look after his young daughter, Missy. In return for the solution to her problems, she had a bargain to keep.

It wouldn't be easy. Colter could be so hard and unfeeling. "I don't particularly like myself," he warned her. "It's just as well you know now the kind of man I am. That way you won't expect much from our marriage."

If Natalie had secretly hoped that something would grow between them—the dream faded with his words. Was he capable of love?

Don't miss any of Harlequin's three-book collection of Janet Dailey's novels each with a Texan flavor. Look for *FOR BITTER OR WORSE* coming in September, and if you missed *NO QUARTER ASKED* . . .

Harlequin Superromance®

A June title
not to be missed....

Superromance author Judith Duncan has created her
most powerfully emotional novel yet, a book about
love too strong to forget and hate too painful to
remember....

Risen from the ashes of her past like a phoenix,
Sydney Foster knew too well the price of wisdom,
especially that gained in the underbelly of the city.
She'd sworn she'd never go back, but in order to
embrace a future with the man she loved, she had to
return to the streets...and settle an old score.

Once in a long while, you read a book that affects you
so strongly, you're never the same again. Harlequin is
proud to present such a book, STREETS OF FIRE by
Judith Duncan (Superromance #407). Her book merits
Harlequin's AWARD OF EXCELLENCE for June 1990,
conferred each month to one specially selected title.

S407-1

H A R L E Q U I N
American Romance®

ABOUT THE AUTHOR

Margaret St. George knows about roots, about the fighting
spirit of this country's immigrants and settlers. Her own family
had its origin in England, and its American roots can be traced
to antebellum Virginia. Her great-grandparents left the east
after the Civil War and journeyed by covered wagon to Kansas,
where they raised their family. Making that long trip was their
marriage bed, the first piece of furniture Margaret's great-
grandfather bought, just as Jamie Kelly did. That bed now rests
in Margaret's home in Colorado, a testament to her ancestors.
Its nicks and scars tell the hundreds of stories of hard times
and the courage it took to endure them.

Margaret is a veteran novelist, of both contemporaries and
historicals; this is the third book she has written set in the turn-
of-the-century, an era to which she is inexplicably drawn. She
has a unique ability to create and bring to life memorable
characters with an unsurpassed wit. Margaret is a member of
Mensa and a past president of the Romance Writers of
America. She and her husband and two sons live in the
mountains of Colorado.

CARU-1A

Take 4 bestselling love stories FREE
Plus get a FREE surprise gift!

Harlequin Intrigue

Two exciting new stories each month.

Each title mixes a contemporary, sophisticated romance with the surprising twists and turns of a puzzler...romance with "something more."

Because romance can be quite an adventure.

Intrg-1

Romance, Suspense and Adventure

The Cowboy
JAYNE ANN KRENTZ

What better way to end a series about the search for the ideal man than with a cowboy—the enduringly popular image of the perfect hero? In June 1990, Jayne Ann Krentz brings us the third book of her exciting trilogy LADIES AND LEGENDS— THE COWBOY.

Kate, Sarah and Margaret, the three longtime friends you first met in THE PIRATE and THE ADVENTURER, are reunited in THE COWBOY—this time to see Margaret off to her mysterious encounter with Rafe Cassidy. Shrewd businessman on the surface, proud cowboy at heart, Rafe *is* the man Margaret daren't admit fantasizing about, her favorite hero come to life and waiting to make amends for the past....

THE COWBOY—available in June 1990!

T302-1